ROMANCE AT ALMACK'S

"Do you come to Almack's often?" James asked.

"Not often," Rachel answered. "I attended occasionally for my mother's sake before my father's illness. Mama finds much pleasure in society."

"And you?"

"Not as much."

"I, myself, had a devil of time securing a voucher for this evening," he said. "I found a friend who had an invitation, only to discover the thing was not transferable."

"I was surprised when I got your note saying we could meet here. How did you finally manage an invitation?"

"I called in a long ago favor. From Lady Jersey."

"Oh," Rachel said. The foremost patroness of Almack's did not give out vouchers indiscriminately. Rachel was secretly impressed that Sally Jersey was obligated to Mr. Ware, but she had no intention of letting him know. The man was too self-assured as it was. Too handsome and too . . . oh lord, she would not have it. He was awakening needs that she had dismissed as unnecessary in her life, but she would never succumb to his magnetism. Never. . . .

—from LADY OF INTRIGUE, by Alice Holden

WATCH FOR THESE ZEBRA REGENCIES

LADY STEPHANIE   (0-8217-5341-X, $4.50)
by Jeanne Savery
Lady Stephanie Morris has only one true love: the family estate she
has managed ever since her mother died. But then Lord Anthony Rider
arrives on her estate, claiming he has plans for both the land and the
woman. Stephanie soon realizes she's fallen in love with a man whose
sensual caresses will plunge her into a world of peril and intrigue . . . a
man as dangerous as he is irresistible.

BRIGHTON BEAUTY   (0-8217-5340-1, $4.50)
by Marilyn Clay
Chelsea Grant, pretty and poor, naively takes school friend Alayna
Marchmont's place and spends a month in the country. The devastating
man had sailed from Honduras to claim his promised bride, Miss
Marchmont. An affair of the heart may lead to disaster . . . unless a
resourceful Brighton beauty finds a way to stop a masquerade and
keep a lord's love.

LORD DIABLO'S DEMISE   (0-8217-5338-X, $4.50)
by Meg-Lynn Roberts
The sinfully handsome Lord Harry Glendower was a gambler and the
black sheep of his family. About to be forced into a marriage of con-
venience, the devilish fellow engineered his own demise, never having
dreamed that faking his death would lead him to the heavenly refuge
of spirited heiress Gwyn Morgan, the daughter of a physician.

A PERILOUS ATTRACTION   (0-8217-5339-8, $4.50)
by Dawn Aldridge Poore
Alissa Morgan is stunned when a frantic passenger thrusts her baby
into Alissa's arms and flees, having heard rumors that a notorious
highwayman posed a threat to their coach. Handsome stranger Hugh
Sebastian secretly possesses the treasured necklace the highwayman
seeks and volunteers to pose as Alissa's husband to save her reputation.
With a lost baby and missing necklace in their care, the couple embarks
on a journey into peril—and passion.

*Available wherever paperbacks are sold, or order direct from the
Publisher. Send cover price plus 50¢ per copy for mailing and
handling to Penguin USA, P.O. Box 999, c/o Dept. 17109,
Bergenfield, NJ 07621. Residents of New York and Tennessee must
include sales tax. DO NOT SEND CASH.*

AN EVENING AT ALMACK'S

Four Captivating Stories
of Love among the *Ton* by

Donna Davidson   *Teresa DesJardien*

Alice Holden   *Isobel Linton*

Zebra Books
Kensington Publishing Corp.
http://www.zebrabooks.com

ZEBRA BOOKS are published by

Kensington Publishing Corp.
850 Third Avenue
New York, NY 10022

First Printing: September, 1997
10 9 8 7 6 5 4 3 2 1

Printed in the United States of America

Contents

Katie and
the Captain

Donna Davidson

Dedicated to Gregory L. Alt
For years of guidance, friendship . . . and fun!
Thanks to
Dale McCann, critic partner, friend
Allan Davidson, historian husband
and to daughters
Ann Alt, final reading editor
Robin Pascoe, for her clever insight

One

A wild, keening wind howled through the narrow opening of Katie's window. She rolled over on her pillow to catch the smell of the storm as it blew across her face, knowing that nothing would awaken her faster than the scent of the ocean in turmoil.

She didn't want to miss a moment of this momentous day. She opened her eyes—and stared. *What on earth . . . ?* She leapt from her bed and hurried to lift the bottom pane to its fullest height. Leaning out into the wind, she scanned the horizon.

Huge clouds churned across the sky—evil, black shadows with jagged ridges of scarlet blazing from a sun struggling to rise. The raging power of a storm was on its way into their harbor and would soon fill the entire horizon. And when the sun rose . . . *it could be the most breathtaking scene she had ever painted.*

Did she have time before Ryan came today?

"Hurry," she whispered, pulling open her wardrobe. Throwing off her nightgown, she pulled on her younger brother's castoff pants and tossed his old shirt over her head. The interlaced strings in front should have been tied, but for now they would have to dangle, as they did, to her knees. Troy's old coat and scuffed boots finished the task.

She knelt down and reached partway under her bed. One tug on a cloth handle pulled her painting bag out. She reached again, rooting around blindly for the canvas-stretched boards she prepared on house-bound days. "Not a small one," she muttered, rejecting one after another. Finally she felt the weight of a larger board and dragged it out onto the oval rug. "Yes," she whispered, sliding it into the bag and rushing from the room.

As she entered the stable, her stallion whinnied a welcome. "You love a storm, don't you, Rembrandt?" Eyes bright with excitement, he tossed his head and moved restlessly inside the stall. Holding a fistful of coal black mane, Katie opened the door and led him out into the courtyard. "Easy," she said, stepping onto her mounting block. Sending a frantic glance at the changing sky, she clutched her bag tightly and threw her pants-clad leg over Rembrandt's bare back.

Moments later they were flying toward the top of Witch's Hill.

From the summit, she could see the entire sky streaked with color. How fitting that these storm clouds should explode into a crimson inferno on the most wonderful day of her life. A keepsake to show her children: *a painting of the morning Ryan came to ask for her hand in marriage.*

They would *celebrate* his note had said, he had an *announcement* to make. While her brothers wagered over the puzzle, she'd kept a smug silence. She'd known immediately what Ryan meant. When he returned from India last week, she was the one who felt his brotherly hug tighten as their eyes met and clung. She heard his hoarse whisper, "Katie," and she *certainly* was the recipient of a kiss that changed everything between them. And today, Ryan would be here to give a name to that wonderful moment.

Katie turned a full circle, finally choosing the view of the harbor. With the churning sunrise as a backdrop, she painted Rembrandt pawing the air, his muscular male power embodying the force of the storm. She worked furiously, sobbing in frustration as the sky grew from glory to glory. By the time she finished and was on her way down the hill with the captured sunrise clasped in one oil-stained hand, frenzied blasts of thunder heralded the promised storm.

Hurry . . . Ryan mustn't see her like this. A girl on the brink of a betrothal wanted to look her best. She had managed to greet his return from India last week properly dressed, with pins and ribbons to hold the thick mass of hair off her face. Her brothers had teased her mercilessly, asking who had snitched their hoyden sister and sent them a lady in return. She hated to think how her hair looked now, hanging loose to her waist, wind-tangled and paint-streaked from pushing it out of her eyes.

She didn't want to think of the outburst that would result if her grandmother caught sight of these clothes. The duchess had come to celebrate her birthday yesterday . . . *"Seventeen and still unmarried, poor girl"* . . . and, to everyone's relief, was returning to London today. Katie hadn't let her grandmother see her looking like this for years. Nor did she let the prudish duchess see her paintings, not since she'd shocked her with a scene portraying newborn kittens fighting over their mother's teats. Heavens, the old lady draped the legs of her furniture lest they seem too blatantly human.

Katie led Rembrandt to his stall, rubbed him dry, and rewarded him with a generous helping of oats. Thunder echoed against the walls of the stable and the smell of rain hitting dry cobbles filled the air. Clutching her bag in one hand and tipping her painting upside down with the other, she dashed for the house. As if waiting for her, the storm hit, drenching her to the skin in an instant. The warmth of the kitchen welcomed her as she slipped inside.

Caught . . . she knew immediately that her grandmother was in the room, for her brothers rose at her entrance, a courtesy reserved for the duchess's presence. What on earth was she doing in the kitchen—a room she was far too haughty to enter—and what the devil was she doing up so early? Although theirs was an early-rising household, the duchess stubbornly kept London hours, sleeping at least until noon.

Katie leaned her bag against the wall and went to the end of the table. "Good morning," she said, kissing her grandmother's cheek.

The duchess was not smiling.

The room quivered with unease. She looked at her brothers, but their focus was elsewhere . . . then she knew what gave the room such strong vibrations. She sent her gaze swiftly to the other end of the long, scarred table, and as always, the impact of Ryan's presence hit her like a powerful blow.

A brown-haired seafaring man with sun-squinting lines framing his eyes, Ryan had matured greatly on his last trip. Not just the size and strength of his body—for life at sea stripped the youth from a boy, toughened him, and returned him to the land muscled and older than his years—but now he carried a sense of command on those broad shoulders as if he'd been born with it.

She wanted to rush to him, to bask in his delight in seeing her . . . but something was wrong. By the time she recognized the fury in Ryan's face, his voice filled the room. "Where the hell have you been, Katie? No one knew where you were."

Why was he angry? She slid the painting onto the table while she tried to make sense of his words. As Troy picked it up to study, Katie attempted an answer. "I meant to be here when you arrived, but the sunrise was too wonderful to miss."

"It's Rembrandt," Troy said, awe and wonder in his young voice. "He's challenging the storm." Proudly, he handed it to his grandmother.

"Heaven save us, Katherine," the duchess gasped, tossing it onto the table as if it were filthy. *"What is this obscenity?"*

Shocked and hurt, Katie reached for her painting with some vague idea of rescuing it, but Johnny snatched it up and whistled aloud. "Never seen anything like this."

George leaned across the table and took it from Johnny. At first glance, he gave Katie an amazed look, then held the painting at arm's length. "Powerful," he pronounced. "Hard to believe a young girl painted this." He slid it down to Ryan.

As Ryan reached for it, the duchess exploded. "No decent female would have painted that. This is just one more example of the barbaric way she's being raised. What if someone *saw that?* She'd be ruined!"

"What's wrong with it?" Troy asked, confused as was Katie.

"Everything! Ladies do not paint barbaric pictures of raw nature, Troy. They paint *watercolors*—pretty flowers and landscapes—innocent drawings that reflect their refinement."

"Ryan," Troy called down the table, clearly determined to reverse the slur against his sister, "what do you think?"

Katie's gaze flew to Ryan's face. Indeed, what did he think?

"The duchess is right." Ryan's eyes narrowed as he examined the painting. "Society ladies paint pretty little flowered things. If one of their debutantes painted this, she would be labeled vulgar and indecent."

He turned to Katie. *"Where* did you do this?"

Wounded beyond reason, Katie began to tremble. Ryan had always loved her work, had encouraged her to paint. Had he changed so much that he cared more what London society would think? *Cold . . . she was so cold.* "From the top of Witch's Hill," she replied, moving toward the cavernous fireplace and its roaring fire.

"You went alone?" Ryan asked. "The stallion was gone when I arrived. I thought you might have sold the bad tempered brute— but I can see from *this* that you rode him out into a storm."

Nodding, she slipped off her coat and draped it over the nearest chair. Then, needing the warmth on her back, she turned to face him.

"Katie," he said tightly, "a lady doesn't—" He broke off to glare fiercely at her unlaced shirt. *Oh, blast . . . in her haste this morning, she'd completely forgotten to tie the strings of the shirt.* Quickly, she clutched the fabric to close the gap, but the damage was done.

"I was covered and I was alone," Katie said, close to tears. "And," she added, hoping he would understand, "I'd never seen a sunrise like the one this morning, I did it for—"

Katie winced as Ryan tossed the painting onto the table.

He turned to look at her two elder brothers—tall, heavily-built shipbuilders—speaking in a low, deadly voice. "You see nothing wrong with the actions of your sister? George . . . Johnny? You live in a seaport filled with sailors who expect to encounter loose women wandering the streets. If they were to spot your sister all alone, looking like a savage gypsy with her wild hair hanging to her waist—"

He broke off, clearly frustrated at their lack of response. *"Look at her!"* Ryan roared. As one, the brothers turned to look—*really look*—gawking as if they had just found weevils in their biscuits.

Johnny blinked. "I'll be damned."

Katie's fingers entwined tightly at her waist and pressed hard against a growing knot of pain. He thought her a *savage?*

Her brothers stared at Ryan. Neither of them had ever heard this tone from their friend, Ryan, whose family had tipped limitless wealth into the Alden coffers over the years. "The townspeople don't see anything wrong with her, Ryan."

"Of course they don't—your neighbors still see her as a little girl who wears her brother's castoffs. You'd be in for a hell of a shock if you dressed her up and took her to London where they *train* the girls to be helpless. The men would take one look and be falling all over themselves to protect her for fear she'd break." At their confused expressions, he explained. "Can't you see how *fragile* she's built?"

George just shook his head and looked helplessly at Johnny.

Disgusted, Ryan lifted his coat off the back of his chair. "Since no one here knows what the hell I am talking about, I will give you a warning, one you can understand, one with nice sharp teeth in it. *So listen to me very carefully."*

As one, the men gave Ryan their complete attention.

"If you don't do what I am going to tell you, I will use my family's influence with the East India company, and your business will be affected for the worse. Do you understand that?"

At the mens' shocked nods, Ryan continued. "I want absolutely no harm to come to Katie while I am gone, especially not because of your neglect. When I come home, I want to see this girl safe, untouched, and protected down to her smallest toenail . . . in fact, I'd like to see her transformed into a lady who would not dream of riding off alone in her brothers' old clothes."

He paused. "Do you understand *that?"* He slipped on his coat, watching to see both brothers give their nod of assent.

Katie gasped inwardly. *He was leaving . . . now?*

Ryan looked at her younger brother. "Are your bags in the coach?"

"Yes," Troy said eagerly.

"Make your goodbyes, then, and let's be off. I should have left an hour ago."

Troy grabbed Katie and enveloped her in a huge hug. Katie

clung to him, confused and dismayed, barely able to speak with her throat closing up, aching. . . ."Where are you going, Troy?"

"I'm going to be Ryan's cabin boy now that he's a captain." The men stood to bid Troy goodbye. As he gave them each a back-slapping hug, Katie frantically plucked the one clear thought from Troy's words.

She looked at Ryan. "You've been made captain? That was your announcement?"

He nodded. "I've got the *Elixir*."

"That's what you've been doing in London this week?"

He nodded again. "I'd forgotten how it was when my father was alive—passengers coming to look the captain over to see if they want to sail with him, dinners with the other captains' families—I thought I'd never get away."

"Well, then," she whispered, unable to bear any more, "Godspeed." Far too close to tears to risk another word, Katie picked up her painting, intending to leave.

"Katie," he said softly, "this isn't what I planned. I never dreamed I would get a ship and would have to leave so soon. I thought there would be more time."

When she didn't answer, *couldn't answer,* she could see his jaw tighten, not with anger, but with resolve. "You're angry with my threatening your brothers, Katie, but if it means sacrificing your goodwill to keep you from harm or disgrace, then so be it."

He tipped his head. "Will you at least say goodbye?" he asked, moving toward her—then stopped as she cringed.

No, not a brotherly hug . . . she could not endure it.

A stillness settled between them, not an easy one, but painful with unsaid words . . . then Ryan extended his hand. "May I have the painting, Katie?"

Dismayed that he would take it from her, she backed away toward the heat of the fireplace. As his face darkened at her movement, she realized his purpose. *He wanted to destroy it. She would not let him touch it . . . instead, she would do it herself.*

She turned and threw it into the fire.

She was glad to see the flicker of pain on his face—and glad to see the flames devour the painting. She could never look at it again without remembering how Ryan saw her. She was a wild aberration, not a candidate for marriage. As a child, she'd been amusing, but as an adult she was a disgrace.

She sent a last glance over his stunned face—and prayed she would never have to see him again. Ryan watched the painting burn for a long, anguished moment, then he turned to look at her as if asking why she had done it. She lifted her chin and glared at him.

His jaw tightened with anger. Abruptly he turned and strode from the room.

Katie's tears began to fall as her brothers tried to smooth over the awkwardness of seeing their sister cry. Darting uncomfortable glances toward her and the burning picture, they quietly discussed the day before them, avoiding the subject of Ryan entirely.

The duchess, sitting in state at the head of the table, had no such compunction. "If you had taken my advice years ago and let Katherine come and live with me, this would never have happened."

"She doesn't want to move to London," Johnny said with the weariness of a repeated argument.

George nodded. "We can handle our own problems."

The duchess persisted. "How will you do that?"

"We'll keep her home."

"Doing what?"

"Hell, how do I know?" George replied, his patience exhausted with the first try.

"Painting," mumbled Johnny.

"And a suitable husband?" When the duchess had her claws sunk into the subject, she never let go.

"She could have any man in town," Johnny said.

"The best she can hope for here is a merchant or a sea captain."

"She won't even consider them as long as Ry—" He grabbed for his glass to cover his slip. Draining the ale in two great gulps, he glanced at Katie to see if she had caught it.

Katie heard him, but loath to disturb a curious numbness spreading inside her, chose to ignore him.

Quickly, George tried filling the gap. "Ryan didn't mean to come down so hard, Katie. After spending a week with all those passengers, seeing how the other captains' wives and daughters . . . and finding you like this . . . he probably thought you wouldn't fit in."

"Not exactly that you wouldn't *fit in*," Johnny said quickly, "but you know how top-lofty those passengers are . . . how they would treat someone like you."

George broke in. "It's just that captains are treated like royalty."

"Hell, Katie," Johnny said helplessly, "you hate dressing up."

Katie ducked her head, lifting her fingers to her lips to keep from crying out. With every revealing remark, she realized that even her own family saw her as Ryan did.

"Exactly," the duchess added, eager to join the attack. "A girl living in this town—this household—only worsens her lot in life, exposes herself to danger. I told your mother as much, but she wouldn't listen, and now she's dead."

The duchess's voice deepened. "If you cared anything for Katherine, you would see to her refinement, before it is too late. Send her to London with me, and I will do it for you."

Her words fell into a thoughtful silence. Alarmed, Katie looked up to find her brothers exchanging significant glances, listening seriously to the duchess for once. *They wanted to send her away?*

"It would solve the problem with Ryan," George murmured.

Johnny agreed. "And keep her out of trouble."

"Then you will do it?" the duchess asked, excitement in her voice. "I'll take her today if you wish."

Johnny looked at Katie. "What do you think?"

"You want me to go?"

"We don't know what to do with you, Katie, and I don't think Ryan was fooling. So, will you go?"

Katie managed a silent nod, stunned by their eagerness to see her gone. If her brothers wanted to be quit of her, what else could she do?

Flushed with her success, the duchess took charge. "Go tidy

yourself, Katherine. Pack only what you require for the journey.
Your wardrobe is totally unsuitable for London."

Katie wandered away in a daze, desperate for the solitude of
her bedchamber. Sitting before her dressing table, she proceeded
to soak her tangled hair in oil to more easily scrape off hardened
bits of paint. Through the sheen of tears, she watched her reflection with distaste—the tanned skin the duchess decried and the
freckled nose that screamed *urchin*—perceiving at last the girl
Ryan saw.

What a fool she had been, racing out this morning to paint a
sunrise to give to Ryan, a scene to display fondly to her children,
so she could tell them that *this was the day your father proposed*.
How had she spun the tale to herself? He'd kissed her when he
came home last week, and from that she'd woven a betrothal . . .
and before that—during all the years of her childhood—she had
declared she would grow up and marry him, and from Ryan's
amused silence she had plaited an agreement between them.

She had loved him from the day she first saw him, when she
was six and Ryan twelve, and her brothers brought him home to
visit. Then, when his widowed father died at the helm of his
ship—and since Ryan already spent half his time running tame
in their house—it seemed only sensible to his aunts and uncles
that Ryan make the Alden home his land base. After all, they
had assured each other, since he'd followed his father's example
and gone to sea at eight, he was aboard ship more than he was
at home.

Never in all those years, especially after her own parents'
death, had Katie changed her mind about her place in Ryan's
life, and in weaving her childish dreams, she had missed the
obvious truth about herself.

She was not suitable for Ryan. Not good enough, especially
to be *Captain Ryan's* wife. Not compared to those captains'
daughters with whom he had dined. Or was there one *special*
captain's daughter, one special, *refined* captain's daughter?

More tears threatened the girl in the mirror. She hated that
reflection, hated those freckles, hated the smell of paint in her
hair. *Savage.* She wiped away those sniveling tears, those signs

of weakness. Wiped them away forever. *Grow up, you silly little fool.*

Without giving herself time to change her mind, she knelt by her bed and rooted underneath for what had been her treasures . . . ah, there it was, the box of sketches and paintings she had saved. Quickly dragging it to the hearth, she lifted each one to examine for the last time—and ruthlessly fed it to the fire.

A sketch of Ryan standing on the deck of a ship, his deep-set turquoise eyes smiling back at Katie. Other pictures followed. Ryan's teasing face as he told a tale she was too young to question; Ryan asleep on a rug under a tree. Ryan, Ryan, Ryan . . . then there were none left.

Staring into the flames, she envisioned another painting, this time of herself. Perhaps framed by the wrought-iron arch emblazoned *Alden Shipyard*—the incredibly wealthy Alden shipbuilders. Or better yet, as the granddaughter of the Duchess of Wakefield on the grounds of Wakefield Hall.

Or best of all—at Almack's, sought after, adored, admired.

And should that gorgeous, wealthy, refined Katie . . . no, *Katherine* . . . just happen to meet a certain captain in London, how fiercely he would regret having tossed her aside.

With tears almost blinding her, she gathered up her palette and her brushes and tossed them atop the funeral pyre.

Turning her back on the flames, she began to pack.

Two

Blast Ryan!

Surely he had cursed her with his words. As an experienced seaman, he knew better than to release such an irresponsible pronouncement upon her head. But, no . . . he must call her *fragile . . . helpless,* and put the idea into the very atmosphere. He must declare that men would be falling all over themselves to protect her for fear she'd break.

No sooner than he left, it began. Things were proceeding just as Ryan had predicted. Upon exiting the ducal coach, strangers rushed to help her over minuscule puddles, and upon entering coaching inns, men of all stations jumped up and offered her a warm place near the fire.

By the time they arrived at the duchess's townhouse, Katie knew she was forever cursed. "Lord love you, Miss Katherine," said the duchess's butler, "you're no bigger than a butterfly. I'll have another feather tick added to your bed at once." He turned to the housekeeper. "Will you see to it?"

The housekeeper crossed her plump arms across her bosom and took one head-shaking look at the newcomer's slim form. "Tea at once," she announced firmly. Katie could see the on-slaught of cream-filled pastries in her future.

At dinner, two footmen drew thoughtful frowns from the duchess when they silently vied over the honor of offering Katie food from their respective trays. With an impatient shooing motion, the duchess cleared the room of servants and skewered

Katie with an impatient stare. "I don't know what you're up to, Katherine, but don't think you can get away with it."

"I am doing nothing, Grandmother. It's Ryan's curse. He set it into motion, and now I'm burdened with it."

"You will explain this nonsense at once."

Katie shrugged. "Sailors call it *demons unleashed*. Once a powerful curse escapes into the universe, it follows the unfortunate soul forever."

"Ridiculous superstition!"

"Do you think I like it any better?"

The duchess sniffed, thus ending the discussion.

Even the duchess's halls were elegant, Katie thought, stepping into the corridor outside her bedroom. Oriental runners cushioned the polished floor and bowls of flowers adorned small giltwood consoles along the wall.

Katie hurried her steps to keep pace with her newly assigned maid. "Where are you taking me, Anna?" Chattering voices reverberated from a room just beyond them. "I'm not ready to meet guests."

"French magpies," Anna muttered, raising her nose in the superior manner that infected all the duchess's servants. "They are Camille's seamstresses, and they haven't stopped talking since they arrived this morning."

"What are they doing here? Who is Camille?"

Anna moved closer and lowered her voice. "They're setting up a temporary sewing room. They're here to create your wardrobe."

They stopped outside the door. "Camille is the reigning designer in London . . . he is a *man*," Anna whispered, "but he hides behind a woman's name because the English are so prudish. Her Grace said she won't have you scuttling into the back room of his shop like the rest of the ladies. She's ordered him here. He's not to leave until you are fit to be seen."

Anna opened the door and the magpie seamstresses fell silent. A fussy little man with a half-ring of black curls connecting his ears came trotting toward her. "A little dryad," he crooned, with a look of adoration spreading over his face, "a wood nymph."

"Oh, no . . ." Katie turned to escape, making it halfway through the doorway before Anna caught her arm.

"Don't leave," Anna hissed. "Her Grace is coming."

"I think he wants me with tea," Katie moaned. "Add cream and strawberries, and I'm the pastry of the day."

Anna giggled.

"There you are, Katherine." The duchess's voice bellowed down the long hall. "Why are you dawdling out here?"

Katie rushed to meet her. "Can't we go to the shops and buy my dresses, Grandmother?"

"Nonsense," she returned, propelling them back into the sewing room. "Camille," she barked at the still-quivering designer, "this is my granddaughter, Katherine Alden."

"Jacques," the designer begged, donning his manhood for the object of his worship. He waved her toward a round platform in the middle of the room, but suspicious, Katie balked and refused to move. The duchess heaved an exasperated sigh and pushed her forward. "You *stand* on it Katherine, so the girls can measure you."

That seemed not quite so alarming, so she stepped up on the box. Immediately, one girl scurried around behind and began unbuttoning Katie's dress. "Wait a minute," Katie shrieked, clutching the front, "there's a man in here."

"One wears less at a ball," Jacques assured her. "After all, you still have on your chemise and petti—" The designer staggered backward as the girl yanked Katie's dress down.

Katie closed her eyes as little yelps filled the room. Underneath the dress, Katie wore a rather tattered, full-length suit of underwear that her brother Troy had discarded.

Camille-Jacques fainted.

That night Katie considered crawling home and forgetting the entire scheme, but the thought of Ryan hearing she only lasted one day in London stiffened her spine. Nothing, she vowed, could be as important as making Ryan eat his every word, preferably choking with regret.

The next morning, wearing a hastily-purchased chemise and petticoat, Katie found herself once more standing on the round platform. Surely, she thought, the humiliating fiasco of yesterday could never be matched. Snickers followed her all over the house, and she wasn't so ignorant that she didn't know they thought her the veriest country bumpkin.

No chattering accompanied the measuring ceremony, only tut-tuts from Jacques as her measurements fell short of even her proclaimed status of *sylvan beauty.* "Don't worry," the duchess said, with her critical eyes on Katie's diminutive bosom. "The Wakefield women are late bloomers."

And gulls sing like nightingales, Katie thought, with a swift glance at her grandmother's splendid figure. They were nothing alike. Where the duchess was a tall, haughty brunette, Katie was a little blonde whom others tended to pat on the head. Where the duchess's imperious voice *commanded,* should Katie's soft tones reach the length of a dining room table, they were ignored. She and the duchess shared only one thing: the desire to transform Katie into a lady.

Which, she discovered a few moments later, would require more of a sacrifice than she truly wanted to make. "Why must I wear a corset? There is nothing to tighten up."

"Exactly," Jacques cooed as he watched his women pull on the laces, "how are you to have *hips* if the waist does not go *inward?* Of course," he mused, with one finger tapping his pursed mouth, "one might produce curves with wax . . . or padding."

"Absolutely not," Katie insisted, blushing to the roots of her hair, but Jacques was not listening. He stepped forward and began flinging lengths of fabric over Katie's shoulders, alternating one side with the other.

Katie eyed the faded pastels with distaste. "New petticoats?"

Jacques's left eyebrow snapped a surprised notch upward. "Gowns, Miss Alden. I seek to complement your coloring."

"I have no coloring of my own. I only *reflect*," she retorted, for color was something she understood very well. "Try something a shade darker. Like that," she said, waving at the leaf-green walls, "or the draperies," which were the color of the ocean.

When Jacques's outraged right eyebrow jumped up beside its twin, Katie pointed imploringly to a vase-full of luscious, deep pink roses. "That color?"

Jacques held his hands up in supplication, his eyes skewing to the duchess. "Your Grace?"

"Carry on, Camille," the duchess said, "my granddaughter is new to London and has no sense of style."

After several miserable weeks, she'd had enough of London. "Grandmother," she said one morning at breakfast, "how long is this going to take? I've had dancing lessons and memorized the use of all the dinner forks. My wardrobe takes up an entire dressing room, and I have finished the book about titles."

"Your dancing master has completed his lessons? How many dances do you know?"

"It's such a waste of time, Grandmother, truly. The silly man won't teach me anything but the waltz."

"Katherine . . ." the duchess drawled with a glint of suspicion, "whose idea was that?"

"His idea, of course. He says that I am too frail to learn the more energetic dances, that I will need my partner to *hold* me lest I faint. I told him that since I never wore my corset while dancing, he needn't worry about my passing out, but after that, he stopped the Boulanger and only wants to waltz."

While the duchess turned purple—something Katie noticed she was more prone to every day—Katie continued her list. "I have looked in your stables, Grandmother, and there are no decent riding horses. I would send for Rembrandt, but it seems a waste when I'll only be here a few more weeks."

The duchess rose from her chair. "Follow me into the parlor, Katherine." She sailed grandly from the room.

Katie stood and pushed back her chair. Two new footmen stepped forward to assist, ready to catch her should she falter. She shook her head and waved them away. "Stow the coddling, men, else the duchess will dismiss you as she did the footmen you replaced." She had warned them; it was all she could do.

In the parlor, the duchess indicated the chair Katie was to take. "What's this nonsense about going home in a few weeks?"

Katie sat gracefully without looking down at the chair, a feat that had taken an entire week to accomplish. "You don't think I can do it that soon?"

"Do what, Katherine?"

"Become a lady. Do you want me to read more books? Perhaps you should hire another dancing master so—"

"You are not going home, Katherine."

Katie thought of protesting, but something about the way the duchess looked at her—almost pityingly—made her speak with caution. "You want me to stay for the season, then?" She could manage that.

"Didn't your brothers tell you?"

The sick feeling grew, and all she could manage was a faint shake of her head. "Tell me what?"

"You're to live with me now, Katherine. We discussed it while you were packing. They gave me custody, complete legal authority over you so you couldn't go running home and ruin everything."

No . . . her brothers would not do such a thing—there must be some misunderstanding. "But, I came willingly."

The duchess's chin rose. "It's true that you came without protest, but we had already reached an agreement. You were to have come to London in any case."

She gave Katie an exasperated look. "I allowed your mother far too much freedom, and look where that led. She ran off with your father without consulting me, ruined her figure with child-bearing like the veriest commoner, and then went sailing into the ocean with your father when every fool knows how dangerous that is . . . if I had held the reins more firmly, she would be alive now, living the life she was meant to live."

She sent a fond glance toward the portrait over the fireplace, her hard features softening for a moment. "Sometimes it's hard to tell the difference between you." She glanced back at Katie in a calculating manner. "Now that I have *you* here, I won't make the same mistakes again."

Katie stood up and gripped the back of her chair so tightly that her fingertips ached. The pain supplied an edge back into reality. "I can go home to visit my brothers, can I not?" *And tell them to undo this terrible wrong.*

"Not until I am satisfied."

She took a shallow breath. "How long will that take?"

"Any sane person would have sent you here indefinitely, but your brothers would only agree to keep you here until Captain Adams's return. I am confident, however, that you will see that this is where you belong."

Katie backed away, her fingertips still on the chair. "Did you know Ryan plans to be away for four years?" When the duchess nodded without surprise, a caustic bitterness flowed through Katie, a welcome relief to the aching grief. "No one trusts me . . . I'm to be a prisoner?"

This time the duchess's composure flickered briefly, but she was made of sterner stuff than Katie. "Do not be melodramatic. These are the terms your brothers agreed upon. They are terrified that you might destroy the family business with your tendency for wildness."

Katie wasn't going to stand for it. "Then you send them a note. Have them come here and tell me that in person. Say that if they do not come—at least one of them—I will turn the town of London upside down."

Before the week was out, George arrived.

"I'll stay in London," she said earnestly. "When I have learned to be a lady, I want to leave."

"Katie," he countered, "if you come home, you'll only revert to your old ways. We'll come visiting as often as we can."

"Ryan's not going to come checking on me, George, at least not for more than a brief visit. By the time he comes home to some cozy little captain's daughter, we will no longer matter to the great Captain Adams."

George sighed and pulled a wrinkled paper from his pocket. "Here's a note he sent us before he left London. It says that should he be killed while away from England, his uncle will check on the situation and take the appropriate action against our family."

She snatched it from George's fist and read it with growing horror. "How could he do this, George? I thought he was our *friend* . . . he *lived* with us."

"True, Katie, but Ryan has never been *easy*. He's been raised to be hard. If he wasn't, he wouldn't last a day with a command."

She knew it was true: Ryan would never relent once he trained his sights on a goal. "Then send me Rembrandt. At least give me something."

He shook his head. "The duchess won't hear of it. Rembrandt is not a lady's mount. Surely," George said sadly, "you can grow up enough to do your part? After all, what girl doesn't want to wear pretty dresses and dance her nights away?"

"Katherine Alden, what are you doing?" Her grandmother's voice came from out of a fog. Katie opened her eyes only to find the duchess's scowling face above her—and the sound of titters echoing in her ears. "You fell asleep at a *ball,*" the duchess hissed, "how *could* you do such a thing?"

Katie tried to straighten up from the head-drooping slump she'd relaxed into, wincing at the stiff pain in her neck. She pulled her feet back under the chair where they belonged and realized that one leg had no feeling. She wiggled her toes and little slivers of pain began dancing all through her leg.

"What have you to say, young lady?" The duchess wanted her pound of flesh in the form of an abject apology.

"I am sorry, Grandmother, but it's well after midnight. The purpose of darkness is to sleep."

"Ridiculous country habits! If you would not rise with the

servants, you would not find this so difficult. You must change your ways, Katherine. I shall institute a new regime of your time at once."

"And so," she told the young gentlemen crowding around the long kitchen table, "you mix the ale and rum together." Setting the pewter pitcher down, she reached for the poker that lay partway into the hot coals. "Then you plunge the hot poker into the mixture and, *voilà tout*," she exulted as the familiar aroma rose with the steam, "you have dog's nose!" She poured them each a dot and waited for their approval.

"Splendid," said Peter, one of her eager swains.

"Delicious," added Edward, a more serious admirer whom the others had coaxed into coming with them.

"May I have more?" Roger pleaded. "I swear, Miss Alden, you are such a little bundle of surprises." Roger liked his food and was constantly roasted by his friends for considering the family chef over the charms of the daughters of the house.

"Here," Edward said, taking the poker from her hand, "that's too heavy for you. I'll put it back."

"Katherine Alden, what are you doing?" The duchess had tracked her down . . . once more.

"It was a hot night like this," Katie said, "and the sailors had just caulked the deck that day. On warm nights, they sleep out-side—"

"On the hard deck?" Roger asked, raising his voice to be heard over the music. "Isn't that uncomfortable?"

"You wouldn't know the difference," Peter said, waving a fan to cool Katie's face, "however, you might roll off the edge into the water."

Katie smiled, as even Roger laughed at that amusing picture.

"So, what happened, Katherine?" This from Edward who liked things kept in order. He didn't approve of them hovering in the corner while mothers waited for them to ask their daughters to dance, but he couldn't resist Katie's lure . . . **Ryan's** curse, Katie thought.

She grinned. "They awakened to find their clothes stuck fast to the pitch. And, for their negligence, the sailors had to do their morning tasks with their clothes still glued to the deck."

The duchess stepped before them. *"Katherine, have you lost your mind?"*

While the men scattered like a flock of startled birds, her grandmother clutched Katie's fan that Peter had hastily dropped into her hand. Intent on setting down the proper edict for the crime Katie had just committed, the duchess said, "From now on, you are to stay by my side at all times. Your dancing partners may return you to me after each dance."

The fan fluttered at hummingbird speed. "They will think you are *fast,* Katherine."

"That's just it, Grandmother. No matter what I do or say, they cannot see me as anything other than a helpless little doll."

"I cannot imagine why," she said, eyeing Katherine's figure, "you have outgrown everything you own twice over." It was true, for as her grandmother had promised, the Wakefield women bloomed late, but *bloom they did.*

"I can't think why you must chance losing the good opinion of your friends with such occasions as these, Katherine."

"It eases my homesickness when they beg for stories, Grandmother. They love it. Such adventure never touches their lives . . . many of them are first sons and cannot go to war, and they are bored with boxing and bear-baiting and cock fights."

"You should be flirting with gentlemen and conversing with ladies. Have you not found any girls with whom you can make friends?"

Katie thought back. "The Wainesworth twins are friendly now that I'm *on the shelf,* and Edward's sister seems to like me."

"Marcia . . . yes, she's a lovely girl. You know, Katherine, Lady Layton and I have been talking about you and Edward."

"Grandmother . . ." Katie protested, but the duchess, as always, was in no mood for suggestions.

"Edward would make a lovely husband, and he doesn't seem to mind your . . . incidents. No matter what mischief you are involved in, he still hangs on the fringes of your court."

"Grandmother, I don't want to marry Edward."

"Nonsense, Katherine. You would be perfect for each other. Other than your occasional lapse, you have accomplished wonders since coming to London. It is a confirmation of your progress that Lady Layton would consider you for Edward."

It was true, Katie thought bitterly, she had come a long way. She was the model of propriety, agreeing with all, while agreeing to nothing. No man interested her as a life partner, for they wanted her just as they saw her, and the girl they saw was no one Katie knew.

The duchess looked up as Katie's next dance partner strolled toward them. "I have accepted an invitation to Lady Layton's house party. Perhaps it might become a betrothal party as well. At least you might *try.*"

Such conciliatory words, Katie thought, when the duchess's *suggestions* were nothing more than commands. She was determined to root out every trace of Katie's former life and replace it with one of her own choosing. The battle between them was unnecessary, but no matter how Katie agreed and compromised, it was not enough for the duchess.

The alarming fact was that she had always won. When Katie resisted even slightly, the duchess's displeasure resulted in a swift display of power.

When, in the first year of Katie's life in London, she discovered Katie taking her mount out for a wild gallop in the park—even at daybreak with no one about, and even with the requisite rider trailing behind—the duchess forbade it, sold the horse, and fired the servant. When Katie declined to give up a friendship with a girl who shared Katie's sense of adventure, the poor girl's family was suddenly forbidden vouchers to Almack's.

Tighter and tighter the duchess wound her silken net. Only in compliance could Katie find relief.

As Katie went on to the dance floor, she pondered the duchess's words. She *tried* to like her life; she truly did. She danced at Almack's and loved the beauty of the waltz; she pretended all those flowery compliments were real. She read newspapers, looking for phrases, words that pleased her. She spent hours at museums, grateful for their farseeing founders and for the Prince Regent's enthusiastic support of culture. When she filled her mind with treasures of the past, and the beauty of artists' works, she could feel her spirit floating freely.

Each day, she looked for moments, conversations, small things of beauty that would feed her soul or make her laugh. But—just as when reading novels, living in the heroine's world until the last page—the return to her own existence was harder to face than before she began.

She didn't know why, but each morning she felt as if one more particle of Katie Alden had slipped away. She had the frightening feeling that one day she would look into the mirror and no one would be there.

Three

A small, dark-skinned boy sat on the woven-mat floor and tugged rhythmically on a long rope, thus powering the overhead fan and furnishing a breeze to the office of Malcolm Adams. Head cocked in confusion, the boy watched the waiting captain overheat himself with typical English foolishness. If only, the boy thought, the captain would stop pacing back and forth, he might enjoy the coolness of the room.

Ryan halted, alerted to his uncle's return as the older gentleman noisily made his way down the long hall. A genial man, Malcolm had a lively greeting for all those in his peripheral vision and a half-dozen demands of his male secretary who followed him to his office door. Shooing his assistant away, he turned his attention to Ryan.

"Don't stand," Malcolm barked as he bustled into the room. "Family, you know . . . sit down, sit down."

Ryan went right to the point. "How can you do this to me? An early return is fine with me, but not at the price of taking the Chawtons."

"Lady Chawton asked especially for you—"

"She doesn't give a damn about my sailing skills, Malcolm. She's got four marriageable daughters, and she thinks that if one of them can compromise me on the ship home, she can marry her off."

"But, my boy, they're some of the loveliest girls in the realm, and wealthy as well. Their father is an earl and he's on the East

India Company Commission. You should be marrying *up*, not down, Ryan."

"Up, meaning what, Malcolm? Rank, wealth, influence?" At seeing Malcolm's pained expression, Ryan softened his attack. "Half my time is spent catering to the wishes of ladies such as these, and I would rather be keel-hauled twice than to be harpooned for life by one of them. Do you have any idea how boring they are?"

"Ryan, as your father's son and a man who has won much respect on his own merit, your post as captain is just the beginning of a promising career with the family. Having a woman with the right pedigree is paramount."

"If I want pedigree, I'll buy a damned fox hound." He ran his hand through his hair. "I've come to know myself well enough to understand that I need a woman with fire and intelligence."

His uncle looked at him closely. "And have you met such a creature, or is this just some seaman's fantasy?"

Ryan walked to the window, gazing absently at the frenetic activity aboard the *Elixir*. "I'm not sure myself. There is someone from my past whose kiss . . . well, perhaps with the passing of time, I have made more of it than was really there, but I intend to find the truth of the matter when I return home."

Edward, his hand protectively beneath her elbow lest she fall over a tuft of grass, guided her toward the ladies painting class on the green expanse of rolled lawn. "You seem restless, Katherine. Is the sun too bright for you?"

"Not at all," Katie murmured from beneath a wide-brimmed hat Camille-Jacques had insisted upon. "There is nothing I would rather be doing." *Except, perhaps, to run screaming through the woods.*

Lady Layton had devised a marvelous week for her house party, her annual cultural extravaganza for the young guests. They were to participate in the three daily activities she had planned. In the evening, they practiced a dramatic rendition under the strict direction of a professional director. In the afternoon, they were creating a tapestry, a difficult skill being taught by a team of artists from Scotland. Katie found those two activities delightful.

The morning activity was another matter.

Again, Lady Layton's goal was to stretch the talents of the young people. Whereas ladies usually dabbled in watercolors, she had decided they must learn to work with oils. She had imported the renowned Paul Moreau, under whose tutelage amateur painters seemed to blossom. Once a year, connoisseurs flocked to his gallery to discover new artists, and to buy, investing in work that might someday increase their fortune.

Each morning Edward had urged Katie to participate, and each morning she had firmly abstained. *One more morning and it would be over.* They wove between the dozen easels propped up on the lawn, stopping now and then to admire some young lady's work. It was wonderful, but a torment all the same.

"You're doing wonders, Mr. Moreau," Edward said genially.

Moreau, a kindly gentleman who seemed to have endless patience with the amateur painters on the lawn, lowered the brush in his hand and smiled at them. "With such a lovely view, it would be difficult for the ladies to fail." He motioned to the empty chair near his own. "Your place has remained vacant all week, Miss Alden. Won't you join us?"

Katie found suddenly that she could not catch her breath. "I do not paint," she managed, looking up at the drifting clouds as if distracted, while in truth, she could not seem to inhale enough air. This was her worst *attack*, as she privately named this strange occurrence.

Moreau looked at her strangely, but unaware, Edward was adamant that she participate. "It's the last day, Katherine, just try it."

"No, truly, I cannot." Even though her fingers itched to lift brush to canvas, she could never submit herself to ridicule again.

"My mother will be hurt if you don't try." Firmly, he lowered her into the chair. *Dear heavens,* she thought as the fragrance of oils wafted toward her, *don't let me fall apart now.*

"Lord Layton," she heard Moreau say, "would you be so kind as to ask a footman to bring the ladies some lemonade? The sun is a bit warm . . ."

"Of course." Lord Layton, the perfect gentlemen, immediately left to accomplish his gallant task. Curious that Moreau would make such a request of his employer, Katie turned to look at him. Moreau had procured a bottle from a wicker basket near his feet and was busy filling an earthen cup with water.

"Take this," he murmured, "before you swoon."

Gratefully, she sipped the cool water. "How did you know?"

He dismissed his insight with a charming Gallic shrug. "Why do you not paint, when you are so obviously an artist?"

Katie studied his kind eyes. "What makes you think I am?"

"You examine the paintings, stopping at the most promising. Then you look at the sky or trees, whatever they are painting, with a calculating look that another artist recognizes."

She finished the drink and handed it back to him. The water helped her to relax. "Very astute."

He gave her a lopsided smile. "Perhaps you found yourself overcome . . . with the longing to paint?" Very smoothly, he handed her his own palette and brush. Before she could think, they were in her hands. "Give me something, Miss Alden," he said, removing the blank from her own easel and replacing it with his own partly-finished canvas. "Quickly, before your young man comes back. A cloud . . . a tree . . . anything."

As he turned away to give her privacy, she looked at his painting. A surge of blood rushed to her head, almost painful in its intensity. Moreau had begun a landscape, but not a gentle rendering. Strong, dramatic. Alive.

As if someone else were holding the palette and wielding the brush, her hands moved in the old familiar pattern. The world disappeared as she worked to complete the background—and as revenge for Moreau's trick—to mischievously place his wonderful profile in his own painting.

His hair waved naturally, thick, grey-streaked ebony. The corner of his eyes drooped a little like a tired hound, but his mouth lifted at the corners, fuller on the lower lip than the top. A little nick marred the upper lip, a common detail for a sailor, and she found herself wondering how he had acquired it.

Katie worked as one possessed, and the face seemed to draw itself. Edward returned, spoke for a moment, but she blocked him out of her mind, and he finally drifted away.

Lifting her brush from the last stroke, Katie sat transfixed by the portrait she had blended into the instructor's landscape. Moreau took the easel and brush from her fingers, waking her from her trance. As he studied her work, Katie blinked and looked up to examine her surroundings. Little had changed, save the slant of the sun. Ladies around her were drifting away while servants dismantled the outdoor studio.

"May I keep this?" Moreau asked, pleased when she nodded. "My wife will be enchanted."

She needn't ask what he thought of it. She knew it was good, as if her painting skills had grown along with her, as if she had never stopped working while she was disciplining herself to live in a world in which she could not thrive.

He handed her a clean rag from his table. When she began to clean her fingers, he took it from her and wiped her cheeks. "Tears," he said. "You've wept through the entire painting."

He waited while she composed her thoughts, *tried* to compose them, but could not seem to make sense of what had happened here. As he stood so quietly beside her, she felt a great outpouring of affection for him, as if they had been friends forever.

"Once in a lifetime," he said, as if he understood, "a teacher finds a pupil with such greatness. It is the reward of a life's work." He handed her his card. "I work from a studio in my home. Come and meet my wife and our children. We'll talk. We'll eat. My house will welcome you."

"Thank you," she said, looking beyond him toward Layton Hall where the duchess stood tapping her feet. *And should I do that, Mr. Moreau, the duchess would destroy you.* No, she would let this incident quietly fade away to nothing.

* * *

The subject of Katie's painting dominated the dinner table.

"Katherine," Edward began, "how is it that you have hidden your wonderful talent from us all this time?" Before she could answer, he shot a question at the duchess. "Was it a surprise to you as well, or did you already know of her skill, Your Grace?"

The duchess had an answer ready. "She painted in her youth, Lord Layton, but with maturity, has left it behind."

"I wish I could draw like that," Letticia Wainesworth said. "I could do sketches of my nieces' darling faces." Letticia was a kindly, plump girl with a fondness for sweets.

Rosalyn, her identical twin, had a better idea. "Perhaps Katherine would do it for us."

"Oh, please say you will, Katherine. They are coming into town next week." It was tempting. Sketches were so straightforward, and it would please her to grant such a gift to her friends.

"I shall come and watch," said Marcia, Edward's sister, fresh out of the nursery and on her way to breaking several hearts.

Katie sent a questioning glance at the duchess, and at her nod, she gave in. "If Grandmother will allow it, I should be happy to do so."

On her left, Sylvester, Lord Tippin, joined the conversation. "Where is this famous portrait you painted, Miss Alden?"

"I gave it to Mr. Moreau. He said his wife would like it."

"Too kind," he returned, meaning it in the fullest sense. "I would like to have seen your work." *And pronounce it not good enough?* As the reigning art critic, cruel words were Sylvester Tippin's weapon of choice. He did not lower himself to penning a column, but let himself be *quoted* as the expert everyone believed him to be. *Ridicule,* as Katie had learned, was far more feared in society than the sharpest sword.

Katie gave him the kindest look possible, for he was one of her disappointed suitors, and she felt uncomfortable for having refused him. "Had you seen the painting, you would have known how inadequate my skills are."

"Still," he persisted, "might we convince you to sketch some of us this evening? A fitting ending for our week's endeavors?"

Clearly, Sylvester couldn't bear to have any artist saunter into his sphere, be judged *talented* without his even seeing the work in question. Without the evidence before him, he was powerless to put his stamp on it, thus retaining his own place as the reigning authority.

"Oh, *do*," said Edward's sister, Marcia.

Katie sent another questioning glance toward her grandmother. If the duchess disapproved, Katie had no intention of stirring up trouble for her friends.

"Sketches will be fine," the duchess replied, hiding her displeasure.

The gentlemen bypassed their cheroots and port, choosing instead to join the ladies for their last evening together. Peter and Roger tucked her into a nest of *protective* pillows on a settee near the fire, and Edward produced charcoal and a sketching pad. Letticia volunteered to be first, and the rest assembled nearby.

Katie could feel herself unwinding as she worked. She found the barriers to friendship dissolving as bubbles of joy rose inside her, an almost giddy elation. She looked up once to see the duchess watching her intently and promptly schooled her face to a less cheerful expression.

Having held himself aloof from the female furor, Sylvester finally strolled over to sit beside Katie. Although she told herself that his opinion meant nothing to her, she still tensed as he leafed through the sketches.

"Very tolerable," he said, halfway through the stack. Smiles broke out among the ladies, and the gentlemen nodded as their own enthusiasms were verified by Sylvester's condescending approval.

"I shall do one of you, Sylvester."

He frowned and shook his head. He was not a handsome man, and he did not wish to appear in an unflattering light. "I never sit," he said. "I cannot remain quiet that long."

"Nonsense," Katie said, echoing her grandmother's favorite expression, "if others must suffer, so shall you." She did a caricature of him, giving him a handsome beard to hide his weak chin and a French beret for artistic style. Putting a quizzing glass in his hand, she portrayed him leaning slightly forward to examine a painting on a wall, with one brow elevated as he pondered its value. With a few clever strokes, she had given him the authority he loved and an aura of unquestionable dignity.

When she handed it to him with a grin, he lifted the sketch into the air. "Ah," sighed the ladies.

"Exceptional," Sylvester said. "You are a deviously clever girl, Katie." An odd thing to say, Katie thought, and an odd tone of voice. She looked into his eyes, surprised to see that he no longer had the awed, adoring look as before. Instead, she suspected that Ryan's hex no longer plagued Lord Tippin, but that he saw beyond that barrier.

"I shall grow a beard at once," he announced grandly, "in honor of Miss Alden's sketch."

Marcia turned to Katie. "Do you paint watercolors, Katherine?"

She shook her head. "I have never done so."

"You must take lessons," Rosalyn said. "Letticia and I took them from Moreau last year. He's a marvelous teacher."

"I shall consider it," Katie murmured, appalled at the very thought. She had no intention of even trying it. The further she stayed from painting, the less she would be disturbed. After today, she knew how a moth felt, and had no desire to get any closer to that particular flame.

Edward spoke up. "I think you might enjoy it, Katherine."

Katie bit back a cry of dismay, yet was amused by her grandmother's face. What a coil for the duchess. Should she snuff out Katie's little dip into the world of watercolors, she would earn Edward's disfavor—and Lady Layton's as well—for to the Layton family, artistic skills *made* the lady.

The duchess nodded her head. "I do not mind watercolors, Katherine." Then Katie's heart sank as the duchess's enthusiasm kindled. "Your own mother excelled in the art. I believe I shall insist."

Katie felt as if she were being swept along by some unseen

hand of destiny. The question would always be, was the hand benign . . . or something else entirely?

Two weeks later, Katie approached Moreau's home with great apprehension. Moreau's surprise and delight at seeing her—and his wife, Cherise's pleasure in meeting the author of Moreau's portrait—lifted Katie's spirits. Somehow, in that moment, her longing for home abated.

True to the purpose of her visit, Moreau introduced her to watercolors. On her third lesson, he sat down beside her. "Tell me why you confine your time to this. You have a passion that would be better served by oils. Why do you not *paint?*" She considered fending off his inquiry, but instead surprised herself by telling him the story of her life. At the end, his scowl was fierce. "This I will not allow, Miss Alden. You must contrive somehow to fulfill your destiny."

"I cannot . . ."

"Of course you can. Where is the urchin who painted the sunrise that fateful morning? Have you killed that delightful, impetuous child?" When he saw how distressed she became— actually wringing her hands without realizing it—he pushed even harder. "Can you not feel her dying inside you?"

"Yes," she whispered, relenting at last.

Four

At two bells after midnight, Ryan leaned against the rail, watching the moonlight skim along the water beside the *Elixir*. "Troy," he murmured, "do not leave me alone, not for a moment. I swear, if pirates were swarming over the rail, Lady Chawton would be culling their crew for prospective husbands."

Troy chuckled, then cocked his head with a thoughtful look. "Before going to India, I had no idea how you affected women, Ryan. I don't mean the Chawton girls, but all the rest. If they're not after a wedding ring, they're eyeing your bed for size." He looked out to sea. "What more could a man want?"

"Indeed. . . ."

A laugh, a kiss, the expression of a dreamer . . .

"I'm glad I'm too young for the nonsense of marriage."

"If they succeed in cornering me, I shall tell them how wealthy you are, and then see if they care about your age."

Troy leaned over the railing to watch the white waves fan out from the bow. "If they come after me, I'm jumping overboard."

Katie looked up as Moreau came in to check her progress. He had assigned her to his upstairs studio, with a northern light and a shelf full of supplies. The contemplation of dividing her time between watercolors and oils lent serenity to the former and indescribable joy to the latter.

The duchess was, indeed, getting her money's worth.

"Moreau, I had no idea there were so many colors of paint. What I had was nothing compared to this . . . I spent half my morning *mixing* to see what I could produce." She looked at the scene on her easel. "I'm afraid I haven't done much."

"Let me see . . ." Moreau stood behind her to study the sea view she had begun. "Continue, if you please." Katie proceeded to paint at her standard pace, which was nothing less than furious.

"Such passion," he said, chuckling. "Emotions drive, and this is good, but first the *technique*. Remember what I have taught you."

Katie fought the impulse to create spontaneously. Never had she dreamed that to learn, she must first learn to go *slowly*. The hours passed, Moreau's very breathing warning her when she erred. When her time ended, she felt as if she had climbed to the top of a mountain to pick a very small, precious flower.

"Moreau, how soon will I learn, *really* learn?" she asked as she cleaned her brushes.

He laughed softly. "The question is how long will I be the teacher and you the pupil."

The duchess stood unmoving, entranced, as a footman hung Katie's watercolors on the wall. Why, Katie wondered, had her simple work taken on such importance for the duchess, so much that she would disturb the decor of her parlor to hang a half-dozen pictures?

The duchess traced a finger along one of Katie's watercolors. "She was very talented—your mother—but when she eloped, I removed all traces of her from the house."

"Does it help to make me . . . as you wanted her to be?"

The duchess's lips trembled briefly, and Katie wondered if the old lady even realized she was not alone. "I think sometimes when I look at you, that I can hear her forgiving me."

Cherise sat sideways on the window sill, one leg swinging freely. Across the room, Moreau sorted through the stacks of

Katie's paintings, rearranging as he moved around the perimeter of the room.

Katie followed along, her head pounding from lack of sleep. "So many . . . I thought I would paint the pictures in my head . . . a few I thought . . . and then I would be free."

Moreau stilled and turned with an alertness that always amazed her. She'd been rambling, but he had caught something deeper—the thoughts that were disturbing her sleep.

Katie gripped her hands tightly at her waist. "I have become a monster, Moreau. A greedy one, I think. I look out my window in the morning . . . and it calls to me . . . a cloud, an old man sweeping the street, even staggering drunkards coming home from their revels. I can barely contain myself, and I know there is no end."

"And this dismays you?"

"Where am I going, Moreau?" she said, sweeping her hand toward the paintings. "Why am I doing this?"

He frowned, considering her impassioned question for a long, thoughtful moment. "You are an artist. Why do you question it?"

"I cannot give them away, I cannot sell them. You must admit that some of these would shock my friends, destroy my reputation. My grandmother would be hurt . . . and should Ryan find out, my brothers' business might be destroyed."

She began to pace. "I thought I would get it out of my system, but with each day, I become more addicted to creating scenes that *call* to me."

"Do you wish to go back to the empty life where I found you?"

Could she? Could she stop *looking* at things, smother the scenes in her head? She had done it before, but had almost died in that closed, windowless place.

"What shall I do? Keep painting forever because my imagination keeps filling up? Perhaps my grandmother is right, too much thinking gives a woman fever of the brain."

She looked around, laughing softly. "Moreau, imagine what

will happen when this room is so heavy with paintings that they crash through to the floor below."

"Katie," Moreau said gently, "that is not why you suffer—a simple matter of *things* and *space*—you suffer because you do not know why you must paint." He paused, looking into her eyes. "Do you?"

"Because I am driven, selfish . . . a wild savage who thinks only of herself."

"No, my dear—those are others' words, words of people who see you from outside . . . not from inside where you are." He bent down and lifted up a painting. "Why did you paint this?"

She examined it, immediately deluged with the feelings that had driven that work. "It filled my mind . . . like music, it haunted me . . . I could not leave it unborn within me."

"Chère, will you trust me if I tell you what that means?"

She looked into his kind eyes, eyes that she had recognized upon their first meeting; eyes that saw her work as she did. "Yes, I would trust you."

He took her hands in his. "Katherine, it is simple. This is a gift. A gift to you because as a child you were willing to let it into your heart, and a gift from you to others who cannot create such things themselves, but who hunger to see the world through eyes such as yours."

He tipped his head and sighed, almost sad to tell her the rest. "What makes it difficult for you is that you were free to let it grow as you wished all your life, and then you were told it must die. But the gift is full grown as you are. Indeed, you are *one with the gift."*

She struggled for words, overcome with emotion as realization came. "I cannot give it up, can I Moreau?" The truth of his words sunk in, as roots of a growing tree spiraling deeply into the ground. Peaceful, she thought, but lonely.

"Thank you," she said simply. Then after a moment, she sought a lighter theme. "However," she said with a teasing grin, "we still have the fate of your floor to worry about."

"That is what I was doing," Moreau returned, "ridding my house of this *weight."*

"Kay-tee," Cherise said, staring at the paintings beside her, "you have not signed the oils . . . ?" At Katie's horrified expression, Cherise's hands fluttered to calm her down. "Not *your* name . . . no, a *man's* name to disguise who paints this work."

At Katie's look of confusion, Cherise grinned. "For the *showing,* to *sell* them at the gallery next week . . . did you think we would only hang your watercolors?"

Katie groped for the nearest chair. "You are showing my *oils? For sale?" Oh, to see her oils on the wall of a gallery . . . to have someone approve enough to buy even one . . .*

"You see, my love?" Cherise called to her husband. "Kay-tee does not stick up her nose to money."

"More importantly, Cherise," he said, shaking his head fondly at his wife's candor, "her gift must fulfill its purpose."

Ryan and Troy waved cheerfully as the Chawton carriage rattled slowly away. Still hoping for another chance at Ryan, the four girls trailed invitations behind them, harsh noises indistinguishable from the squawking sea gulls flying overhead.

Ryan sighed in relief as the carriage rounded a corner and disappeared. "Are you anxious to be home, Troy?" The boy had matured enormously, and Ryan was looking forward to seeing the family's reaction to his size.

Troy grinned. "I can hardly wait. And you?"

"Of course," he said smoothly. "I'm looking forward to seeing everyone." *And to test the memory of that kiss.*

"I'll feel better after this business with Katie is over. I don't think they have any idea what a son of a bitch you . . . sorry, Ryan."

"You have a right to be concerned, Troy." He turned toward their own waiting coach. "Ready? We have a long trip ahead of us."

Troy's maturity fell away as their coach turned up the drive of the Alden home. Leaning out for a glimpse of the hound he'd left behind, only Ryan's rescuing hand kept him from tumbling out.

They awakened the house upon their arrival. In turn, George yelled for the cook, who roused the rest with equal fervor.

As Ryan waited for Katie to make herself presentable, he looked around the room. It seemed good to be home, he thought, taking in the comfortable furniture that was too old to be fashionable, but not old enough to be valuable. Katie's mother had papered and draped the rooms, and judging by the faint bit of color left, it hadn't been touched since. Solid mahogany stairs connected the four floors and lined the walls. The carpets were new from India, sent home by Troy.

As food and drink covered the table, the men sat down to eat. Ryan struggled to be patient, but halfway through, he lost his temper. Standing abruptly, he started toward the door. "I'm going up to get Katie. She's not going to ruin Troy's homecoming with a case of the sulks. Or," he asked, turning back to send a piercing look at them, "are you hiding something from me? Has something happened to her?"

George stopped with his fork in mid-air. "What are you talking about? Katie's not here . . . she lives in London now."

Stunned, Ryan shook his head. "What in the devil is she doing in London?"

"Hell, Ryan," Johnny said, "you're the one who said she had to become a lady. Said you'd ruin us if she didn't."

"Don't tell me you packed her off to London to stay out of trouble? When did she go, Johnny?"

"The day you left. She burned all her painting things . . ."

"Terrible stench," George reported with his mouth full.

That stopped him cold. *She burned her painting things?* "She said she would never leave home. How did you get her to go?"

"We made a deal with the duchess. Katie wasn't up in the boughs over it, but she didn't fight us either."

George frowned at the memory. "Later, when she found out she had to stay until you got back, she balked. Sent for me . . . crying . . . but, I told her she had to stay there. Near broke my own heart to do it, but after that, she dug in and made the best of it."

"All that time with that old harridan," Ryan said. "Katie must be miserable."

Johnny shrugged. "The last time we went calling, she looked pretty happy to me. The place is swarming with suitors—and not wharf-side sea dogs either—there's dukes and earls chasing after her."

Troy had been with Ryan long enough to know when the subject needed changing. "It's time for bed, lads. We'll talk about it in the morning."

"Never mind talking," Ryan said, in a voice no one questioned, "we'll go to London in the morning. I have to see what's happened to Katie, and Troy has been blathering for months about seeing the sights."

Ryan watched them go up the stairs. *Damned bumbling idiots.* How, he wondered, could Katie's brothers build ships with such excellence, keep impossible schedules, and with great cunning outbid their competitors, when they could not handle a mere slip of a girl?

Katie was going to scream if the ancient coach didn't move a little faster. The diabolical duchess had sojourned to every watering hole in the south of England, *taken the waters,* and was at last wending her leisurely way back through London.

When Katie agreed to let Moreau include her oils in his showing, she had forgotten her grandmother's annual pilgrimage to rejuvenate her health. Too contrary to go with the *ton* and limit it to one simple location, the duchess conducted her own grand tour.

Now Katie had missed the opening of Moreau's gallery, missed the triumph—or tragedy—of reviews, and in her enforced ignorance had suffered agonies as her pendulum of confidence swung back and forth.

Still, excitement filled her, made her feel *alive,* eager to see her work on the walls of a London gallery.

The following morning Katie's patience had not improved. She had managed to contain her excitement through breakfast and lunch, but now Edward was on his way to take her to Moreau's gallery.

She had invited the duchess to come view her watercolors, but that lady wanted no part of a public showing, insisting that it was *too common,* a snobbery for which Katie was extremely grateful.

"My word, Katherine, you are *pacing.* What is wrong?"

"Nothing," Katie replied, stopping before the fireplace. "A mere surfeit of energy after our long journey yesterday."

"Nonsense, Katherine——" She stopped, frowning at the sounds emanating from the hallway. Heavy footsteps, voices . . .

A footman barely managed to reach the parlor doorway ahead of the boisterous crowd behind him. "Your Grace's grandsons," he announced breathlessly as they pushed past him.

Her brothers here? She laughed with delight as George reached her first, lifted her up and twirled her around. "Katie, my girl . . . when are you going to grow up?"

George turned to greet his grandmother as Johnny reached for her. "I swear you haven't gained a pound," said Johnny, swinging her into the air. By now Katie's head was whirling with their rough nonsense.

"Hello, Katie," Troy said behind her, laughing as she turned in surprise. "D'you remember me?"

"Oh, *Troy* . . . you've grown up. And you're home *early!*" Katie threw herself at him, laughing and crying all at once.

As Troy enveloped her in a fierce hug, she heard the poor beleaguered footman announce, "Captain Ryan Adams."

She gasped. *Ryan, here?* And what had she been doing when he came in? Swinging around the room with her skirts halfway up to her knees, squealing like a child. Trembling, she composed herself, pasted on a serene expression, and turned to face him.

Ryan stepped into the room—and could only stare. By the stars, never in all his thoughts of Katie had he imagined that the fledgling beauty he'd beheld on his last trip home might be enhanced to this startling degree. The only resemblance she bore to the urchin he'd left behind was the diminutive fragility that so resembled Katie's mother.

Should she don male clothing today, no one would mistake that lush female figure for a boy's. And her hair . . . the snarled paint-flecked tangles of old now shone and tumbled in a cascade of golden curls down her back.

Her brothers had kept their promise—perhaps not as he had intended, but this Katie was everything he'd hoped to find on his return—he was more than satisfied.

Something else niggled at him, *pleased* him . . . the laughter he heard as her brothers scooped her up for a twirling hug . . . the very sound he'd been listening for these past years. And should he kiss her once more . . . would the magic still touch him, fulfill his fantasy?

He intended to find out.

Katie returned Ryan's scrutiny. Wearing his captain's uniform, he stood apart from the others, a powerful man with skin the shade of oiled teak, unfashionably long hair tied back with a leather thong, muscular legs planted firmly as if standing at the helm of a ship. And the expression on his face as he studied her—and let her study him—how did a man ever master that *stillness,* that *waiting?*

She had imagined this moment of meeting, but had forgotten one ingredient: the power Ryan's presence held over her. All those years of loving him, of thinking he was hers, returned to her now. This must be how a seaman sworn to stay on the land must feel when he smelled the ocean breeze—or how a man sworn off rum might suffer when his friends broke out the grog. Her old feelings for Ryan rekindled at the sight of him as if she were starved and suddenly presented with a feast.

She gave her weakening brain a brisk warning shake. Was she going to revert to the foolish girl who had concocted illusive daydreams, when this was the moment for which she'd given almost four years of her life? Her brothers were at risk should she fail . . . as was her own wounded pride.

The duchess stepped between them. "Good day, Captain Adams."

Ryan gave the duchess a bow, grand as any that Katie had

seen. "Forgive our manners for arriving without warning, Your Grace, but we were so anxious to see Katie."

"Indeed," the duchess returned, "that was very apparent."

"We've come for a visit," George boomed out with no finesse at all, "and to make sure Ryan's satisfied with Katie." He pounded Ryan on the back. "Did a good job, didn't we Ryan? Her hair's messed a bit, but otherwise she's neat as a pin."

Blast George! Had he no tact at all? Katie's fingers flew to her hair, tucking and pinning to restore her usually smooth coiffure.

Johnny joined in. "Never see her without her shoes these days. Rides like a lady, wears a velvet dress, and sits sideways on the horse."

Troy chimed in, grinning man-to-man. "As pretty as all those women who have been chasing you, eh, Ryan?"

George grasped Katie by the shoulders and turned her to face Ryan directly. "So what do you think, Ryan? Are you through being mad at us?"

"George," Katie protested, as a wave of heat poured into her face, "have you no manners?"

Johnny waved his approving hand at Katie. "See what we mean?"

"Well?" asked George, waiting for Ryan's response.

Heaven help them all, Katie thought with a swift glance toward the incensed duchess, she was going to kill her brothers. How could they treat her like this?

She watched Ryan's amused face, daring him to say anything derogatory about her. She could see the laughter rising up inside him—and the irresistible urge to stir her up just a bit himself. "I don't know," he mused with a grin. "I've never seen a *lady* flying in the air like that." Katie's brothers roared.

"We're all right, then," said George.

She didn't mind the laughter. If she were not the victim of her brothers' bragging, she might have laughed herself. But something else was on Ryan's mind. She knew him well enough to recognize a serious undertone, a secret agenda behind the facade he presented.

Smiling genially, he sent another glance slowly over her. "I might have to watch her for a few days to be sure." *Oh, blast . . . what did the wretch want now?*

Troy, ever the peacemaker, sensed her distress. "Well, that's all right, then. We will be here a few days . . ." He stopped and turned his youthful charm toward the duchess. "Shall we stay here with you, Grandmother?"

"Of course you must stay," the duchess replied graciously, wide-eyed with horror at the very idea, "you're family after all." *And Ryan was not,* Katie thought with relief. The duchess had no intention of including Ryan in this cozy reunion.

"There you are, Ryan," Troy said cheerfully, "I told you m'grandmother would welcome us. Stay and talk to Katie, and we'll hurry back down for tea." Before the duchess could concoct a way to graciously oust Ryan, Troy had the servants taking their bags upstairs and Katie's three brothers were pounding up behind them.

"Katherine," the duchess said, pulling the bell for Troy's anticipated tea, "I believe I shall go up and see that they are comfortable." Amazed, Katie watched the duchess rush out of the room.

Beside her, Ryan chuckled. "She's probably snatching breakables out of their rooms as we speak."

Katie couldn't help it, she laughed.

"Ah, Katie . . . I've missed you."

Careful, she thought, pulling back from the lure of that endearing expression. She must not weaken at a little kindness as if all the nights of tears and all the days of stifling misery had never happened. Deliberately, she looked away to break the spell—and to put her thoughts in order.

She had always envisioned the end of her term in London differently. Upon hearing of Ryan's return she would go home, and sometime later Ryan would drop by to check on her. She would, of course, be the perfect lady. Dressed as a lady, speaking as a lady, her manners perfect. Like all her London suitors, Ryan would fall all over himself to gain her favor, be overcome by his own curse. She would treat him graciously, as a friend of old.

Brokenhearted, he would regret losing her all his life. A lovely happy ending.

He had not conformed precisely to her plan, but that did not mean matters could not proceed in much the same way. Only the locale had changed. Indeed, she should be grateful, for like a figure in a painting, she would only be enhanced by the backdrop of London.

Shaky defenses in place, she lifted her head and faced Ryan once more. Giving him her most gracious smile, she extended her hand. "Welcome home, Ryan." As his warm fingers grasped hers, bowed over it . . . he *kissed* it.

With one simple touch, a maelstrom of sensual feelings swirled within her. Sensing her reaction, the wretch looked into her eyes—and smiled as if whatever he wanted were already his.

Five

Well, Katie thought, she was not going to be intimidated. She was Katherine Alden, granddaughter of a duchess, with a dozen suitors and the respect of the *ton*. She would *drown* him with refinement.

She withdrew her hand and smiled gently. "Sit down, Ryan. Tea will be here in a moment." As he complied, she floated to a settee situated across a table from his chair, grateful for every moment of training she had endured at her grandmother's exacting direction.

"Troy has grown so much . . . it's as if he left a boy and came back a handsome young man." A modulated tone, she thought, an innocuous subject. Perfect . . . let his little captain's daughter do better.

Ryan blinked. Blinked in surprise, Katie thought. He was no doubt expecting a giddy, childish conversation, but instead was receiving a taste of London manners. "You've blossomed in London, Katie. When George told me you had moved here, I was sure you would be miserable."

"Not at all, I find it suits me very well." Another bland reply to warn him off a subject unwelcome to her. A gentleman would retreat.

He frowned, but ploughed rudely ahead. "George said you cried and begged him to come home."

Had the man no subtlety? "Really?" She looked away as if

trying to recall an unimportant event. "I believe I was homesick for Rembrandt."

"You didn't miss your brothers?"

I was brokenhearted, distraught. They were far too eager to see me gone. "They had a business to run and were concerned about the problem you had just presented to them. They came to visit as often as they could. Then, too, my life here was so very busy."

"They were worried over my threat," he retorted in a harsh voice—then switched subjects. "They said you burned all your painting things."

Traitors . . . her blasted brothers were idiots and traitors! She shrugged charmingly. "Putting away childish things for something far more important."

He fell silent, staring at her as if he couldn't fathom the change in her. Neither of them tried to talk as servants entered and silently arranged the repast. Katie poured tea into a cup. "What will you have in your tea, Ryan?"

Ryan frowned. "Plain and strong, as you very well know, Katie." She gave him a vapid smile. He swore under his breath and reached for a sandwich.

She took a delicate sip of her own tea and left the rest alone. The last thing she needed was to drop pastry crumbs down her front while Ryan was watching.

A lady, however, never let a silence grow. "What sort of things did Troy wish to see here in London?"

Ryan shrugged. "Astley's, Gentleman Jackson, that sort of thing. I think he wants to see some poor watchman get pushed over in his kiosk—bloodthirsty little devil."

Katie tipped her cup and hurriedly sipped, lest she laugh aloud. When she was sure she could speak, she pursed her lips. "Totally inappropriate, of course. I shall speak to him."

That marked the end of Ryan's patience—a commodity always in short supply—she could feel him withdrawing as she watched. *Excellent.* Perhaps he might leave sooner if he were bored beyond bearing.

The doorman returned to the parlor. "Lord Layton."

She rose abruptly to her feet, her mind whirling. *How could she have forgotten? She was due at the gallery. The Moreaus were waiting for her.* Out of habit, she managed to glide to the door, her shaky hand outstretched for Edward's air-kissing salute. "So lovely to see you, Edward."

Edward looked from her to Ryan, clearly wondering why this unknown man was sitting so cozily in Katie's parlor. "Edward," she said, "may I present an old friend of the family . . . Captain Ryan Adams of the *Elixir.*"

Ryan stood to return Edward's bow. A heightened energy seemed to have invaded the room as the two men eyed each other. She could feel them measuring each other against some male guide only they understood. "Please be seated," she said. "My brothers are upstairs and will be down shortly. Troy has been serving on the *Elixir* and has just come home this morning."

Edward looked up at the sound of thundering footsteps. George plodded into the parlor with his brothers close behind. The duchess straggled in, a harried expression on her face. Troy spotted the meal arranged before Katie and rubbed his hands together in delicious contemplation. "Tea" he exulted, kissing the duchess's cheek. "Thank you, Grandmother." The duchess nodded, trying to mask a small pleasure at Troy's youthful affection.

The duchess headed for a chair near Katie, her face breaking into a smile upon seeing Edward. Edward arose and bowed, and after they exchanged courtesies and the duchess sat down, Edward turned to Katie. "Katherine, my dear, should we postpone our visit to the gallery?"

Thank you for that rescue. "Yes, I am afraid we must. I shall send a note to Moreau." Lifting the tea pot, she reached for a cup.

"Here," Edward said, sitting down beside Katie, "that's too heavy for you." Before she could protest, he seized the pot from her hands and proceeded to do the honors. Although this was not an unusual occurrence, Katie could have expired from embarrassment.

Ryan—as did her brothers—gaped at the sight, but spoke of

the matter at hand. "Are you missing some important event, Katie? You needn't, you know."

Edward answered for her. "An art gallery is having its annual opening. Katherine's work is being shown."

Alerted to this interesting information, her brothers slowed their eating to listen to the conversation. Edward and the duchess watched Ryan . . . and Ryan watched Katie. *Could this possibly get any worse?*

Ryan turned to Katie. "Are you painting again? George said you had given it up."

"She's taking lessons," the duchess replied. "Watercolors."

Ryan looked surprised. "Watercolors?"

"She's very good," Edward said firmly. "She does sketches and caricatures as well. Moreau is featuring her sketches at the gallery."

"My sketches?" Katie yelped. "He's showing my sketches, too?"

"Oh, my," Edward said, "they were to be a surprise, and now I've let it out."

The duchess spoke. "I have decided to attend." *The very last thing Katie wanted.* Katie carefully set her expression into an amiable mask. She'd done it a hundred times over the last few years. She would need it today, and she suspected, even more in the coming days.

"Katie's brothers and I would love to go," Ryan said, just as if the wretch was head of her family. "Shall we all go together?"

"Excellent," Edward replied, without blinking an eye.

Blast it! Why must Edward's manners be so impeccable? She didn't want these people—especially Ryan—anywhere near the gallery. She doubted her brothers would recognize her work, but Ryan had spent too many hours at her elbow while she painted, and would spot it in a minute. No matter how friendly Ryan might appear now, he would view her dramatic oils as proof that he had been betrayed and invoke the infamous threat.

This was truly a nightmare.

* * *

Chaos reigns, Katie thought as the two coaches finally arrived at the gallery. By the time her brothers met Edward, finished tea, pounded back up the stairs to change for the outing, and argued amiably over who was to go in which coach, she was practically hysterical—silently, of course. Now as they strolled into the gallery, Katie surrounded by the duchess and five males—her brothers' casual attire and enthusiasm far different than Edward's *au courant* wardrobe and suave London boredom—she felt rather like a celebrity who had collected her entourage by lottery.

The wonderfully elegant gallery exceeded her expectations. Chandeliers hung from the ceiling, and diverse paintings covered the vaulted walls. Patrons wandered slowly, murmuring together, or simply stopping to study a favorite. At the far end a crowd clustered at one corner. Such a strong, silent *life* in the room.

Katie sped her glance swiftly over the walls. *Where were her oils?*

"Kay-tee," Cherise squealed across the gallery, hurrying to meet her. Moreau smiled indulgently at his wife, following along behind. As their affection surrounded her, Katie's spirit fluttered with pleasure.

"Come meet my guests," she said, as Moreau and Cherise approached. "You know the duchess, and this is George, my eldest brother . . ."

Edward greeted Moreau with chagrin. "I let it slip about her sketches, Moreau. You might as well lead us to them first."

More squeals emanated nearby as the twins spotted Katie. "Katherine, you must see your sketches," Letticia trilled. "We gathered them back from all our friends."

Rosalyn added her bit. "Sylvester gave them a wonderful review, but what could he say since his own sketch is on the wall as well?"

Katie could feel Ryan's intent observation. What was he thinking? Had he been only teasing, or did he truly suspect she might not live up to his demands? Did he have some mental checklist as he watched her every move? Thank heavens for her friends whose chatter would surely verify that she was widely received by members of the *ton*.

Sylvester strolled into the long gallery from a side room, surrounded by a coterie of artists eager for his opinion. Edward murmured to Ryan, "Sylvester Tippin is a very knowledgeable critic of art. His opinion can break an aspiring artist, so Katherine is fortunate to have garnered his approval of her work."

Ryan, Katie noticed with amusement, seemed unimpressed.

"Katherine, my dear," Sylvester called upon seeing her, "how very naughty of you to miss your own opening." Once Sylvester gained the ascendancy of a conversation with his little scoldings, Katie always had the illogical urgency to apologize for something. Her response was always to counter with an assault of her own before she gave into that urge.

"I understand you gave my sketches a good review, Sylvester. Are you ill, or did you mean it?" Sylvester's eyes narrowed with grudging approval. Beside her, she could feel Ryan stiffen. She glanced quickly sideways to see why and found his eyes shuttered against her scrutiny. How she wished she knew his thoughts . . .

Her brothers entertained themselves as they moved slowly along the wall beside them. Should they like something, such as scantily-clad women, it got an approving nod; otherwise they doubled over in laughter, cheerfully pointing out one defect after the other. She found herself wanting to nudge Ryan, to enjoy the spectacle together. Sad, she thought, that those days were over.

As their little crowd grew and moved with them and grew again, she gave up her attempts to make them known to one another.

Moreau, who moved a little ahead to lead the way, turned a corner into an adjoining alcove. "Your sketches are just in here, Katherine."

A calming peace fell over her as she and the duchess stood before her displayed work. She had created drawings with as much character and humor as possible for her friends. Their generosity in loaning them back to surprise her—to honor her—touched her deeply.

"Clever puss," George said. Johnny nodded, too fascinated to comment. Surprised, too, Katie thought with a little thrill of pride.

"Can you sell sketches like these?" Troy asked.

Katie laughed. "I've never thought of it. These were gifts to friends." As her brothers commented on particular sketches, Katie waited for Ryan's opinion.

"Charming," Ryan murmured, almost as if distracted, as if something were lacking. "Where are your watercolors?"

Moreau answered. "Our ladies' watercolors are in the other alcove. We also have our refreshments in there . . ."

"Splendid," Troy replied eagerly. "Lead the way."

Moreau gave Katie a smile at Troy's excitement and drew the others out behind him.

Ryan's stride lengthened as they approached the spot where Moreau waited. Then, standing back from the wall, he examined her watercolors. Katie swallowed nervously as he stood so still, so *unmoved* before her work. What was wrong?

"Lovely, my dear," Edward said, "I especially like the country church. The young man looking into one window and seeing his sweetheart beyond the one opposite, so clever of you . . ."

"Thank you, Edward." Katie's mind wandered from Edward's continuing comments as she watched Ryan. True, her work was somewhat different and stronger than the other watercolors, but not in any way offensive. Yet, waves of palpable emotion emanated from Ryan; she could feel it in the small distance that separated them. Was he disgusted with her work?

What was he thinking?

Ryan examined each watercolor with intent concentration. *Where the hell was Katie in this work?* He had counted on being able to find her here. During all their years of growing up together, her art revealed her thoughts as a weather vane reported the wind's direction.

So where were the indicators here? As if she had directed someone else to paint these for her, only the craftsmanship showed through. Some cleverness, some whimsy, but *no emotion.* The sketches had more life to them, as if she were playing at the time . . . but *gently.*

Katie looked back at Ryan. He reciprocated her searching look, and sauntered forward to join her brothers near the front of the group.

"Come now," Moreau said, "we will return to the great hall to see the winners of the competition."

Katie frowned. "Competition?"

Dropping back to walk beside Katie, Cherise's expressive hands fluttered. "Prizes give the showing *flavor,* Kay-tee, as the spices in a sauce." She tossed her head and intertwined their arms. "You will see for yourself."

Katie's gaze flew in every direction as they neared the winner's wall—evidently the end where the crowd was congregated—but had not yet found her own work. As each space yielded no sign of her paintings, Katie's throat began to dry up. *It wasn't possible . . .*

Sylvester was there before them, explaining to his friends those qualities that made the winning art worth his distinctive praise—and to let them all know that he had served on the judges panel.

"The winner," he said, his dramatic voice carrying down the hall, "has shocked all of London with the power of his painting. It's almost chillingly real, and the subject often controversial—"

"I can't read the name, Lord Tippin. Who is this chap?"

"Savage . . . K. A. Savage."

She had won? The judges had chosen her work as the best in this entire gallery? Her heart soared. . . . She looked into Moreau's kind eyes, so elated, so full of pride, sharing their precious moment together. *Thank you, my friend.*

"Let's go see," George bellowed, turning his focus on Sylvester's words of praise. Prizes were something George could appreciate, perhaps add his opinion on the matter. As a cheerful, light-hearted flock, they all moved in the direction of the winner's wall.

"No . . ." Katie clutched Cherise's hand as her gaze flew to

her work featured on the wall behind Sylvester. "My family must not see this," she whispered frantically, "especially not Ryan. It will ruin *everything.*"

Cherise stopped and cast her clever glance at Katie's group moving so inexorably toward the infamous corner. "Well then," she said, closing her eyes, "we shall stop them, no?"

With a dramatic wail that echoed throughout the hall, Cherise executed a perfect opera-house swoon all the way to the floor.

Six

Leaving Troy asleep in their room, Ryan stepped out into the hall. The moment of truth—and the end of Ryan's patience—had arrived. After suffering a week under the tyranny of their sister, George and Johnny—cowards both—had decamped at midnight, leaving Ryan to submit their farewells. Troy declared he would rather face a mutinied crew than spend one more day at the mercy of this new Katherine Alden and her everlasting refinement.

Katie, the little admiral, had organized excursions all over town, leaving them exhausted at the end of each day. For Troy's sake, she took them to Astley's to see the circus and the Royal Exchange to see the vaults where the East India Company stored their pepper. George and Johnny chose Tattersalls for horses and a tour through St. Mary's of Bethlehem hospital to observe the insane. Katie leaned toward culture, and they suffered more museums and botanical gardens than a man needed in a lifetime. They attended musicales and plays and—may he never suffer through one again—the opera.

Never could he get Katie alone. Each day she seemed to gather additional strength to fend off his attempts to speak privately. The duchess, too, was determined to keep them apart. He'd laughed aloud when he'd gone upstairs their first day, for although there were several empty bedrooms, she had assigned him and Troy a room together.

What astonished Ryan was Katie's cool aplomb. An opium-eater could not have maintained such coolness under fire.

Sometimes, she seemed the very replica of the duchess with her mannerisms and tone of voice. It set his teeth on edge, made him want to shake everything she'd learned out of her and find the old Katie somewhere inside.

The first time he met her—baby teeth missing, hair uncombed, barefoot—she scolded him for stepping on her drawing. At the manly age of twelve, he found criticism highly embarrassing and demanded to know why she was covering the front steps with dirty charcoal. George and Johnny only laughed and bid him skip around her as they did. Each brother reached down and affectionately mussed her hair. When he grinned and added a snarl or two as well, she retaliated with a smear of charcoal across his polished boots. It was, of course, love at first sight.

He wasn't ready to give up yet. If she was in there, he was going to find her . . . and the time had come. He grasped the handle of her bedchamber door and turned the handle.

Katie dreamed Ryan had come back from his ship and was kissing her on the cheek. "Katie, open your eyes."

She sat up abruptly, staring at his laughing face. "Put on your riding habit and boots," he said. "I'll be in the stables."

"Are you out of your mind, Ryan? It's the middle of the night."

"Shh, you'll wake the duchess. Wear this under your habit," he said, tossing a package on her bed. "Rembrandt's waiting for you." Grinning, he left.

Rembrandt? Katie untied the string, immediately recognizing Troy's old trousers. *What on earth was Ryan up to now?* She scampered behind the dressing screen and made a swift toilette, threw her clothes on, and before she had time to change her mind, hurried to the stables.

"Here he is," Ryan said as she entered.

Katie couldn't believe it. "Oh, Rembrandt," she crooned, throwing her arms around her horse's neck.

At last, Ryan thought, *a small break in Katie's perfect demeanor.* He might learn to like the damned stallion after all. He chuckled. "I thought the hero got the hug."

She stepped back, eyeing Ryan with distrust. "The hero gets a hug, but the villain gets a black eye if he doesn't explain what he's up to."

Pleased with yet another sign of his old Katie, Ryan spread his hands in token of his innocence. "I brought you a gift—and I'm challenging you to a race." When she couldn't find a retort, he explained. "The gift is for a lady. The race is for this gallant villain," he said with a bow, "who knows he cannot lose."

"As with the downfall of most villains, your ego will be your undoing."

"Shall we discuss the stakes of this race?" he asked innocently.

Utterly confident, Katie laughed. "Since I'll be claiming the prize," she said, as Ryan tossed her up on Rembrandt's back, "I'll have the fortune you brought back from India."

He smiled as he mounted his own horse. "Agreed . . . and your penalty for losing? Shall I ask for your stallion?"

She leaned over to pat her stallion's neck. "Anything but Rembrandt."

He guided his mount closer and held out his hand. "Your word?"

She slapped her hand in his. "My solemn word." Then, with an exuberant laugh, she nudged Rembrandt into a trot. When they reached Hyde Park, the race was on.

An hour later they rode slowly back to the stables. "Where did you get that blasted horse, Ryan?"

"An Irishman I know. He raises them for racing."

She sighed. "And my penalty?"

"I want to be alone with you tonight—on my terms."

Katie gave Ryan a furious look and spurted Rembrandt to a gallop. After all the misery he'd handed her, now he had the nerve to insult her with such a demand? *Or was this the last test?*

Without effort, he kept behind her. She could still hear the steel behind his demand . . . could feel his unyielding determination in the night air. She ignored him in the stable as she rubbed Rembrandt down and Ryan did the same for his own horse. She was *never* going to speak to him again; she only wished he might give her the same consideration.

Her nerves began to unravel as he strode beside her up the stairs, and fear struck as he stopped beside her door.

"Just because I rode Rembrandt doesn't give you the right to invoke your threat on my brothers, Ryan. This ride was your idea, and this *last* trick—to test my morals—is despicable."

"You little idiot," he said furiously, "do you think I *wanted* you to fail? Hell, you succeeded beyond anyone's expectations, and the last thing I would deny is that you are a lady. All I ask tonight is an honest conversation between us . . . and we'll see where that leads."

"Still," she replied cautiously, "you cannot come into a lady's chamber. If you try to, I shall scream, and the duchess will come."

Smiling, he leaned toward her, bracing his hand on the wall above her head. "And the result of that would be . . . ?"

Furious, she fairly hissed at him. "Don't you understand? That would ruin me . . . is it worth compromising yourself as well?"

"If necessary," he said smoothly. "I'll be back in ten minutes to collect on my debt. And, Katie . . . change into a dress. I have no plans for ravishment," he drawled, watching her widening eyes, "except as a final option."

She raised her chin. "I would fight you to the death, Ryan."

His head came up . . . challenged . . . and with a look that curled her toes, he moved closer. *Close* beside her, so close she could feel the heat from his body and the scent of wool and fresh night air—and the scent of his skin. Raising his fingers to her cheek, he trailed them down the side of her neck. "Would you really, Katie?" he mused, as her breath quickened at his touch. "I wonder. . . ."

Then he proceeded to show her what he meant. His large hands cradled the sides of her head, his fingers thrust into her hair. With her secure in his grasp he leaned forward slowly, giving her plenty of time to struggle. She could feel the heat of his face, his breath on her skin, as his mouth angled over hers. With the barest hesitation, he pulled her mouth hard against his own.

Hot, his mouth was so hot, so urgent as it began to move. As if searching for something hidden, his kiss deepened and slanted. A low growl rumbled in his throat, a triumphant sound as her lips opened in surrender. She leaned into the kiss, fell limp as he tasted her lips.

"Not a fantasy," he murmured against her mouth, sinking back into the kiss once more. His mouth moved again, leaving his imprint behind as, shuddering, he pulled away from her. "Look at me, Katie."

Languidly, she opened her eyes. He studied her face for a moment, giving none of his thoughts away. He stepped back. "Go in, *now.*"

Shaking, she rushed into her room. She knew Ryan; he did not make empty threats. If she did not let him enter, he would not be above breaking down the door. She gathered what she needed and made her way to the dressing area behind a screen. As she washed and donned her most concealing dress, she knew she was in trouble.

The wound he dealt her years ago had formed a shield of sorts, protecting her feelings while giving her a place to hide when Ryan came home. Sure of her ability to hold him at bay, she'd waged a two-pronged battle against him, one to seek her revenge, to show him what he had thrown away, and the other to prevent his hurting her anymore. Their friendship was over, she had told herself, she wanted him out of her life. Over and over she'd chanted that incantation until it was as real as the air she breathed.

But the warm, powerful presence of Ryan—no matter that he stood back, watching, never intruding, never touching her—had weakened that shield this past week, made it precariously vulnerable.

And tonight, he'd come in for the kill. How brilliant was her enemy, to offer an innocent ride on Rembrandt, an innocent wager. Lulled, she had agreed—and lost. With that devastating kiss, she discovered the one thing she had hidden even from herself.

She loved him—had never stopped loving him.

She should have seen it coming.

The loneliness that she had foreseen at Moreau's had grown enormously since Ryan's arrival. Every day, she more desperately missed the old friendship they shared. Ryan had encouraged her as a child, had shown a sincere interest in her growing progress. Indeed, Ryan's interest inspired her to paint the infamous sunrise. Ryan used to say he could find her in her painting, knew what she was thinking, knew even if she were ill or sad by the rendering of that day. Ryan had been her comrade, her playmate, her confidante, and there was no one to take his place.

As that loss loomed larger with every dueling conversation between them, the more desperate she was to send him out of her life. For, as if a foolish dreamer whispered into her ear, she found herself drifting off into romantic scenarios where they loved and lived together.

Such a dream was impossible. Were she to give herself to Ryan, he would only continue where the duchess left off. The duchess's rule had constrained her into compliance—Ryan would crush her. He was no longer the twelve-year-old boy whom she amused. The captain of a ship at sea needed to be the harshest taskmaster in the world, for in that isolated kingdom, only his invincible strength kept him in command.

Far more heartbreaking would be the havoc Katie might create for Ryan. When he discovered that she still painted in secret, their love would wither as if it had never flourished at all. Or should she be found out, disgraced . . . it would surely affect his reputation, harm his career.

The seeds of their destruction would lie just below the surface, waiting only for a little moist sunlight to bring them out into the open.

Life was never going to be the dream she'd hoped for when she painted her sunrise. If she could just get past the agony of seeing Ryan every day . . . *and the finality of seeing him go* . . .

she might get used to being a vagabond of sorts, forever living a life of duplicity.

A soft knock brought her rushing to the door. He swept an assessing glance about the room and strode to the fireplace. With swift economy, he soon had a blazing fire warming the chamber. She watched silently while he stripped covers from her bed and made a cozy nest on the hearth.

He sank down easily and waited for her to join him. She hesitated, but the fire drew her. *Ryan* drew her. She was decent, after all, she thought as she drifted down beside him, *compromised,* but covered to the chin.

He looked at her. "Give me your hand, Katie." He held his hand out to rest upon his knee. She hesitated. Giving in to this simple request felt like the first step toward the unknown, a willing permission of sorts. He waited quietly, unmoving. As if of its own accord, her hand slipped into his. She didn't know until that moment that he'd been holding his breath, but his sigh gave him away. Her hand almost disappeared as his fingers folded over to secure the link. *Like a door softly closing.*

The maneuver brought their shoulders together. How many times had they sat exactly like this before a fire as they were growing up? How brilliant Ryan was at disarming her. It was almost a reenactment of how they closed each day at home.

"Where shall we begin, Katie?" he said finally. "Perhaps you'd like to get the name-calling over with to clear the air."

That brought a smile. "I hate to waste one before I need it."

"Questions, then," he said, with a returning smile. "We'll keep talking until there are no more . . . you first."

She hated to start. She had so many secrets, it seemed dangerous to even open her mouth. "Very well . . . why did you come to London with my brothers? Why are you here?"

He grinned. "After our kiss, you ask me that question?"

Blushing, she shook her head. "I want a serious answer."

Ryan gazed into the fire. "I didn't like the way we separated when I came home last time. I wanted to put things right between us, to mend the anger. Then, too," he said, "I had some unfinished business."

"To see if my brothers had kept their bargain."

"That, too," he said, "but that was not all." He looked directly into her eyes. "When I came home, we kissed. It touched me. I thought it moved you as well." Musing aloud, he reached for the poker and stirred the fire. "I wanted to spend more time with you, to see what that meant . . . where it might lead."

He had meant to court her? She had not mistaken the kiss?

He let the poker fall idle. "You know what happened next—I had time only to rush home and say goodbye, snatch Troy for cabin duty, and," he said, looking down at her, "hope for another kiss, a moment to talk. Instead—"

Instead, you found the girl you had kissed was a little gypsy who wandered the streets alone—and you knew she would never do. She pressed her fingernail hard against her thumb, praying the pain would hold her steady.

He sighed. "I didn't intend to hurt you, Katie. I had only minutes to secure your safety. The price I paid was your anger."

"I wasn't angry because you were *worried* about me, Ryan. I was angry over your opinion of us."

Instead of immediately responding, he looked into her eyes as if searching for something beyond her words.

Ryan's grip on her hand tightened. "After I left, I realized that in all fairness, if I hadn't come home to find you all dressed up that first day . . . kissed you and thought you were all grown up . . . I might not have blinked an eye over you chasing a sunrise."

He raised her hand to his mouth. Gently kissing it, he said, "I wanted to get you alone tonight to ask your forgiveness, to clear the air between us—and to ask you to marry me."

Paralyzed with shock, Katie closed her eyes as every emotion she had ever felt for Ryan did wild and bloody battle. Out of the tumbling chaos, one completely irrational thought emerged.

"Now that I wear dresses and no longer chase sunrises, I am acceptable?" She ripped her hand out of his. "Now that I am *housetrained,* you want to marry me?"

Damn, Ryan thought, why was she angry? "Katie?"

"You waited a week to ask me. I suppose you needed to see if I was the real Katie Alden?"

He laughed in relief. "So you caught on to that, did you? Well, you had me worried, but I can't tell you how glad I was to see—"

"Ryan, I'm not going to marry you." She scrambled to rise.

"No, you don't, Katie," he said, pulling her back to his side. "You're not going to throw a tantrum and separate us for another four years. Just calm down and explain what you're mad about." He pulled her close. "And after that kiss, don't pretend you don't love me."

"How dare you imprison me, Ryan?"

He pulled her chin up so he could see her face. "You love me, admit it."

Tears crept down her cheeks. Her fury seemed to have dissipated, and a great sadness taken its place. Her voice was husky, but firm. "Trust me, Ryan. I can never marry you."

He pulled her into his arms and kissed her hard. The little devil was lying, but he knew her mind was made up, that *she meant every word*. She tried to fight him, to keep her mouth stiff—but at last, she softened. . . .

He broke off as the door opened. The duchess had found them.

Seven

Swift and silent as a snake, the duchess struck. No matter that she caught them kissing, that Katie was well and truly compromised, she ordered Ryan out into the night. No servants were called. Only Troy awakened when Ryan packed his bag to leave. Indignant, Troy hauled his own empty bag out from under his bed, intending to follow Ryan. As Katie and the duchess stood in the doorway watching, Ryan murmured into Troy's ear, and nodding, Troy returned his bag to its place under the bed.

Ignoring the duchess, Ryan looked long and hard at Katie, but she said nothing. At that moment, she felt sorry for the men under his command. Finally, face shuttered, he turned and left.

The duchess recoiled at Troy's angry face. Her voice shaking with rage—and fear, Katie knew—her words fell into the silence Ryan left behind. "Katherine left that kind of life. She'll not return to it again."

"Ryan's rich," Troy said fiercely. "His family may not have titles, but they are far more important than Lord Layton . . . or you." Troy's venom drove the duchess from the room.

"She's afraid," Katie explained. "She lost our mother to a shipping family, and she doesn't want to lose me."

Troy gave her a harsh look. "So you are going to send Ryan away when you know he loves you? You've gotten as mean as *her.*" He slid into bed and pulled the covers over his head. As she turned to leave, his voice echoed out from his cave of blankets. "He'll marry someone else, and you'll be sorry."

* * *

Ryan strolled toward Katie's watercolors, mocking himself for doing so. She didn't want him. It didn't matter why. He could curse himself for bungling and losing her, but it wouldn't change the fact that she had said no.

Why was he here this morning? What was he looking for?

After a sleepless night, he knew something was terribly wrong, *missing.* How could she melt in his arms, touch his heart so deeply without loving him?

He called himself a fool, but came to the gallery just the same. He stopped before her array of watercolors, running his gaze over each one. He had always been able to find Katie in her work until now. He moved closer. Damn, he barely found them interesting. They were just like all the rest on the wall, charming little scenes designed to match the color of a chair.

He ran his gaze over the first: a small girl below a tree reaching up for her kitten. Above her on a branch, a boy with a teasing grin held it out for her to catch—all pastels, faint clouds, a charming house. On second glance, he had to admit he liked the way her pictures told a story with so little effort.

In the next, a young girl stood on a hill looking out to sea. Her hat, a floppy straw, was falling off her head, and beyond . . . *beyond were the sails of a ship, balanced up and down for coming into harbor.* How clever Katie was, for at first glance, the sails looked like clouds. How many times had he and Katie lay sprawled on Witch's Hill watching just such a scene?

But what was the story here?

He went back over it, searching line and shade, looking for the mystery. He sighed happily when he found it. In her hand— the one holding the hat in place—was a letter, hidden among the ribbons and flowers that adorned the hat. He remembered that dress . . . that hat . . . and that letter. She'd run to meet him, had been the first to arrive, brandishing the letter he'd sent almost a year before.

The little witch was a genius. His face creasing into a grin, he went back to the first painting. The story was evident . . . .

then he remembered the incident perfectly. The boy, of course, was his own devilish self, and that particular kitten had left a scratch on Katie's ear that never quite disappeared.

Grinning now, he moved to the third picture. He almost passed it by since it was a London drawing room scene. Then he stopped and studied it closer. The room was filled with people, a party of sorts. The central character—a girl surrounded by admirers—looked as content as the cat who got the cream. Only her eyes were . . . looking to the side where a rough-hewn fellow stood apart, full of longing, but knowing he would never qualify for her attention. *How dare she put his face on such a pathetic character?*

Then he began to laugh . . . and couldn't stop, no matter how absurd it was to stand alone in an empty room and roar like a man demented. Still chuckling, he moved to the next, wondering with the faintest bit of hope, if all her pictures cataloged their lives together.

They did.

As Ryan contemplated, realized what it meant, he heard a shuffling of feet at the doorway. Moreau stood there, watching him like a fond father who had caught his young son doing something very clever. "Deceiving, are they not, Captain Adams?"

"Aye, as is the artist."

"You are not offended?"

Ryan frowned. "I like them far better than the bland rendering I saw at first glance. Did she tell you the hidden stories?"

"My wife recognized the pattern before Katherine realized what she had done. She was . . . very upset. I wondered why, but never asked. I did not wish to burden her with anymore."

"Burden her with anymore? What are you trying to say, Moreau?"

"I am concerned about your Katherine Alden."

"As am I." He sensed that Moreau was a friend, but knew without asking that he would never divulge Katie's secrets, should he be privy to them. And his wife . . .

Ryan's heart began to pound as he remembered . . .

"How is your wife, Moreau?"

Moreau looked confused. "My wife?"

Ryan persisted. "She fainted last week when we came here with Katie. She . . ." He broke off. *Damn, how obtuse he had been.*

Although Moreau's wife executed her swoon with exceptional grace, Ryan should have recognized a humbug when he saw it. How many times had the Chawton girls pulled that little trick on his ship? And Katie's face as she watched her friend's dramatic gesture was . . . not alarmed . . . but too comical by half. What mischief was Katie involved in now?

Why the swoon? What had it gained Katie? All her friends had met her family, so she was not ashamed of them, indeed, she had thrown them together at every opportunity. No, the only thing changing at that moment was their venue in the gallery.

He strode out of the alcove, passed a surprised—and amused—Moreau, and headed down the length of the enormous room to where they stood when the swoon occurred. He slowed down, looking from side to side as he moved closer to the end. He could hear Moreau's footsteps a short distance behind him.

The one thing he noticed was that the walls here held only oils, so why was he looking for Katie's work? It made no sense. George said Katie had burned her things. Katie had stuck her impudent little nose in the air and claimed she'd left oils behind, gone on to more important matters.

Had she lied to him?

His mouth twisted. She'd damned well lied about not loving him, so why would she stop at other things as well? He slowed down, almost at the end. His heart sank . . . he hadn't found anything. And now he was at the winner's wall that the little rooster, Sylvester, had been crowing about. Surely, if her things were here, the critic would have known about it . . . and her friends would have been squealing their heads off.

"The winner," he murmured, looking up at the ribboned painting—and stopped. "What magnificent work," Ryan said in awe, his throat tightening with emotion. Warning himself not to rush to a conclusion, he read the small signature in the corner.

K. A. Savage.

The painting was incredible . . . and it was Katie's.

A ship endangered by a violent storm at sea, her passengers fearful for their lives. A shade of darkness here, a slash of color there, and the people came alive, movement, emotion . . . so much emotion.

Ryan could not move, could barely breathe. "Katie is your student? You taught her to paint like this?"

"No one could teach someone to paint like this, Captain Adams. I only shared a few skills she had not yet learned." He paused. "Such empathy is unusual in one so young, but Katherine is rather like a . . . a reflecting mirror. She absorbs life, then vibrates it back into her work, only more brilliantly. For some people, that reflection is too exact, too powerful, but she can do nothing less."

Ryan nodded, his eyes moist. "Katie is *luminous*. To be with her is to be more alive yourself."

"You do understand," said Moreau. "That is good."

"Has it been well received?"

Moreau chuckled. "Do you see that little card in the corner? That tells the patrons that the work is sold." Moreau waved his hand toward the other featured paintings. "As are all the rest of her work."

"There are more?" His gaze sped across the wall. Painting after exquisite painting stunned him. Ryan moved slowly, stopping at each picture, soaking up the incredible energy emanating from her work.

A couple saying goodbye at dockside. He sad to leave, but anxious to be gone, leaning toward the vitality of departure. She seeing the ship as her rival, already missing him, knowing she has already lost his interest, and might lose him forever to the dangers of the sea.

How often had Katie watched departing ships, sensed these very feelings in the woman left behind, suffered with her?

A family in the woods. One infant asleep. Parents touching, looking into each other's eyes, hoping the child will stay fast asleep so they might freely caress . . . she ripe and fertile, he virile, robust. Yearning, lust . . . another child next year.

This wonderful scene would surely shock the sensibilities of her peers, yet he felt himself longing for just such an earthy richness of life.

Horses. Rembrandt with a harem in the wild, his teeth at the neck of a chosen mare.

Ryan chuckled. No wonder she sought anonymity.

An old man sprawled in a doorway. Once strong, valiant. Threadbare clothes, buttons missing, shoes tattered. A winter dusk. Coming to steal from him are children . . . cold, hungry children whose needs are more desperate than his. His eyes watching, without hope, knowing he will let them take it all.

Silence carried him to the last painting.

Another shipboard scene. Night. A glowing phosphorescence spinning from the moon across the water to give life to the lonely man at the railing. He longing for what he cannot have, and in the shadows of the golden waves . . . the face of his love.

Ryan reached for the back of a bench nearby and lowered himself onto it as if he had aged beyond the strength to stand. He had no doubt who the man in the moonlight was. As if reaching across the ocean into his mind, Katie had captured a scene he had enacted night after regretful night on the *Elixir.* The face of his love was clearly Katie with her hair flowing free and wild.

"I will pay any price for this one, Moreau. Tell the owner that his investment has already exceeded his wildest expectations."

Moreau's kindly face looked worried. "It might not be easy."

"I will have this, Moreau. Let me know if you cannot convince them." He glanced back over the grouping. "How long has she been painting these, Moreau?"

"A few months only," he replied, moving forward to stand beside Ryan. "She fought against it . . . even now, she finds it painful."

"Painful . . . why?" Even as he asked the question, he knew the answer. *"K. A. Savage* . . . I called her a savage gypsy. So she thinks that's how I see her, that I hate her work?"

Moreau looked down. "More than that, I think."

"She wants no one to know these are hers?"

Moreau nodded. "To protect her brothers, to save the duchess shame." He shrugged. "To safeguard the lonely place she lives in from attack."

Dear Lord, had he driven her to this? "It is my fault, Moreau. I shall tell her that I approve. I'll go away so she needn't be reminded."

Moreau grasped Ryan's shoulder, his voice urgent. "And with that grand gesture, you leave her trapped between two worlds, content with neither, guilty with both." At Ryan's frown, Moreau's voice gentled. "Only you can free her, Captain Adams. The question is, will you do it?"

"The question might better be," Ryan mused, "if I have the faintest idea *how* to do it."

Moreau stood. "Come home and dine with me. We shall put our heads together—and ask my wife."

Dancing. Some other brokenhearted soul must have invented dancing, Katie thought, as she moved through the steps of the quadrille. It lifted the spirit like nothing else. A feast for the senses. Lovely dresses flowing, music vibrating life into one's blood, laughter, flirting. Lives changing with the snap of a fan, a kiss in an alcove, eyes meeting across a room.

She had worn her favorite dress, a soft pink, to cheer herself. And today, in rebellion of *something,* she had purchased a silk shawl meant for a courtesan, with every shade of bright pink possible. Lo and behold, only the duchess had been shocked.

Edward lightly touched her elbow as they left the floor. "May bring you some lemonade, Katherine?"

"That would be lovely. I shall wait for you here."

She should be returned to the duchess, but that lady was across the crowded room. Katie chose an empty chair near the wall and sat down. She watched her young gallant go, one more perfectly suitable gentleman of whom she was only *fond.*

She found watching people an excellent distraction. She liked to arrange them into a picture in her mind, expressions on a face, lines that revealed the past. She wove stories about them and was continually surprised at how often her observations told an authentic story.

She let her eyes drift along the chain of chaperons lining the walls of the room. So revealing to watch their expressions at a new piece of news, such as now when they all—like a swarm of birds changing direction on a beat of a wing—looked toward the entrance.

Then the buzz began, the sharing of exciting news of some shocking person who dared to enter Almack's. . . .

She looked down at her toes, wiggled them to see if they were still capable of voluntary movement. Across the way, a whisper began, as it often did, and seemed to be coming closer. She looked up—shocked—to see Ryan coming through the crowd like the unrelenting prow of a ship, straight toward her.

His words filled the distance between them. "Well, Katie, a fine chase you've given me, trying to catch up with you tonight." Strong fingers clasped her hand, leading her swiftly away.

"Ryan," she protested, as he pulled her into the middle of the crowded dance floor. Couples milled around, chatting, moving on and off the floor. The orchestra began a prelude for the waltz to let the patrons know what was coming next. "How did you get in here, Ryan?" She sent an examining glance over his clothes—sure it would be all wrong—finding him entirely correct with the obligatory white knee breeches, white neckcloth, and a dress coat with long tails.

"Did you think I would not come after you, Katie?"

"Ryan! I'm talking about the voucher you need to get in here—" She stumbled as the crowd ebbed closer, and Ryan, the wretch, slid his arm tightly around her waist. "Has the duchess seen you? You've got to get out of—"

"Katie . . . be quiet." He looked down at her and shook his head as if he didn't know what to do with her. "If you would just stop *thinking* and close that damned *mouth* that gets you into so much trouble, we might just get through this." She fell silent, shocked that he would speak so sharply to her. "Good,"

he said, as the music started, "don't say another word about the damned voucher."

He swung her into the waltz, his gaze never leaving hers. Predatory, she thought with a chill. As if he had her marked and purchased, and was planning his next step.

"Troy's moved onto the ship," he told her. "Says he's had enough of females to last him for a long time." Then he was silent once more as they swung around the floor. With a subtle shift of hands, he pulled her closer, tightened his hold on her waist, guided her with more control.

It made her furious that he should be so adept. "That was the move of a master, Ryan. Have you been taking lessons?"

His lips twitched. "The social life in India takes up much of a captain's life," he explained. "I could dance in my sleep."

"Have you been to Almack's before? Is this another thing you can do in your sleep?"

Laughing, he shook his head. "Someone stopped me on the stairs to check my clothes and my voucher."

"Mr. Willis," she explained. "He's very nice."

"I expected him to whip out a ruler and slap me on the hand."

"Don't be so irreverent, Ryan. If you have a voucher for Almack's, it means you are liked, that they *approve* of you."

Ryan tipped his head forward to murmur softly, "I approve of you, Katie. I'd hate to think they are more important than I."

She couldn't think of an answer to that, didn't dare tell him how she really felt. "It's elegant here, Ryan. I *love* Almack's."

He looked at the ceiling. "It's a large room for dancing, I'll grant you that. But," he said with a teasing grin, "how many slippers have you worn out on this uneven floor?"

Incensed, she scowled at him. "Who let you in here, Ryan? Did you rob someone to get a voucher?"

Pleased to have stirred her up, he swung her faster as they turned the corner of the room. "Since you will not let it alone, I will explain. Getting a voucher took the snap of a finger . . . I am in great demand, you know. You might worry about that, Katie, in case you turn me down too often. When you decide to have me, I might not be around."

She swallowed hard and looked away. How was she to endure thinking of that for the rest of her life?

"Katie," he crooned softly, "I'm only teasing." Then he paused, and she knew his next words were calculated to give her a message. "My family is very powerful in the East India Company, Katie. The people here tonight come begging to us, wanting to send their sons to India to make their fortunes. The Company is what makes England a power in the world, and outside of London, the patronesses of Almack's are simply not important at all."

His hands shifted once more to bring her closer—so smoothly, it was hard to see the movement. The music slowed and wound to a close. With a steady grip on her hand, he led her to a corner chair and sat down beside her.

Turning on an angle, he took her hands and leaned forward. "Last night we misunderstood each other, and I intend to put it right before another moment passes."

She looked around, her eyes wide. "Here at Almack's?"

"Look at me." The moment she did, she was caught, could not look away. "I did *not* spend the time last week checking to see if you meet the social standards for a captain's wife. I was trying to find the real Katie behind that damned facade you'd wrapped yourself up in. You've been so cold and distant that I didn't know who you were. Bringing Rembrandt was my last hope. If you didn't crack last night, I was going to admit that the Katie I knew was gone forever. When I saw you riding in the park, I knew we had a start. Then our kiss . . . *kisses* . . . I knew you loved me then."

He felt her stiffen, but when she did not argue, he continued. "In India, I was deluged with invitations. I could have had any woman I wanted, Katie, marriage or not. They were well dressed, well mannered, biddable, and ready to please the highest bidder. If I wanted someone *housetrained* as you so cleverly described yourself, I didn't have to come home to find her."

Ryan looked up as Edward handed Katie a glass of lemonade, then extended another glass to Ryan. "Perhaps," he said with a meaningful glance at their clasped hands, "this belongs to you."

With a respectful nod, Ryan took the glass. "It always has, Lord Layton." Edward gave them a short bow and strode silently away. Ryan caught Katie's eye. "He's a good man, Katie, but he's not for you."

She squared her shoulders and tried to pull back her hands. When he wouldn't let her, she subsided. "Ryan," she said softly, "I had no intention of marrying Edward."

"I know," he replied, smiling grimly at her start of surprise. "You didn't intend to marry anyone, did you, Katie?" Her eyes closed as if he had struck a blow. It wrung his heart, but clemency was not part of his plan.

"I am not intimidated by London society, Katie, and I won't be ruled by it. If my wife did something outrageous, she would be talked about, that much is true. But if she *needed* to do it, felt strongly about something that would offend the people here, my love would never waver."

"Why are you saying this, Ryan?"

"What I'm trying to tell you is that a little scandal here is not going to shake the world I live in." He studied her for a moment—still so tense and worried—and sighed.

"Let's talk about your painting."

Katie shuddered as a stab of fear shot through her . . . what did he know?

"I went back to the gallery today," Ryan said. "Even though you insisted, I could not believe that you didn't love me, and I was hoping to find the answer in your work. Then those devious watercolors fooled me . . . until I saw they were the story of our lives, yours and mine."

"Oh, no . . ."

Raising a brow, he gave her a reproachful look. *"K. A. Savage."* he said, as her mouth fell open in dismay. "A clever jab at me, I suppose, and well deserved. I like it, though; it's a good name to keep you buffered from the prejudices of the *ton*. But, Katie . . . how could you hide them from me? In all our years together, have I ever been ashamed of you?"

"How dare you ask that, Ryan. You called my sunrise indecent and tossed it on the table . . . you were going to destroy it, so don't tell me you were not ashamed—"

"Katie, stop it. I wanted that painting to remind me of you. It was priceless . . . when I used the word *indecent,* I was reporting what the *ton* would call it." He leaned forward. "Think back . . . I was agreeing with your grandmother, not condemning it myself."

She fell back in her chair. "I burned it."

He nodded. "It broke my heart." He pulled her hands closer, almost, Katie thought, as if he feared she might attempt to escape. "I hurt you, Katie, and I will be forever sorry to have caused you even one tear." He gave her hands a small, meaningful shake. "It's time to forgive me, Katie. It's time to give me back your friendship, to offer me your love."

Tears filled her eyes, but she managed a small nod, searching his face to see if he understood. All around them, people's eyes were fastened on their behavior, their linked hands, Katie's tears. The duchess would be so very outraged.

Katie wanted to leave but felt compelled to let Ryan lead her where he wished. As the music began again, he leaned back to watch the dancers, seemingly content, still holding her hand in the space between them. "What else, Katie?"

"Did you *like* my paintings?"

Surprised, he looked sideways at her. "I've never seen anything like them in my life. They are incredible . . . exquisite."

"We can keep them secret—"

"Katie . . ." He looked into her eyes with the greatest love and just a little amusement. "Remember when you came to London and everything seemed bigger and there were so many new things to learn? In a small town, ideas tend to flow in a small stream without much diversity. In a larger town like London, the stream is wider, the ideas more widespread. In the *world,* though, there is no end to differences.

"The English community will always see you through the vision they are used to, and signing the name *Savage* to your work is fine if you wish. But the world . . . the world will love your work."

"Ryan . . ." She tried to tell him how she felt, but her throat was closing up. It seemed so unreal, so impossibly wonderful.

"What?" he said gently. "You finally are ready to say you'll have me and now you can't *talk?*" He pulled her to her feet and put his hands on her shoulders, their foreheads almost touching.

When he saw tears fill her eyes, he leaned forward, and pressed his lips against hers, hot and sweet and very, very sensuous. Gasps filled the air around them, but he never relented until she gave him the sigh of surrender he wanted.

He leaned back to put the distance of a breath between them. "All I've ever wanted was you, Katie."

"And I you," she whispered.

He slid his arm around her waist. "Let's go brave the duchess and tell her our good news. Your brothers want you home, and we have a date with the vicar."

Scandalous

Teresa DesJardien

One

Clara Northdon glanced again across the ballroom at Almack's at her handsome, sandy-haired betrothed dancing in the
arms of another woman and decided it was beyond time that
she spoke to him. "I will not be neglected," she vowed under
her breath.

"What did you say, my dear?" Phyllis Roswell asked, inclin-
ing her head toward Clara's shoulder in an invitation for confi-
dences.

Clara transferred her gaze to the dark-haired woman who was
supposed to become her sister-in-law and who was already her
dear friend, and hesitated a moment. Perhaps it might be better
to wait to speak to Lawrence until they were in a more private
setting, away from his sister's perceptive scrutiny. Any little flaw
in the fabric of Lawrence and Clara's engagement was readily
apparent to Phyllis, who was not always loath to offer her opinion on the matter.

Clara would have murmured that it was nothing, but unfortunately the music ended and, as the dancers offered one another
bows and curtsies, Clara clearly heard Lawrence solicit a second
dance from his partner, Miss MacKenzie.

"But Lawrence has not yet danced with you!" Phyllis said
with a frown. She turned to Clara, seeking confirmation. "Has
he?"

"No," Clara mumbled, feeling a blush spread to the roots of

the tiny blonde ringlets that her maid had cleverly hot-ironed along her browline.

"Well, you must speak to him about that!" Phyllis instructed, casting her brother a dark look. "Or, if you prefer, *I* will go and—"

"No!" Clara interrupted. "I will do it." Certainly it was past time someone spoke with Lawrence about his increasing dereliction of duty toward his own fiancée, but as much as Clara admired her friend, an older sister's rebuke would hardly soothe troubled waters.

For the truth of the matter was, things had not been quite right between Clara and Lawrence for some months now—since February, in fact, when she and Lawrence's families had returned from the country to take up residence in London in anticipation of the Season. Their reunion, she thought, had been a happy, eager one, even though Clara had last seen Lawrence only a short while earlier, when he had come to visit her family's country estate for a week. But somewhere between that first call Lawrence had made upon her in London and today, a span of a mere handful of weeks, a coolness had developed in how they behaved and spoke with one another.

Clara took a step, intending to cross and put her hand on Lawrence's arm, to request a few moments' speech with him, but the object of her agitation stopped her cold by turning his back to her.

Clara gasped and was only just saved from crying out a verbal protest when she saw that he had pivoted to greet his two best friends, and that the three of them then turned to approach where Clara and Phyllis stood.

"Oh, no," Phyllis said, with a dry but tolerant tone reserved especially for the foolish friends of younger brothers. "Here is Trouble, and more trouble."

It was an old joke, and Clara could only summon the smallest of smiles to acknowledge it. "Trouble" was the nickname for Terrence Tarkington—the origin of which had never been clearly explained to Clara, but to judge by the sweet-tempered, short, plumpish man's unfortunate habit of landing incessantly into scrapes, an explanation had never seemed necessary. "More trouble" referred to his crony, Mr. Bertram Adams, who was as tall and whip-thin as Trouble Tarkington was short and rounded, and whose talkative nature would have been tedious if he did not possess a fine sense of humor.

The three men greeted each other with their usual raillery, and Clara knew that for at least a little while she had lost her chance to take Lawrence aside, for she had no desire to draw attention to her intent by interrupting the threesome's badinage. She sighed to herself and silently rehearsed what she meant to say to Lawrence: "I must point out to you that any number of times now you have failed to solicit from me the first dance. I must further point out that people expect us to go into dinner together, and yet the last few times we have met you have failed to come and find me . . ." Would Lawrence take offense? It seemed he did so rather easily these days, Clara thought as she chewed at her lip.

". . . Do me the honor?"

She looked up, belatedly realizing that the conversation had finally come around to include the ladies. Trouble Tarkington had been speaking to her. "I am sorry . . . ?" she said with a little grimace of apology.

"Wanted to know if you cared to dance," Mr. Tarkington repeated with his usual pleasant smile.

Clara glanced toward Lawrence and shook her head in seeing that he was already moving away toward Miss MacKenzie to claim his second dance with her.

"Yes, thank you, I should very much like to dance," Clara said to Mr. Tarkington, and hoped that her annoyance did not show on her face. Let Lawrence take offense! she thought grimly to herself, for she would not wait one more day, not even one more hour, before speaking to him about his poor manners, despite friends, sisters, or even the difficulty of finding a quiet corner in Almack's itself.

For now, however, she had a dance to share with Mr. Tarkington. One might suspect that the taller, more angular Mr. Adams might be the more graceful of the two friends, but the truth was that Mr. Tarkington had been born to the art, making dancing with him a pleasure. Neither was he a gentleman to demand much deep conversation as they went through the formations of the dance, so between those occasions where the pattern brought them together long enough to chat lightly, Clara was able to devote most of her attention to observing Lawrence as he danced with Miss MacKenzie. The two smiled and spoke and laughed as they passed one another, but such light flirtation was not what disturbed Clara.

Everyone knew—had known for ages—that she and Lawrence were betrothed, so Miss MacKenzie could not even hope to attract an offer from him. What disturbed Clara was that Lawrence's light flirtation used to regularly come her way as well . . . and yet it did so with noticeably less and less frequency. When of late Clara had swallowed her pride and put herself forward, playing at being the coquette, it seemed to her that Lawrence became tight-lipped and even less inclined to return her banter.

Why? Was it the change in Lawrence's status? Could that have caused the unspoken rift between them? Certainly it had changed the way many people purported themselves around him.

Lawrence Roswell had become Lord Travers some nine months ago, a second son who had unexpectedly inherited the title, estates, and plump pockets that had been his perfectly healthy older brother's—until that gentleman's untimely death from accidental drowning while sea bathing in Brighton. It was not to be wondered at, of course, that Lawrence's ascendancy had also brought with it a rise in his social reception: now he was no longer merely a second son and soldier, but a viscount. Could his elevation have caused the estrangement that seemed to grow daily between them?

She did not want to believe that. Lawrence was no parvenu. He would not dismiss her merely because his status had increased and hers had not . . . would he?

She did not miss his regimentals, even though Lawrence's handsome oval-shaped face and excellent physique had appeared to advantage in his uniform. No, she could not regret that he'd had to give up being an officer in the Army, not in this time of war with France. The lists of missing or fallen soldiers tacked up in public places and the news sheets too often filled with military obituaries were enough to make her happy that Lawrence had left his military profession behind. It was not leaving his one-time occupation that she questioned, but rather that he had instead taken up a new, grander one: that of an owner of a sizable estate, a peer.

It had been perfectly right and seemly that a second son (with a reasonable quarterly allotment supplemented by his soldier's earnings) should wed the daughter of a knight (who meant to supply a reasonable—if not grand—dowry along with his daughter's hand). But now there was an inequality in their standings. Lawrence was a viscount with land and monies . . . and Clara was yet a knight's daughter, with what now seemed a rather paltry dowry that would lend little to her betrothed's estate. The inequality was not enormous, nor unusual, and the agreement so long-standing that it was truly no cause for distress . . . surely?

She wondered . . . but, truth to tell, it was not even that Clara might resent just a little her betrothed's advancement in life (for if she were his wife, then his advancement would become her own as she was made his viscountess). But that was the rub, for what she truly wondered at, what she increasingly noted, was the time that had slipped away, the promise that had yet to be fulfilled, the marriage that had yet to take place.

And at the very least, Clara grumbled silently, *even if the betrothal stands firm, we have learned to take each other for granted.*

There was no way to argue away the truth of that fact, Clara thought with a grim little *moue*—and there danced Lawrence, cavorting with another woman as though to prove Clara's very point!

"Do you mean to visit the tables tonight?" Mr. Tarkington threw at Lawrence, as he and Miss MacKenzie were brought near by the pattern of the dance.

"No, he does not," Clara answered firmly in Lawrence's stead.

Lawrence threw her a curious glance. "It seems I do not," he said with a wry smile for Mr. Tarkington's benefit. "Can you tell me, m'dear, why I do not wish to game tonight?" he asked of Clara.

There was a kind of cautious light in the way he gazed at her, and Clara felt herself blushing as though he had censured her. However, there was no time to answer his inquiry, for the dance moved them away from one another, and Clara was glad for it. She wanted to speak with him, but she was not sure she wanted the entire world to know her intent. What they had to say was surely private—and possibly even hurtful—and she preferred that their conversation go unremarked.

Well, at least now Lawrence was aware that the wind was blowing in a new direction tonight. Was it a good thing or poor that she had lost the element of surprise? Once upon a time she would have claimed to know what Lawrence's responses would be to any number of given situations, but with the cooling in their association had come a change in his demeanor—or had it been the other way around? The important thing was that their comfort and enthusiasm for one another's company had spiraled downward with increasing rapidity. Lawrence might become cross just when everyone else was enjoying a bit of sport, or suddenly utter a taciturn remark, or even abruptly excuse himself to leave an event. Well, Clara was done with concerning herself as to how he might act should she dare to question his plans for the future—she *would* speak with him, tonight!

As she finished the dance with Mr. Tarkington, Clara pondered the course of her betrothal to Lawrence. Their families had talked of an engagement for years before Lawrence had ever asked for Clara's hand . . . how long had it been since he'd asked anyway? Good heavens, could it be going on four years already?

Of course, Clara had been only fifteen when a sixteen-year-old Lawrence had taken a first kiss from her lips and had pledged to marry her. It had been wildly romantic at the time, even though (or perhaps because) both had known it would be years before their parents saw fit to allow an actual marriage to go forth. It had been two more years before Mama had conceded Clara was to leave the schoolroom and make her debut in Society.

There had been no hurry to marry then, of course—not with a whole season of gaiety ahead of them. Then Lawrence's father had died and that had required six months of mourning, and then his beloved brother had perished, and the black weeds had been donned once more. . . .

Now here Clara was, only two months away from turning twenty, still unmarried, still pledged to Lawrence . . . and still left to wait on the sidelines as that jackanapes danced with a succession of other women!

Five minutes later, when the music had come to an end, Clara cringed, certain everyone must hear Lawrence's jovial laughter as he left the floor with Miss MacKenzie on his arm. A glimpse at Phyllis, who was also exiting the dance floor with her partner, proved that even she appeared bothered by Lawrence's seemingly deliberate inattention to his own fiancée. It was quite enough.

Clara reached down to lift the front edge of her skirts just enough to give her ease of movement, and proceeded across the floor with a haste she would normally not exercise at such an august gathering. Their conversation would not be put off one minute longer!

"Lawrence!" she called, as she approached his side.

"Lawrence!" came another female voice, and Clara turned to see with a resigned sigh that Phyllis had followed in her wake. Well, Clara meant to speak to Lawrence alone, and she would frankly tell Phyllis so, if it came to that.

"Yes?" Lawrence turned from Miss MacKenzie to Clara with still a slight smile to the set of his mouth. It was such a nice mouth, too, Clara thought, as she felt her displeasure grow instead of dissipate under Lawrence's too-belated attention. She took a deep breath, reminding herself that he could be such a dear man, very thoughtful and considerate . . . that is, she reminded herself, when she managed to capture his attention!

"How do you do tonight, Miss Northdon?" Miss MacKenzie asked.

Clara clamped down her impatience and returned Miss MacKenzie's nod and small curtsy. "Fine, thank you," she answered, aware of the distraction in her voice even as she answered Miss MacKenzie's additional inquiry as to her health. "And you, Miss MacKenzie?" she forced herself to ask politely.

"Very well, thank you."

The pleasantries went on a bit longer, with inquiries after one another's family members, but finally there came a polite pause, and Clara was more than ready to fill it.

"Lawrence, will you stroll with me—" Clara started to suggest, but she never got to say 'to a quiet space,' for at that moment Trouble Tarkington and Bertie Adams swept down upon their small party.

The greetings had all to be exchanged once more, and Clara could not keep from shifting her weight impatiently from one foot to the other. She wished their little talk was already done and behind her. If she thought about what she meant to say too much, she might find reasons to delay for another day or two. She meant to ask Lawrence to set a date for their wedding. After all, she was nearly *twenty* already—most of her girlfriends had been married two years past!

But what of love? whispered a small voice in her head, which made her frown. Once upon a time, Clara had been absolutely certain that she loved Lawrence and that he loved her, too. But now . . . ? Could it be that whatever charms she possessed no longer captured Lawrence's regard? Well, Clara thought sadly, if that were the case, the sooner she knew it the better—for both of them.

"My, but you are a cross-patch tonight!" said the very tall Mr. Adams down at Clara.

All eyes turned to gaze at her, and Clara felt yet another blush creep up her face. "I am not!" she said, with a petulance that only proved his point.

The irony must have struck Mr. Adams, for he turned to Phyllis to say in amusement, "You did not tell her of the wagers being laid down, did you?"

Now it was Phyllis's turn to blush, and an annoyed light sprang into her eyes. "Wagers!" she scoffed, moving to stand next to Clara, taking up her friend's arm to twine her own with it in a show of alliance. "I think any man foolish to wager on such a thing, for Lawrence is sure to marry first. The other two of you do not even stand betrothed!"

Clara had heard for weeks of the various wagers concerning Lawrence, Mr. Adams, and Mr. Tarkington. The three of them were the closest of bosom beaux and had long since carried the title of *"Un Fredon"*: "three of a kind." The Bachelors Three, yet another wag had dubbed them.

It had only been a matter of time after such a label was placed on them that a series of wagers should be entered in the betting books to be found in various gentlemen's clubs. The wagers consisted of particulars as to which of the three would be the first to marry, and when, and to whom—any marriage thereby, of course, breaking up the *Un Fredon* alliance of bachelors.

"Certainly I have heard of the wager," Clara said to Mr. Adams, not quite able to keep a note of asperity from her voice. "But, as Phyllis notes, I cannot imagine why anyone should care to lay a wager on a matter that is clearly all but settled. Unless, that is, Mr. Adams, you guard a secret from us? Is there soon to be news of a Mrs. Adams?"

"No! No indeed," Bertie cried, laughing. "I've no plans to thrust my head into parson's mousetrap, and if Lawrence tells you otherwise, he's a liar! Now on the other hand, Trouble here would just as soon be married."

"Me? I dare not!" Mr. Tarkington cried, his eyes wide.

"Indeed not," Phyllis agreed. "For it is generally believed that once one is married, it is time to cease falling in love with every girl one meets."

"Exactly my dilemma, Miss Roswell," Trouble agreed wholeheartedly. He cast her a sideward glance. "And, er, Miss Roswell, might you have a dance free that I might secure?"

Phyllis laughed. "Now, Mr. Tarkington, you simply must not think to flirt with *me!* I am betrothed this past sixmonth to Sir Godwin, as you well know."

"Can't harm a thing to try," Mr. Tarkington said with a cherubic smile.

As Phyllis laughed and nodded her agreement that Mr. Tarkington could have the next waltz, Clara turned back to Lawrence . . . only to feel her gaze narrow once more as she saw that Lady Esther Berridge, only daughter of the Earl of Cotwarring, approached Lawrence's side, her hand reaching to touch his arm in a familiar fashion.

"Lord Travers, how lovely to see you here tonight," Lady Esther greeted him. She had a pleasant face, but her real glory was the mass of dark black curling tresses that, Clara knew with a spark of envy, had no need of nightly curling papers or hot-irons.

"And to see you as well, Lady Esther," Lawrence returned. "How do you find the company tonight?" he inquired, a common enough question, but Clara felt a sting that he did not turn at once to include her in the conversation.

"Thin, I should say, Lord Travers. There is scarce a man here tonight worth dancing with. Yourself excepted, of course," Lady Esther said, and Clara felt herself stiffen at the note of coy invitation the comment included.

"Yes, well, I," Lawrence hemmed, obviously having heard it as well. "I should be honored if you were to grant me the next dance," he finished, and Clara hoped it was not just wishful thinking on her part that he sounded less than enthusiastic. But perhaps she was mistaken after all, for Lawrence took Lady Esther's hand on his arm to escort her to the dance floor, with nary an excuse nor even a glance in Clara's direction.

Despite the fact that Clara shared the dance herself with Mr. Adams, by its end her disgruntlement had turned into something darker and less capable of being tamed.

All equanimity fled once she glanced to find that Lawrence shared his smile with the cloying and vexatious Lady Esther—

who, everyone knew, stood on the very precipice of being refused admittance to Almack's.

Lady Esther's entire family was a gathering of eccentrics—
wealthy, yes, but also undeniably peculiar. The earl was wont
to loudly sing out song lyrics, should anyone be so foolish as
to utter a pairing of words that inspired him; Lady Cotwarring
only ever spoke in a whisper—perhaps in a vain hope of avoiding inspiring her husband's habit; the girl's brothers were forever
offering to meet others in a duel for imagined wrongs; and
everyone knew that the arguably fetching black-haired Lady
Esther herself was far, far too desperately interested in being
married. Two betrothals had ended in dissolution, and although
it was publicly said that Lady Esther had requested the betrothals be ended, it was far and wide believed that the two gentlemen
in question had cried off, no matter the harm to their honor.

Clara could have forgiven Lawrence for dancing with the
chit—indeed it was very Christian of him to give the poor girl
a dance—if only he had not spent the entire time smiling and
laughing with her. Then he lingered at Lady Esther's side, chatting amiably with both the girl and her brother, Sir Randall
Berridge, whom everyone knew to be a boor.

"So you come back to me," Clara said in a tight voice when
Lawrence at last crossed Almack's ballroom to her side.

"Eh?" he said, blinking in the manner of a man caught in
surprise.

She did not deign to explain the obvious. "Will you ask me
then?" Clara demanded without preamble.

"To dance with you?" Lawrence asked, still obviously puzzled.

"Of course! But, too . . . What I mean is—!" Clara cried,
her tone and temper rising. She *had* meant a dance, but she
suddenly decided she was done with waiting, done with subtlety, done with trying to maneuver Lawrence into a quiet corner. He could set a firm date for their marriage, now, here,
regardless of the fact that they stood near the center of the room.

"Clara, you are not making the slightest bit of sense,"
Lawrence told her, as he reached out to snag a glass of wine

from the tray of a passing servant. "One for you?" he asked her over his shoulder.

"No!"

Lawrence lifted a hand, to dismiss the servant and seemingly also to signal a lack of willingness to fight with Clara. "My dear girl, if you are ready to leave, you have but to say so, and I will call for the carriage."

"No," Clara repeated, and then she remembered Lady Esther's touch, and she decided to put her hand on Lawrence's arm as that hoyden had done. "Lawrence," she said, struggling for composure, "I really think we need to talk about the date."

"The date? Oh yes, the boating! Well, I meant to talk to you about that. You see, my cousin Alfred has broken his wrist, and so will not be in the competition, so I do not think I care to go—"

"No, Lawrence! I mean our wedding! We really must talk about our wedding." There, she had said it!

"Oh," Lawrence said, looking momentarily nonplussed. "Are we not marrying in the summer?"

"This summer?" Clara asked, for it was already May. "I could not possibly—"

Lawrence's face went suddenly blank. "I see. The following summer, then."

"No, Lawrence," Clara said on a deep sigh. Her stomach roiled as she pondered if next summer would arrive and he would again be saying 'next summer.'

"I see," he repeated, his entire body going stiff. Was it her imagination, or did he go white around the mouth, almost as if he were sick . . . or angry?

"Well, I cannot say I did not see this coming. You have ever been reluctant to set a date. I understand perfectly that you mean to cry off."

Clara stared. "I—! *You* would not speak of it."

"Of course I would not! A man cannot just up and cry off. Not the honorable thing at all!"

Clara gave an audible gasp—Lawrence had been wishing

their betrothal ended? No! For how long? Oh no, this could not be!

"I have suspected for a long time that your . . . our affections toward one another have cooled and . . . and become something less than one might desire in a spouse. I . . ." He floundered for a moment, and a dark expression crossed his features, although Clara could not have said whether it was caused by pride or regret, even though both emotions warred furiously within her own breast as she listened to his awful words.

He cleared his throat. "I shall offer no impediment to this dissolution." He physically shook himself. "That being said, I will go and see to the carriage, for I hope I am right in saying that neither of us can wish to linger here. Not now." He gave a terrible scowl, and then abruptly sketched her a quick bow before charging away from her side.

Clara looked up, dismayed to find that Trouble Tarkington, Bertie Adams, and Phyllis stood in a shocked semi-circle of stares, with an alarm on their faces that revealed they had overheard everything.

Worst of all, however, was to see that Lady Esther also stood at hand, with a smug smile tilting up the corners of her mouth.

Two

Lawrence waited in the dim light of evening outside Almack's front entrance, using the excuse of needing to call for his carriage as a way to avoid the crowd within. He would dispatch Clara home, with Phyllis to take his place in the coach. He'd ask Trouble to take him home, for then he could avoid sitting across from Clara—he could know the relief of being free of her society.

That was the difficulty, however: he would not really be relieved at all.

Lawrence lifted a cheroot to his lips, having lighted it from the lantern of a footman, but Lawrence was not really interested in smoking. Instead he let the hand holding the glowing tip settle to his side, not sure if the few puffs he had taken from the tobacco had provided even the smallest iota of the comfort and distraction he had sought. He was not really one for smoking, but he had thought it might occupy his hands and give him an excuse for remaining on the street. The truth was, he was too agitated to return inside to the assembly rooms at once, and even when he did, it would only be to collect Trouble, that they might leave. He could not stay, not following that long-dreaded scene with Clara.

He'd known a change in their attachment was taking shape; the encounter he'd been fearing had turned out just as he had imagined. It had been impossible to miss that he and Clara were spending less time in one another's company, that Clara moved through the parties, balls, and routs that made up their days with a gaiety that seemed not to include any urgency, indeed not even the smallest beginning of any plans to wed, despite their freedom from mourning. Her attentions had been light and easy with everyone—just as they were with himself. Light and easy and . . . *unattached,* that was the word.

And now she had cried off! Clara, his best friend, his childhood confidante . . . his love.

He did love her, he knew that. How could he not know it, when each day since he had returned to town in late February had thrust one more heartsick wound into his chest? The sight of Clara dancing in the arms of the biggest rogue in London had alarmed him. Seeing her three nights later laughing and chatting with a handsome major had made him jealous. Indeed, seeing her exchanges with any male under the age of sixty made him long to be the one at her side, the one to make her smile.

Where once they had chatted easily as they had driven through the park or promenaded through an evening's entertainment, the past two months had seen a strange formality grow between them, a reserve that had never existed before. Clara had never said a cross or disheartening word, but there had been some growing impediment between them, something he perhaps should have examined more deeply long before now.

Too late! he thought, his heart in his boots. Clara had cried off from marrying him, and Lawrence had no inkling of why. He ought to have let Clara speak, to say her piece, but the diffidence in her voice, the rigidity of her posture had warned him that bad news was to be delivered, and he had said the words before she could. He had thought they might hurt less that way . . . but he had been wrong.

Perhaps he would walk home, despite the cloud cover that hid the moon's light, for it was a brief enough stroll from King Street to the residence he shared with his sister in Panton Street. Perhaps the exercise would clear his head, let him see more clearly a way to undo the life-altering damage that had somehow occurred this night. After all, not many of the company attending Almack's tonight could have overheard their interplay, just

Trouble, and Bertie, Phyllis, too . . . and Lady Esther, unfortunately. Lawrence moaned, to think how Lady Esther was wont to spread whatever rumor she knew, or even thought she knew.

As if his thoughts had summoned her, Lady Esther's too-familiar trilling call of "Lord Travers!" broke whatever serenity the evening might yet have possessed.

"Lady Esther," he mouthed in greeting as she approached. He hoped she would catch the coolness in his tone, and so choose not to linger at his side.

It was a vain hope, however, as well he might have known. Lady Esther would never let something so minor as someone else's discomfiture or depth of feeling halt her actions, even should she by some miracle happen to be sensible of them.

"I have need of your assistance," she said, and even in the poor light Lawrence could see there was a glitter in her eyes. There was something about her expression, too, that made him feel oddly disconcerted.

"Assistance?" Lawrence repeated.

Lady Esther glanced quickly at the footman, who moved past them, probably having been informed by the Majordomo that another carriage was needed. "Oh, yes," she said, "assistance of a very important nature. You know I have not been made any offers—well, in truth, I have. But only from fortune-hunters and horrid old lecherous men."

Lawrence frowned, struggling to hide the shock he felt at her blunt and unexpected words.

"I will not have them, I tell you!" Lady Esther said, adding a stamp of her foot for emphasis. "And since Papa insists I must marry, and soon, I wish to marry someone comely, someone upon whose arm I should look to advantage. Someone who is still well regarded within Society."

"As I am sure you will," Lawrence said, even as he took a step toward the doorway, in preparation of escaping the girl's nonsensical prattle. What was the point of her assertions? Did she think he would offer for her simply because she wished that someone would? Did she think her seemingly imminent dismissal from the hallowed halls of Almack's could be forestalled by marriage into a less eccentric family?

Lady Esther eyed him up and down, and Lawrence had the distinct impression that he might as well be a piece of horseflesh for auction at Tattersall's. His discomfiture grew.

"Do please pardon me—" he began to say.

"I do *not* pardon you. Remain exactly where you are," Lady Esther said firmly, in the way one might speak to a recalcitrant child or misbehaving pet. "Lord Travers, as you are a gentleman, I am sure I may count on you to remember that fact."

Lawrence frowned, utterly perplexed at the lady's meaning. He tried to form another excuse, but there was again no opportunity to murmur it. He could only stare as Lady Esther thrust her hands into her hair, setting her coiffure and ribbons all askew, and as she then grabbed the bodice of her dress with both hands, and with a most deliberate tug twisted the gown to one side.

"Lady Esther—!" he started to protest. He did not finish, except to give a grunt of surprise, for she crossed the space between them in a flash, casting herself firmly against his chest, her arms snaking up to wrap around his neck.

"I will make you a very good wife," she whispered near his ear.

He tried to thrust her off, but the girl had a strength belied by her slender size, and she clung to him as a limpet clings to a rock. He could not pry one of her hands loose but then she reached to grab him anew on a different part of his coat.

"Oh, sir! Unhand me! You veritable beast! How dare you?" Lady Esther shouted, her tone now filled with distress, even though her expression, so near Lawrence's face, remained perfectly calm. "I am sorry," she lowered her voice to say privately to him, "but I truly am in need of a husband." Aloud she shouted, "Oh sir! I feel I shall faint!" Suiting her actions to her words, she leaned against him, her body limp, as if she would collapse indeed.

Lawrence stumbled back, fighting to keep his balance, but

the contest was lost, and he fell to the pavement before the arched doorway of Almack's, Esther sprawled atop him.

"I will not have it!" he told her from between gritted teeth, knowing full well, if belatedly, the lady's game—she was not the first to think to entrap a husband by executing a public display. The silly chit had not even the sense to do it up proper, for there was no one of consequence to see them, their audience being but two gaping costermongers making their way up the street and a coachman waiting with his horses at the opposite corner.

Lawrence put his hands on Lady Esther's shoulder and pushed, taking advantage of the fact that she had lost her grip on his coat. Half freed from her length, he rolled to one side, and sprang to his feet, spinning to face her. The reprimand on his lips died however, as they both stared down at the profusion of velvet ribbons that had previously laid tied in elaborate bows just below her bosom, but were now at her side where she had twisted the fabric. Even as they both stared with unblinking eyes, several of the ribbons' edges turned a powdery gray, and small puffs of smoke rose to frame Lady Esther's face.

She sat up abruptly and started to pound at the smoking mess, but even as she did, one of the ribbons flashed alive into open flame, and the lady screamed in terror.

Lawrence belatedly dropped his still-smoking cheroot—no doubt the source of this disaster—to the pavement and cursed his tailor for the tight fit that made it a struggle to be free of his coat. After three long seconds it was off, and he cast the superfine over Lady Esther's midriff. He dropped to one knee to slap frantically at the fabric, his efforts causing the lady to scream all the louder.

There was a terrible smell of burnt fabric, and another wisp of acrid smoke seemed to imply that the gown burned still. Lawrence looked up and saw that a handful of people had come from inside Almack's, but that they all were frozen in place, staring at the bizarre sight before them. With an oath, Lawrence realized there would be little enough help from that quarter, but he did spy two large vases of fresh cut flowers on either side of the portal into Almack's. It was the work of a few moments to race to the door, dash the flowers from one of the vases to the ground, and return to the shrieking Lady Esther. He upended the vase, and then gave another startled oath as the water cascaded out—not to fall to the level of his coat, but instead striking Lady Esther directly on the head.

Her screams abruptly subsided into little more than watery burbles. The soaking served the purpose, however, for the flood of water had drenched her, not to mention his coat, entirely.

Lawrence knelt beside her, lifting his coat and checking to be sure any hint of fire was drowned. He sighed in relief to find none, and then his breathing became a little shaky, no doubt as much from the shock of the event as from his physical efforts. "Are you burned?" he asked Lady Esther.

She tried to speak, only to pause and lift the back of her hand to her mouth, dashing away some of the water streaming from her hair. She only managed to get out "Ptooie!," but a shake of her head indicated she had taken no harm.

"Lawrence!" came another feminine cry, and he looked up to see Clara, her hand raised to her face in alarm. Behind her the small crowd of round-eyed observers grew by the moment, their voices raised in cries and questions as to what had happened.

"By Jove, he's *attacked* her!" someone in the gathering said loudly.

"I have not!" Lawrence denied at once, his gaze locking with Clara's. She still appeared alarmed, but underneath he saw the shadows of other emotions—too well buried for him to interpret what they might be. If only he could be sure he saw a hint, even just the merest grain, of regret for their earlier contretemps there . . .

Lady Esther began to cry, a blubbering of unintelligible words, and with reluctance Lawrence turned back to her. He could see that she would soon work herself into another screaming fit. Before she could lapse into hysterics, he looked to the growing crowd, but it was clear there was still no one among them inclined to approach and offer assistance. It was up to him, then, to see to it. He bent down to one knee and scooped Lady Esther into his arms, and she gave a squeal of surprise as he hoisted her and rose to his feet.

"For heaven's sake, move out of the way!" he growled at the crowd assembled in the entry portal.

Everyone moved back inside the building, carrying an excited hubbub of noise with them. Once Lawrence was inside the door, the crowd of interested faces parted, and Lawrence walked between them, feeling ridiculous as he sought out a sofa on which to deposit Lady Esther. "Call for a doctor," he said to an agitated Mr. Willis, who had followed in his wake.

The Majordomo nodded and scurried off, no doubt to write a note for one of the footmen to carry to the nearest doctor's home.

Lawrence spied a sofa and deposited Lady Esther on it. He meant to step back, but one of her hands darted out, catching the front of his shirt, and he was dragged down, half-kneeling, half-sitting beside her.

"Lord Travers, how kind you are!" she said loudly.

"Stop this at once!" he said in as low and fierce a whisper as he could manage. He tried to wrench her hand free of his shirt, but she clung tenaciously.

"Of course I forgive you!" was her loud reply, accompanied by a bright smile.

"I said to let go!" he ground out between clenched teeth, but the words made no impression on her.

He would have scolded her in a louder and firmer tone—hang trying to be polite or attempting to save the shreds of her reputation!—but he was distracted by the sight of her gown, which had gone entirely diaphanous in the soaking she had sustained. The crowd had obviously noted this fact as well, for an added round of exclamations filled Lawrence's ear. Why, it appeared as if the silly chit had not so little as a shift on underneath her gown, and it was quite clear she did not sport any stays! "Good gad!" Lawrence said, abruptly diverting his gaze out into the crowd.

"Lawrence!" Trouble called, as he pressed to the front of the crowd surrounding the sofa. "By Jove!" he cried upon spying Lady Esther's *dishabille*.

"Give me your coat," Lawrence demanded, putting out his hand and gesturing impatiently.

"What? Oh yes, I see, of course." Trouble shrugged out of his coat, and Lawrence suppressed a smile as his friend rather gallantly limited his expression to one quick grimace of woe upon seeing his coat spoilt by water stains as soon as it was laid over Lady Esther.

Now she was safely covered, Lawrence met Lady Esther's gaze once more and was shocked to see a small smile shaping her lips as she looked up at him from beneath her lashes. Impudent wretch! He looked away again, only to encounter Clara's wide-eyed and white-faced stare.

"What has happened?" came the strident cry of Lady Esther's eldest brother as he stepped from the crowd.

"There was a fire—" Lawrence began, not looking at the man, but instead staring into Clara's face. Phyllis was at her side, holding Clara's elbow as though to steady Clara on her feet.

"Gadzooks, what happened to you, girl?" Sir Randall cried, stepping forward to take up his sister's hand.

"I am fine. I was not burned, praise God," Esther replied.

Lawrence took the opportunity Lady Esther's distraction offered and with a jerk pulled his shirt free of her hold and slipped to his feet, making sure he was well outside the grasping female's reach. He took a step toward Clara but was frozen in place by Lady Esther's voice.

"Randall, do not let him go! I must thank Lord Travers. He saved my life, you know!"

Lawrence turned his head and started to make a motion to deny that any thanks were required.

"How can I express my gratitude to you for saving me?" the lady cried to him in impassioned tones. "If you had not kept our embrace from turning into a terrible disaster, I should have been killed!"

"Embrace?" he echoed, immediately shaking his head. "There was no embrace."

He heard that word spread outward in a whisper, and mixed with it were others: *ruin, reputation, scandal*.

Lady Esther's hand shot abruptly to her mouth as she gave a gasp, like a child who has accidentally revealed a secret she had promised not to tell. "No, I—I mean, of course, when I tripped and you caught me," Lady Esther said.

Lawrence narrowed his eyes at the disingenuousness of her tone.

"What happens here?" interrupted a Russian-accented voice that at once declared its owner to be the Countess Lieven. Lawrence turned to her, finding that three other of the patronesses who oversaw the weekly propriety of Almack's stood at either side of the countess: Lady Jersey, Lady Cowper, and Mrs. Drummond-Burrell. None of them appeared pleased by the fracas.

"Oh, Countess Lieven! It is the most terrible thing," Lady Esther cried piteously. "Lord Travers was kissing—I mean, I was speaking with Lord Travers, when I tripped against him, and he was holding a cheroot, and my ribbons caught afire, and he most gallantly rescued me! And now I am soaked from head to heel, and I am so very chilled, and—!" Lady Esther made a sound, as though she choked back a sob. "And now I am compromised, and so publicly too!" She picked up the sleeve of Trouble's coat and pressed it against one eye as though to soak up tears, although Lawrence saw no evidence of any.

"Compromised?" Countess Lieven repeated, casting a glance from Lawrence to the white-faced Clara.

"You silly chit!" Lawrence exploded toward Lady Esther, all out of patience with her. "You have manufactured this entire affair, and all in a pointless effort to entrap me into offering for you. Well, I will not do it. I cannot do it! I am already betrothed," he said, not caring to keep any harshness out of his tone.

"No, you are not!" Lady Esther replied at once. Her expression was one of hurt, of girlish earnestness, but Lawrence saw an unmistakably eager light leaping in her eyes. "I overheard your disagreement with Miss Northdon tonight, Lord Travers," she charged. "You said you understood that she was crying off from your engagement."

All eyes turned to Clara, who went an even paler shade as a gasp rippled through the crowd. Lawrence felt all the blood drain from his face as well.

"This is true?" Countess Lieven turned to ask Lawrence.

He could only stare at her, caught between a need to deny anything Lady Esther said, and telling the truth, as any honorable man must.

Countess Lieven turned to Clara. "This is true?"

Clara's throat moved convulsively, but no sound came forth from her bloodless lips. Whispers moved through the crowd, a dark murmuring that marked the fact that neither Clara nor Lawrence had been able to utter a denial.

"It is not true!" Phyllis said in Clara's place, earning an anguished glance from her friend as Phyllis stepped forward, now drawing all attention to herself.

"Miss Roswell," Countess Lieven acknowledged Phyllis, but then she was interrupted by the patroness at her right side, Lady Jersey, who sharply asked Phyllis, "What do you know of this matter? Did Miss Northdon cry off or not?" Lady Jersey glanced with disapproval at first Lady Esther and then at Lawrence. "For if Lord Travers is now free to make this lady an offer, it behooves him to do so, since he so obviously assaulted her person."

Everyone gasped anew, except for Clara; Lawrence saw by the mute hurt in her eyes that she had already pondered the possibility that it was no accident that Lawrence and Lady Esther had been found together alone, outside. Could she really believe he had fled from an engagement to her directly into Lady Esther's arms?

"Lawrence cannot offer for Lady Esther!" Phyllis cried, her voice rising in alarm. To Lawrence's ears it was not so much a statement of fact as a protest against such an alliance—a sentiment with which he heartily agreed.

"Because?" prompted Countess Lieven, and she was echoed by Lady Jersey.

"Because . . ." Phyllis said, with a frantic glance at her brother.

Everyone stared.

Lawrence took a step toward her, shaking his head. It was no good. He could not let Phyllis call Lady Esther a liar, especially not when they all knew the horrid creature only spoke the truth.

"Because," Phyllis repeated. "Because he is already married!" she said all in a rush.

This time no one gasped; all they could do was to stare at the pink-cheeked Phyllis.

"Married?" Lady Jersey scoffed. "To whom?

"Why . . . ! Why, to . . ." Phyllis's blush deepened, "Clara Northdon, of course."

Lawrence made an inarticulate sound as his stare traveled from Phyllis's flushed face to Clara's pallid one. A growing sense of unreality engulfed him as he thought *this cannot be happening*. All these tales, these impossible lies—they could only lead to societal censure at best, ruination at worst. What was Phyllis thinking?

It was a good thing, Lawrence thought from the depths of the uncomprehending fog that filled his brain and seemed to block all ability to think, that his friends stood at hand, because Clara did something Lawrence had never before seen her do: she fainted dead away, into the arms of a very startled Bertie Adams.

Three

"Clara?" Someone called her name.

Even though her eyes were closed, Clara realized someone pressed her hand between his own, and there was a gentle rocking sensation beneath her. She slowly opened her eyes and was startled to find herself laid along a coach's bench seat.

"You fainted." Lawrence, sitting opposite, supplied an explanation.

"We are taking you home," said an unhappy-looking Phyllis at his side.

"How do you feel?" Lawrence asked, frowning.

"I fainted?" Clara asked, in place of an answer. She levered herself against the seat and sat upright. "I never faint."

Phyllis nodded a response. "Well, it . . . it was all a bit much. We thought it best to leave Almack's at once, that there might be more harm to be done from staying than from transporting you while you were yet in a swoon. I pray you do not take it amiss."

It all came flooding back to Clara then: Lady Esther and Lawrence caught alone together; Lawrence so gallantly carrying the sodden and exposed Lady Esther to a sofa, and the jealousy and resentment that had flashed through Clara at the sight; and, worst of all, Phyllis's preposterous claim that Lawrence was already married . . . to Clara.

"I feel a trifle dizzy," Clara murmured, putting a hand to her head.

Lawrence looked as though he would speak, but just then the coach ground to a stop, and the carriage door was almost instantly pulled open by one of her father's liveried footmen. Lawrence climbed down first.

"You are to carry Miss Northdon into the house," he ordered the footman. "She has been taken ill."

"Indeed he will not!" Clara said firmly. She eschewed the hand either man offered and climbed unaided from the coach. She picked up her skirts and hurried into the house, silently fuming that Lawrence had found Lady Esther worthy of being carried in his arms, but not herself! Of course, whispered a small and vexatingly reasonable inner voice, it was just as likely that he did not offer because he had meant to protect her clothing from the water that still soaked his own.

She was not particularly interested in being fair-minded at the moment, however, and so it was with further vexation that she saw Lawrence and Phyllis following her into the house. They even trailed her past the foyer—ignoring the butler's attempts to waylay them until he could inquire if the family were receiving—and into the sitting room, where Mama looked up in mild surprise.

"Ah, you are home already, Clara. How did you find the company at Almack's—? Why, Miss Roswell, Lord Travers!" Mama interrupted herself to exclaim, and she stared at Lawrence's coatless and half-soaked appearance.

"Good evening, ma'am. May I inquire, is Sir Barnabus at home?" Lawrence asked, and even though Clara half-wished he would go away so that she might sort her emotions out in peace, she had to admire the outward calm he displayed. One would never know he had this day broken his engagement, saved a woman from being consumed by fire, and been the center of a hopeless lie issued before and witnessed by the very cream of society.

"Why, yes, my husband is at home," Mama said, her hands rising to her throat as though in anxiety; she no doubt guessed from the strained expression Phyllis wore that the news about to be shared could not be good.

The next half-hour was an exercise in the ridiculous, even though Papa began politely enough. "Lord Travers, good evening." He went on to inquire how it was that Lawrence was so disheveled.

"I put out a lady who was on fire," Lawrence answered.

This statement, sounding rather like a quip, did not sit well with Papa. "Explain yourself, sir."

That the explanation was so peculiar, and the end results of this night's actions so calamitous, did nothing to appease Papa's growing displeasure.

"Do you mean to tell me, sirrah, that you have compromised not one but two ladies this evening? And one of them my daughter?" Clara had never seen her father so red-faced with anger.

A muscle along Lawrence's jaw twitched from being held tight, but when he spoke there was no other sign of upset he might be experiencing. "I maintain that Lady Esther compromised herself. And as to your daughter," Lawrence threw one quick, unfathomable glance at Clara, "I do not believe it can be said she is *compromised* by being regarded, for the moment at least, as having married me."

Papa lifted his eyebrows. "True enough! It is when everyone learns you are not indeed married after all that she will then be compromised—and you cannot deny the truth of that fact, sir!"

Lawrence blew out a sigh and slowly shook his head. "I cannot."

Clara felt her lower lip tremble, but she caught it with her teeth to keep it still. What did Lawrence's solemn tone mean? Was he disappointed that he was not yet free of her company, or dare she hope that, for her sensibilities' sake at least, he regretted the night's folly?

Phyllis was then called upon by Papa to explain why she had uttered such a ridiculous pronouncement of marriage in the first place.

"All I knew was that Lady Esther had the most *avaricious* gleam in her eyes!" Phyllis cried, looking abashed. "It was abundantly clear to me that she meant to entrap Lawrence. We all know how desperate she is to marry! And I could not bear the thought of Lawrence being made to offer for the . . . the peagoose!" It was clear she would like to have used a stronger epithet. "Only think, to have Lady Esther take the place of Clara as my sister-in-law, as Lawrence's bride . . . ! The idea is simply intolerable. I had to act."

Phyllis crossed the room to place her hand on Lawrence's arm, her every look and gesture imploring understanding. "No one was speaking, do you recall? There was that awful silence, and the patronesses staring, and Lady Esther sitting there on that sofa so smug and satisfied as a cat who's been at the cream—well! Someone had to say something. So I stated that you were already married. It just dropped out of my mouth! But I had only served to worsen the situation, and then you both were trapped, and all by *my* stupid tongue prattling on so . . . !" Phyllis's explanation ground to a halt as she pressed two closed fists to her mouth in visible regret.

Papa sank into a chair opposite Mama's. "I daresay it would have been less of a catastrophe if you had but stayed and denied the truth of it, right there and then," he said in a hopeless tone.

"And call my sister a liar?" Lawrence said.

Papa grunted in acknowledgment that Lawrence had been placed in a difficult position.

Phyllis began to cry. Lawrence put his arm around her shoulders.

"Oh, Lawrence! What a muddle. I am so sorry," she said between sobs.

"Shush, my girl, 'tis done. Better not to wallow in regret, but to apply ourselves to finding a solution."

"If one is to be found," Mama said faintly. She and Papa exchanged despondent glances.

No one spoke, the ensuing silence seeming to underscore the hopelessness of the situation. Clara racked her mind for an explanation that would not make all of them appear to be utter fools, and she despaired when not so little as a scrap of an idea occurred to her.

The heavy silence was interrupted by the return of the butler.

"Mr. Tarkington and Mr. Adams have called," he announced. "Are you receiving, sir?"

"We most certainly are not—" Mama began.

"They are privy to everything that has occurred," Lawrence interrupted her to explain. "And perhaps they can tell us what occurred at Almack's after we left so abruptly."

"Show them in," Papa ordered at once.

Clara glanced out the door toward the stairs that led up to her room, longing to retreat to that haven, especially now that Lawrence's friends who had overheard the breaking of her betrothal had come to call. She was kept from giving action to her thought, however, by the unexpected beaming smiles both men wore as they bowed themselves into the room.

"Sir Barnabus, Lady Northdon," both men greeted their hosts. Mr. Tarkington turned at once to Lawrence to declare, "So much for all those wagers that have been laid against you, you rogue! *Un Fredon* is no more."

A disgruntled exasperation rolled over Lawrence's face, but before he could respond, Mr. Adams had crossed to Phyllis. "Brilliant girl!" he hailed her, offering her a bow. "You quite saved our dear Lawrence from a fate worse than death."

"I saved him from Lady Esther perhaps, but I have otherwise ruined his life, and Clara's too!" Phyllis replied, her eyes refilling with new tears.

"What is this?" Mr. Adams asked, twisting to glance at the other gloomy-faced occupants of the room. "Good gad, Trouble, it is abundantly clear they've not figured out the manifest solution to this night's tangle."

"I daresay you are right," Mr. Tarkington agreed, shaking his head as though in amazement.

"Solution?" Papa latched on to the word.

"It is so obvious!" Mr. Adams said on a laugh. He turned to Lawrence, a hand smugly planted on his hip. "Why, you nodcock, all you have to do is marry the girl! Miss Northdon I mean, of course."

"Marry her?" Lawrence cried.

"Marry me?" Clara squeaked. She glanced toward Lawrence,

who glanced back at her, and she wondered if her expression were as startled as his.

"But of course, infants!" Mr. Adams said, and Mr. Tarkington nodded over a wide grin.

"But if we married now, everyone would know we had lied about being married earlier," Clara pointed out the flaw in his logic.

"And so? Everyone will know you lied, but by then the deed will be done. Travers will be safe from Lady Esther's claim of having been compromised by him, your reputation will be secured, and whatever small scandal results from a sudden marriage will all fade away after being nothing more than a nine day's wonder." Mr. Adams beamed at them.

"If only I had a special license lying about somewhere," Lawrence said with a sarcastic tone.

Mr. Adams wagged a denying finger. "There is a problem in the idea of a prompt marriage via a special license, my friend. Trouble and I have wondered what should happen if the archbishop were to refuse to grant you the license, because of some rumor he might hear regarding Lady Esther? A day or two lost is a day or two in which Lady Esther might aspire to some further mischief. No, there is a better plan," Mr. Adams said.

"Tell us more, Mr. Adams," Papa said, a reluctant hint of encouragement overshadowing the concern in his eyes.

"Clara, Miss Roswell, please take a seat," Mama instructed, playing the hostess by thinking of her guests' comfort. As if good manners would solve the problem, Clara thought a little sourly, but all the same she and Phyllis did as they were bid, and the gentlemen found seats as well.

"We have thought it all through. The two of you must go to Gretna Green!" Mr. Tarkington pronounced to Lawrence as soon as everyone was seated. "At once."

Clara's mouth fell open in shock.

"Gretna Green!" Papa bellowed. "No daughter of mine is going to elope! I thought the idea was to *save* her reputation, not damage it further. No, I will not permit it. A special license will serve us well enough."

Clara felt the blood drain from her face as it had earlier to-night. Papa was talking as though he had accepted this prepos-terous idea that she and Lawrence must marry. How could she possibly marry him? Lawrence had made it clear he no longer wished to be wed to her, that his affections had surely soured or turned to some other woman . . . else why would he have concocted an argument that made it look as though Clara had been the one to cry off?

"Well, er," Mr. Adams said, and he and Mr. Tarkington's sat-isfaction slid away as they exchanged apprehensive glances. "I am afraid there is another reason why the utmost expediency is required. I do not believe Travers should remain in London, not even to return to his home."

"By damn, does it ever end?" Papa swore.

"Why not?" Lawrence demanded of Mr. Adams.

"I am afraid that after you left Almack's, Lady Esther's brother, Sir Randall, made it abundantly clear that he meant to call you out, my lad," Mr. Adams said to Lawrence. "Tonight. As soon as you arrive home."

"Bad form," Mr. Tarkington chided the absent Sir Randall. "He ought to just challenge you, Lawrence, and leave it until morning like a civilized man."

This statement earned Mr. Tarkington a dark look from Mama. "He is mad!" she said in protest. "Sir Randall would be imprisoned for dueling."

"Sir Randall does not seem to fear that penalty, ma'am," Mr. Tarkington said, his usually cheery demeanor turning somber.

"Nor has he ever, the damn fool, always demanding satisfac-tion for this imagined offense or that presumed insult," Papa muttered, his brow creased in a frown of disapproval. "I daresay it would serve him well enough to finally be caught out at it by the authorities. Perhaps you should give him the satisfaction he demands, Travers."

"Papa!" Clara cried. "How can you say such a thing?"

Lawrence turned to her, looking at her full on as he had not all night. If only his expression was not so inscrutable, Clara thought with a scowl, then she might have an idea what to say to him. Instead she just stared back, and after one long moment, Lawrence looked away again.

"I was not in earnest," Papa explained, though one could not judge as much from his mournful expression. He planted his hands on his knees, and then he stood, transferring his hands to his hips. "Well, there is nothing for it then. These young jackanapes are only too right, Clara."

"Jackanapes?" Mr. Tarkington repeated in offended tones.

Papa ignored him. "You and Lord Travers will have to marry in haste. Go on and pack your valise then, my girl."

Elope with Lawrence? It was impossible, utterly impossible. Papa would have to be told that the engagement was broken, and it did not matter how much it pained Clara to have to give him the news in front of Lawrence. Clara worked her jaw, but no words came forth.

"And tell your maid to pack a bag as well, of course," Papa instructed.

"Oh, no, sir, there ought be no maid along!" Mr. Adams interjected. He flushed scarlet under the scowl Papa gave him.

"Why ever not?"

"Well, Trouble here and I, we have had the brilliant thought that a maid would not serve at all well in this instance."

"I will be the judge of that," Papa said gruffly.

"Er . . . yes, of course. Well, the thing of it is this. Trouble and I will put it about that Travers and Miss Northdon, er, that is, the new Lady Travers, have gone on a bridal journey, returning to Travers's estate in Salisbury, where they were wed a week ago. Only, of course, they'll travel far north instead, crossing to Gretna Green to marry there. We shall tell one and all that they feared some cousin or other was on the very brink of death, and having already twice donned mourning and delayed their nuptials, they became eager to circumvent any further delays, and so married of a sudden. Trouble and I will swear we were witnesses at the wedding, if you, sir, will be so good as to tell anyone who inquires that you gave your consent to the marriage, as the lady is under one-and-twenty."

Papa scowled and considered for a moment. "I suppose I can

say as much, for I have given my consent this day, if not a week ago. It was always intended these two should marry, for that matter, and I cannot say I understand why no date had been set before now," he huffed.

"Papa!" Clara managed to say, her voice very faint. How could he agree to this, to any part of this abominable scheme?

"Yes, well!" Mr. Adams hemmed, with the smallest sideway glance at Lawrence, a silent acknowledgment of the broken engagement he had witnessed at Almack's. An uncertain look crossed Mr. Adams's features, but it could only be a shadow of the dismay that filled Clara's own.

"If anyone should care to investigate the truth of our declarations that there has been a wedding, they will first have to travel to Salisbury to call upon the vicar there and see if the banns were posted for the proper three weeks," Mr. Tarkington explained, perhaps to cover the ensuing weighty pause.

"However, finding this lack," Mr. Adams hurried to agree, "then they would have to inquire of the Archbishop of Canterbury as to whether or not he issued a special license. Too, there may be pointed questions as to this ailing cousin we mention, and as convenient as that would be if you have such a cousin, I do hope for his sake that no such unfortunate fellow exists. Still, and happily, by the time all of these questions are found wanting, Travers here and Miss Northdon will already be safely wedded in Scotland!" Mr. Adams finished with a flourish.

"There you have it!" Mr. Tarkington pronounced with content. "Given that any inquiries would eventually lead to the truth that Travers has indeed already married, albeit belatedly, I cannot think even Sir Randall should care to pursue the matter then."

"Oh no. I fancy his attention will have already turned in a trice. It always does," Mr. Adams agreed. "Do you know he challenged Byron to a duel last August?"

"No! Lord Byron!" Mr. Tarkington repeated with relish.

"Indeed, but my lord could not be bothered to rise from his bed of a morning, claiming there must be three or four others waiting in line to duel with Sir Randall before him, and so he should not be missed in any case."

"Oh, that's a cracking good one, that is," Mr. Tarkington crowed.

"Answer me this, you puppies," Papa sharply interrupted their banter. "What are we to say when people ask why Clara and Lord Travers did not announce their 'marriage' at once, a week ago?"

Clara cheered just a little, for at last Papa brought a measure of sense to the matter of what was to be done.

"Because," Mr. Tarkington replied, obviously pleased to have an answer at the ready, "they wished to soon have a more formal wedding in Town, now the knot was safely tied before this cousin could stick his spoon in the wall! Thoughtful creatures that they are, they did not care to ruin the effect for all their friends who might want to attend and wish them happy."

"Hm, flimsy," Papa declared, but he added, "though not entirely implausible."

"As much as I could wish a formal affair," Mama put in, "I think a Town wedding would not at all suit, not now. Not after the to-do at Almack's. Almack's, of all places! I shan't be surprised if we are refused entrance when next we attempt to attend," she fretted.

"A small enough price to pay if our daughter is kept from utter ruin," Papa said, a trifle sharply.

"Too true," Mama said to Papa, but then she turned back to her guests. "But, Mr. Tarkington, you have said nothing as to why my daughter ought not have a maid at her side while she travels," she pointed out.

"Ah, of course!" Mr. Adams resumed the discourse. "Because, ma'am, if there is no maid to witness the Scottish wedding, then she cannot be bribed or otherwise made to testify to that fact. And," Mr. Adams looked away, twin spots of color rising to his cheeks. "And if your daughter has no maid with her as she travels with Lord Travers, she will indeed be once and for all truly compromised. Should the tale get about, despite our combined best efforts, no one would be able to gainsay

Travers' obligation to marry your daughter, not under those circumstances."

"It is . . . vaguely logical," Papa conceded, and perhaps he even smiled just a little, although Clara could not imagine why. This was horrible! Everyone was looking relieved and agreeing it must be so, and the real truth was that Lawrence's friends had hit upon the very worst solution possible; forcing Lawrence to marry her! Not even two hours ago, Clara would have said that to marry him was her dearest wish, but two hours ago she had still believed Lawrence loved her, that he wanted her to be his wife. Now she knew better.

"But *I* can be her escort," Mama said. "Oh, I must hurry and pack at once!"

Mr. Adams shook his head. "That would appear very suspect, I fear."

"No indeed, Lucille," Papa joined in. "You must be here to spread the tale of Clara's simple but heartfelt nuptials a week ago, and of our dear sick cousin, er, Robert, who precipitated such haste."

"Oh, yes, I suppose I must. I do not like to lie . . . but I like the idea of earning society's cut even less. I mean to say, after all, Clara and my lord have been betrothed an age, and they *will* marry, so it is but a little white lie as to the timing of the thing."

"Quite, quite," Mr. Tarkington soothed.

Mama drew herself up, a look of determination replacing her concerned frown. "Do not just stand there, Clara," she said firmly but not unkindly, crossing to take Clara's arm. "Come along, my girl, I will help you pack."

"No," Clara said stiffly, her voice as hollow sounding as her legs felt.

"My dear, this is the closest we shall come to planning a bridal affair for you, so I do wish you would let me help you pack—"

"I mean," Clara interrupted her mama, "no, I will not go. I do not wish to go to Scotland!"

"Well, of course not, my dear, but haste is of the essence in this matter. We cannot rely on whether or not the archbishop would be accommodating, and even if he were, we could not then hope to hide the fact that you married later instead of sooner."

"I mean," Clara said from between teeth clenched against despair or tears or both, "I will not marry Lord Travers!"

Mama took a step back in surprise, dropping Clara's arm, leaving her free to gather up her skirts and flee the room.

Clara glanced back once from the bottom step of the stairs that led up to her room, and might have laughed at all the round-mouthed, staring faces turned her way—even Lawrence's—were she not robbed of humor by the pain of her heart slowly breaking in two.

Four

"She will not open her door," Sir Barnabus reported in defeat an hour later, as he returned to the sitting room. He slumped into a chair, scowling at his booted toes as if they had somehow caused this evening's uproar. "I suppose I could have it knocked down, or taken off its hinges perhaps. There may be a master key," Sir Barnabus mused, casting his gaze about as though he would find a key lying at the ready.

Lawrence did not deign to answer. They could take the door down or otherwise bully their way into her room, but that did not mean the woman on the other side would then have anything to say to them. Besides, such a storming-in certainly did not augur well as to any marriage schemes, Scottish or otherwise.

It was past eleven o'clock in the evening. *When will my carriage ever return,* Lawrence thought in agitation, aware it had been at least half an hour since Bertie and Trouble had announced they were retreating, not on foot—as they had arrived—but instead commandeering his coach. They had taken a distraught Phyllis with them, that she might be returned to the home she shared with her brother (and hopefully allay an on-coming headache). Clara had long since taken the key from her maid and locked herself into her room. More than an hour's worth of commentary thrown at her locked door had not persuaded her to come out, not even with the threat of ruination hanging over her head.

There was no point in Lawrence's remaining. He would just have to walk home through the darkened streets and hope the night was not made completely wretched by a footpad's attack on top of everything else. He put aside the fourth cup of tea a highly agitated Lady Northdon had thrust upon him between trips to rap on her daughter's door, decided that in lieu of donning his own still damp shirt again he would return Sir Barnabus's shirt another day, and rose to his feet.

"Giving up, my lord? You could go up yourself and have a try at reasoning with her," Sir Barnabus suggested, but he spoke with a perceptible lack of optimism.

"I fail to see that any logic of mine could succeed where her mother's words failed to prevail," Lawrence said wearily.

Sir Barnabus made a face, indicating agreement. He shook his head and spread his hands in a questioning gesture. "Can anyone tell me why the girl has taken the idea of marriage so suddenly in dislike?"

"It is not the institution, I believe, sir. It is me."

"You? Clara's always had a soft spot for you! She was never happier than the day her mother finally said the betrothal could be announced."

Lawrence lifted his shoulders in a shrug, certainly not understanding the gradual shift in Clara's feelings himself. "Affections can change," he said, finding the words as puzzling when they were said aloud as they were in his baffled thoughts.

Baffled indeed, for even though it was not quite two hours since Clara had cried off from their engagement, there was very little of that terminating conversation remaining in his mind. He remembered bits and pieces, a word here or there, but mostly there remained the sharp pain he had felt in his chest when she had pronounced that they must talk about the wedding. He recalled how her stiff posture and unsmiling face had forewarned him that his suspicions of a declining devotion had proven true. What had happened? Where had he turned wrong? What had he done to cost him the regard of the only woman he had ever imagined as his wife, his love?

Sir Barnabus interrupted Lawrence's thoughts. " 'Affections change?' " he repeated with a disbelieving expression. "Clara's? The girl's as constant as the tide! You are wrong, my boy. It has to be something else . . . but the question is, what? I do not un-derstand this refusal of hers. Did the two of you have a—"

"My lord, your carriage has returned," the butler announced from the doorway.

"Sir Barnabus, do please excuse me. I will, of course, do any-thing necessary to correct this . . . predicament, I suppose is the word. But it is clear to me that Clara has no intention of pursuing marriage to me as the answer. I really must return home then, I suppose, as it grows late."

Sir Barnabus frowned anew, and shook his head, but Lawrence gave him no chance to argue the point. He bowed, turning toward the door almost before he was finished bowing, and stepped quickly from the house.

He settled back into the chocolate-brown leather squabs of his coach, having given his coachman instructions to take him home, and shivered from the evening chill settling on his dampened clothing. Then he groaned at the sudden thought that home might not be quite the haven he sought, for Sir Randall might be await-ing him there. "I'll be damned before I will duel with that half-wit tonight!" he swore.

Lawrence reached for the door, to instruct his driver to deliver him to the mews near his house—he'd walk the rest of the way and crawl in a rear window of his own home, if needs must to avoid Sir Randall—but the door was pulled open for him.

"What the devil—?" Lawrence began, but despite the poor light he immediately recognized the two men crawling in to join him. "Bertie? Trouble? I thought you had both fled home long since."

"Never a bit!" Trouble said. He pointed at Lawrence's chest and then at a bag he had brought in with himself. "We have been very busy, devising a plan."

"As if your last one was so successful," Lawrence said sourly.

"My good man, not every single contingency, such as half-mad young women who suddenly declare they have no wish to be saved from certain ruin, may be anticipated. This plan, how-ever, has no weak points, no way of failing."

"Well, actually," Mr. Adams said, "we could have a difficulty if Sir Barnabus does not care for our idea—"

"Silence, nay-sayer!" Trouble cried. He thrust the valise onto Lawrence's lap. "You will find dry clothing inside, your own in fact. And I want you to know that I have decided not to make it a habit to gather clothing for friends who have homicidal lunatics waiting on their doorstep. That damned fool, Sir Randall, shook his fist in my face and threatened to strike me with his walking stick if I did not tell him where you were! I daresay he will be challenging me to a duel next. That is, after he wakes up."

"Dashed him to the ground, did Trouble. With one blow," Bertie said proudly.

Lawrence gave a lopsided grin. "Good show, Trouble."

Trouble sniffed. "Yes, well, it was far and away time someone taught him some manners."

Lawrence's smile faded and he sighed, hearing with his own ears how tired he sounded. "Well, at least now I can go in my own front door."

"Hardly, sir!" Trouble cried.

Lawrence looked from one of his friends to the other, his gaze narrowing in suspicion. "You do not mean to tell me that you still 'have a plan?' "

"Most certainly. It is quite clear to Bertie and me that your affairs have become terribly muddled, and we feel we can help set things aright, if you should not mind too much a suggestion or two."

Lawrence gave a cautious grunt.

"Tell us, Larry," Trouble said, "despite the to-do with your Clara at Almack's, is it possible you care for her still?"

Lawrence hung his head, not quite able to let his friends see the raw emotion the words conjured up within him. "Yes," he answered simply.

"He loves her still! Told you," Trouble crowed.

"Then you would wish for a reconciliation?" Bertie asked. "If we could help arrange such an event?"

Lawrence closed his eyes for a moment and blew out another sigh. He could tell his friends no, thank you, but whatever it is

I'll have no part in it. He could extract a promise from them that, whatever this scheme was, they would not implement it.

He also knew that the only thing he would find at home was his empty room filled with too many thoughts of hopes dashed, love lost.

He dropped his hands and opened his eyes. "Explain your plan to me," he said quietly.

"I do not think we can exactly explain it," Bertie said. "I think we have to show it to you." He and Trouble traded wide-eyed glances.

Lawrence sat up straight and eyed his two friends with a dawning sense of trepidation. "Here now, Trouble, Bertie! I hardly need to find myself in the middle of a scrape, not now. Not in this matter. Perhaps things are best left to me, to unmuddle them as I see fit—"

"We had best go ahead with it," Bertie said.

"I think so, too," Trouble agreed, bringing a length of rope from his pocket.

Lawrence's unease bloomed into alarm.

Clara, sitting on her bed, lifted her head from where she had forlornly rested it against her knees. Someone was rattling the lock on her door.

Not a moment later, Papa swung open the door, lifting his hand to reveal the small metal device there. "Found the master key," he explained.

Clara pursed her lips and turned onto her hip to face the far wall.

"I do not like to enter uninvited, but I cannot see that I have much choice left to me," Papa said, and his voice was less stern than she would have expected.

Out of the corner of her eye, Clara noted in puzzlement that her father did not approach her side as she expected, but instead moved to her wardrobe. He pulled open the doors and reached in to pull something out, and despite herself Clara's curiosity forced her to turn back to face him. "Papa?"

He did not answer, and she saw that he had her valise in hand. He pulled a folded shift from the wardrobe and stuffed it without any particular care into the valise. He reached to do the same with a pair of silk slippers and then a mixed handful of summer and winter hose.

"Papa!" Clara repeated on a cry, springing from her bed to put a restraining hand on his arm. "What are you doing?"

For an answer he turned to the door—yet open—and called out, "Come on in then."

To Clara's astonishment, Mr. Adams and Mr. Tarkington stepped in. The butler had not taken their top hats, which they tipped from their heads in greeting.

"Good evening, Miss Northdon," Mr. Adams said.

"Good evening again," came from Mr. Tarkington.

"Good evening," Clara murmured in complete bewilderment. Whyever would Papa show these gentlemen to her room?

"I know you will be displeased with me, Clara, but it is all for the best," Papa said, turning back to continue stuffing more items into her valise. "I am doing what will, in the long run I am sure, make you happy. I will not pretend to understand why you have of a sudden decided against Lord Travers, but the truth of the matter is you have no real choice in the matter of marrying him. I am convinced that he will be a good, kind, reasonable husband, and you know that if I was not so convinced I would . . . well, I do not know how else we would solve this dilemma, but it does not matter, because you are going to elope with Lord Travers."

"Papa, I have to tell you—"

He held up a restraining hand. "Enough, Clara," he said to her. He closed the valise and turned to the two other men in the room. "Gentlemen, you may proceed."

Clara parted her lips to protest once more, but was cut off abruptly when a woolen blanket was tossed over her head. She would have shouted in outrage, except that a shoulder was then firmly planted in her midriff, robbing her of breath as she was hoisted from her feet.

"Hurry! Hurry! We do not wish to be seen," Mr. Adams's muffled voice reached her ears.

She was carried out to the hall, down the stairs, and to her further astonishment out the front door of her home, and she struggled all the while.

"Mr. Tarkington!" she reprimanded through the cloth at the figure carrying her on his rounded shoulder. Her arms were pinned by the blanket, but her legs were not, and Clara flailed them with little restraint from her captor. Mr. Tarkington gave a satisfying grunt of pain when her knee sharply caught him in the chest. "Mr. Tarkington, put me down at once! I shall scream. Papa!"

"Clara, dearest girl, please be a good girl and hush," came Mama's voice in a half-whisper.

Mama? Sanctioning this . . . this madness?

"We do not wish the neighbors to take note of what is happening," Mama further cautioned.

"I do not care about the neighbors!" Clara objected into the cloth pressing tightly against her face.

She received no response, but was instead unceremoniously deposited on to a hard wooden floor. At least the blanket went lax as a result, and Clara took the opportunity to fight it off her head. Just as she realized she had been placed on the floor of a carriage, the door was closed, plunging the interior into a gloom that was only faintly relieved by a glimmer of moonlight coming through the windows.

"Hold that door! Now tie it—no, over here!" came Mr. Tarkington's urgent cry from outside the coach.

It was only a moment more before Clara realized there was another occupant in the coach, which she discovered with a shriek of alarm as she bumped into him while attempting to rise from the floor.

"Lawrence!" she cried angrily to his hunched over figure.

"Clara," he greeted her politely, for all the world as if it were a common occurrence for his hands to be tied to his ankles. "I hope you were not hurt?" he inquired.

"No." Clara dashed a lock of her disordered hair out of her face and scowled ferociously at him.

"Good. Well then, m'dear, I can only think you must be wondering what is happening, if perchance you have failed to understand that you have been shanghaied."

"Shanghaied!"

"Well, kidnapped is more accurate, I suppose."

"I want out of this carriage. At once!" She tried to sound imperious, but a scramble to obtain the seat opposite Lawrence probably ruined the effect.

He slanted his gaze up from his awkward position. "As do I. But my good friends have decided it is in our best interests to elope as they had proposed we do."

"It is not up to them," Clara argued. She reached for the door handle. It moved and the door even edged open a bit, but then it was solidly stopped. She made a sharp tsking sound that reflected her utter vexation. "They have tied us in!"

"It would seem it is up to them after all," Lawrence said, in a dry tone.

Clara cast him a dark look for an answer, but then she half-rose from her seat, stretching out a hand toward the roof.

"I should not think there is any purpose in knocking," Lawrence said. "The driver is not my man, Trouble assured me, even though this is my coach. So I must assume the driver has been aptly paid and firmly instructed not to let us out. Well, at least not until we are well on our way."

Clara sank back into her seat. "To Scotland," she said grimly.

Lawrence nodded. "To Scotland."

There was a scraping sound from the top of the coach. "That would be your bags, I imagine," Lawrence drawled, and tilted his angled head at the valise on the seat next to him. "Mine is here, as you can see. Personally delivered by my good friend, Trouble Tarkington, who seemed remarkably cheerful for a man who is going to be flailed alive as soon as I have the opportunity."

"I cannot believe Papa is allowing this to happen," Clara said, unable to find any humor in the situation. She made a helpless gesture with her hands and then let them fall haplessly into her lap.

"He is thinking this is the best way to protect you, I imagine."
Lawrence shrugged a shoulder despite his bonds. "He is right."

"But, wait, I have a thought!" Clara said, hearing the despair
in her own voice. "We could rock the carriage from side to side,
to make it turn over. The driver, or passersby, would have to untie
the door then and let us out."

A sour look replaced any humor that had graced Lawrence's
face, a reproach that came across clearly despite the coach's
gloom. He looked away from her, as if there could be something
of interest in the corner of the floorboards.

"Well, I suppose not," Clara said, deflated. "We would have
to consider the driver, or what the horses might be made to suffer."

It was a poor word choice, for Lawrence could easily have
rejoined: "Not unlike us."

He did not, however, and in the ensuing silence Clara's conscience was at last pricked by the facts. "I suppose I should untie
you."

"That would be most agreeable."

Clara pursed her lips, but she could scarcely scold him for his
sarcasm, given that she had left him tied and bound for close to
five minutes. She reached for the knots at his wrists just as the
driver called to the horses, and the carriage rolled forward. Clara
slid from her seat, colliding painlessly with Lawrence.

He sucked in his breath. Clara quickly straightened away from
him, wounded anew by this evidence that her touch was so unwelcome.

It took her a length of time to undo the tightened knots, during
which Lawrence used some colorful words to describe the other
members of *Un Fredon,* but at length he was freed. Short of
rubbing each wrist and extending his legs with sighs of relief,
Lawrence seemed to have taken no harm—proving his friends
had at least a modicum of sense. Not that one could guess it from
this sorry situation she and Lawrence found themselves in, Clara
thought.

"So then," she sighed with a kind of resignation, as she settled back against the squabs. "What occurs next?"

Lawrence absently scratched at his chin as he considered her question. "I do not know," he answered at length. "I suspect our driver has a specific destination in mind. I imagine it will not prove so distant that we will be made to suffer unduly, but neither can I suppose we will arrive there any time soon. The idea, of course, is that we go far enough from London, that no matter how hard we should try we cannot return to London before day-break—it would be impossible. For, of course, even if we did not have the debacle at Almack's to add fuel to the tattlemongers' flames, as unmarried travelers neither of our reputations can possibly survive a night alone together."

"But when the driver stops to harness new horses—surely we can call out then, and there would be people around to hear our calls, and we could be rescued?" Clara suggested.

"Rescued? The only result would be to make known our situation to that many more people, who would no doubt be pleased enough to spread the tale of our late-night jaunt together. That is no solution at all." He gazed at her, expressionless, remote, seeming very unlike the man whose company she had ever cherished. Where had her friend, her beloved, gone? When had this cold stranger taken his place?

Clara looked to her hands where they lay folded together in her lap and realized she wore no gloves. She had no cloak, no bonnet, and she had no idea if any of those items had been packed into her valise. Worse yet than these lacks, however, was the friendless state she found herself in.

"There is absolutely nothing else for it then but marriage?" she asked, her voice barely loud enough to carry over the sound of the carriage wheels against the road.

"Nothing left but to endure," Lawrence answered, his voice sounding hollow.

Oh, what a terrible, weighty word that was: endure. But what troubled her was that it might not be a word just for tonight, or even to get them through the marriage ceremony that awaited them north of the border. Clara very much feared it was a word to describe the rest of their lives.

Five

Lawrence came awake at the changing sound of horses' hooves striking gravel instead of the dirt of the public road.

Clara startled awake opposite him and slowly sat up as she blinked the sleep from her eyes. The blanket Lawrence had laid over her once she had dropped asleep fell from her shoulders, and she shuddered.

Heaven knew how much time had passed since the long silence that had fallen between him and Clara had led each of them eventually into slumber. It was still dark, however, and he thought perhaps he sensed a pre-dawn chill in the air.

"A posting inn," Lawrence said, giving a nod toward the view outside the window. "Thank heaven for that! At least we will not be made to wait out the dawn in a barn or a shed, as I half-feared."

There were a series of rasping noises, accompanied by a few grunts. "We are being untied," Clara stated.

"Yes." Lawrence sat forward, blocking the carriage door with as much of his body as he could. He did not expect any foul play—their driver was no doubt Bertie's or Trouble's personal coachman—but it was best to shield Clara until their circumstances were established.

The door was pulled open. "Gor! It's m'lord Travers!" Trouble's coachman, Hollings, cried upon spying Lawrence.

"Good evening, Hollings."

"M'lord," the coachman sputtered, "it's that sorry I am! I was under orders, you must know. I thought I just had me a troublesome maid for a passenger! That she'd made a pest of herself an' was bein' sent home-like—!"

"I understand. Do not concern yourself, my good man. I shan't bring charges against you. I am far more interested in knowing what else you were ordered to do."

"Nothin', m'lord! I was to take me passenger here, to the Ducks and Drakes Inn."

"Here?" Lawrence inquired.

"Rushden, in Northamptonshire, m'lord."

"So far as that, eh? Tell me, Hollings, how many hours remain until dawn?"

Hollings consulted a battered pocketwatch by the dim light cast from the carriage lamps. "One, two hours. Thereabouts, m'lord."

"I see," Lawrence said, settling back in the seat to reach for the valise Trouble had brought for him. He opened it and took out the purse he had earlier found there, more than a little gratified that it had been supplied among the bag's contents. He took out a small handful of various coins and passed them through the carriage doorway to Hollings. "Please be so good as to bespeak a simple meal and rooms for Miss . . . Lady Travers and me."

"You're married, m'lord?"

"Here sits my bride," Lawrence answered with a smile and a gesture toward Clara.

"Best wishes are in order then."

"Indeed, and thank you. Now, as to those rooms?"

"Oh aye, sir. Won't take a minute."

Hollings departed, and Lawrence shut the carriage door against the pre-morning chill.

"Was that wise?" Clara asked, her tone flat. "To register as if we were already married?"

"It is in keeping with the lies already told, m'dear. I daresay it would look more peculiar if we registered any other way. This way if we're seen, then there is no assumed name that must be explained away."

One side of her mouth hitched up in a quick grimace. "True enough," she conceded.

Silence fell again, more awkward than ever, and Lawrence thought Clara looked just as relieved to have Hollings return as he felt himself. Still, he did not leap down from the coach at once, instead reaching to take the blanket from Clara's lap and place it around her shoulders. "It appears I must buy you a cloak tomorrow. Well, make that today."

The merest hint of Clara's usual soft smile crossed her face, reminding him of the usual bright reward that would have been his, not so long ago, for his trouble and for the small jest. He could almost understand that she did not love him anymore, almost—but it was beyond understanding that their friendship could have waned to this pale imitation of what it had been for so long.

They went up a set of stairs to what a bleary-eyed innkeeper called "the fine rooms," but the term was generous. Still, the simple sitting room had furniture that looked as though it would not fall apart if you sat on it, a fire crackling on the grate with newly piled wood, and the windows and floors seemed clean enough in the murky light from a branch of candles, so it must suit.

The meal of bread and cheese and beer, brought to them by a sleepily grumpy maid, was as dismal as the silent tension that had grown between them ever since Clara had been deposited at Lawrence's feet some five or six hours ago. After a few bites, Lawrence conceded that his stomach had no interest in food, and it was evident that Clara felt the same.

He rose and crossed to the door leading to the only other chamber, the bedroom. There was a bed with multiple covers thrown back invitingly at one corner. A fire crackled on this room's hearth as well. He nodded, knowing Clara would be reasonably comfortable here.

"We've a few hours to spare before we travel on, so you should get to bed, Clara," he said gently as he turned back to face her, only to discover with a jerk of surprise that she had followed him and stood practically at his elbow.

There was a grim set to her mouth, and her gray eyes were turned a smoky, unhappy hue by the meager light shed by the fire and the few candles.

"One bedchamber. One bed," she said tonelessly. "But why would Lord and Lady Travers require more than one bed?"

"I will sleep before the fire here in this room, Lawrence replied.

"But why?" She gave a little laugh.

Its bitter edge made Lawrence frown, and he wished she would look at him, instead of over his shoulder to the bed. He started to lift a hand, to put it on her shoulder, but it seemed so unlikely that she would accept any touch of his that instead he forced his hand to remain at his side.

"Why should you sleep huddled before the fire, when there is a perfectly good bed here?" She strode into the bedchamber, hands on hips, eyes alight as though from some inner demon. He followed her slowly.

"What difference a few days?" she went on. "We are to marry after but a few weary days of breakneck haste in a coach. Why wait for the bedding? There is nothing to lose, no reputation to steal away, for we are locked into this marriage with no turning back, are we not?"

She turned to face him in a defiant stance, and her words seemed a taunt. Lawrence felt an answering pique fill him, making him press his lips together tightly to keep from responding in kind. He would have turned his back to her, shut the door between them to hide from her scorn and her dislike of him . . . were it not for the single tear that slid down her cheek, clearly to be seen as it mirrored the flickering firelight.

"Clara," he breathed, and then he could not stop himself from crossing the room, from lifting his hand to gently wipe away the tear. "Clara, do not cry."

She leaned into him, her hands against his chest, her forehead to his chin, and gave a sound that was not quite a sob, yet more than a sigh. How good it felt to touch her again, to be allowed within the invisible wall that had sprung up around her.

"I am sorry," he said, and only reluctantly let his hand fall

away from her face. He could not make himself step back, outside of the circle of her arm's reach. "You ought not to have
gone through all this."

She withdrew a little, but only enough that she might raise her
eyes to meet his. "I am sorry, too." She gave him a rueful smile.

"We will find a way to go on," he told her, not really believ-
ing it. How could he live with her, loving her as he did, knowing
that the affection she had once felt for him was gone? Even this
small bridge of friendship restored between them was as much
pain as it was pleasure. How could he live an entire life this
way, near her, in her life, perhaps even a father to her children,
but never a lover whom she held in her heart?

"I suppose we will," Clara said with a sigh. She stepped back,
and Lawrence had to stare at the floor, unblinking, willing away
the pain of rejection that filled him. She might in time become
his friend once more, but he knew the love of this friend would
slowly destroy him.

As if to prove his secret thoughts—to begin his torture immediately—Clara spoke softly and kindly. "In truth, Lawrence,
I cannot see the point of you sleeping on the floor, freezing,
when there is a warm bed big enough for two."

He continued to stare at the floor for one long moment, but
then he forced himself to nod. "It makes perfect sense." But,
oh, what a bitter taste it put in his mouth!

He shook his head, as a condemned man shakes his shoulders
back before mounting the block, and cleared his throat. "You
will, of course, be safe from any attentions by me," he said, not
quite looking at her. "It is important to my personal honor that
the union be sanctified . . . first. Before . . . that is, well, I am
sure you take my meaning."

Was that a shadow of pain that flitted through her eyes? Impossible to tell, for she nodded and turned away.

"I will let you," he floundered for a word, "prepare for sleep,
and when you call I will . . . I will do the same." There was
very little she could say to that, he supposed, so he quickly
bowed himself free of the room, closing the door behind him.

He stood before the fire in the sitting room and thought of

what remorse Phyllis might feel come the morning when she learned of the enforced elopement. He thought of his estate in Salisbury, how he would have liked to wed there in truth, not just in a lie. He thought of his two foolish friends, good lads who thought they had done him a favor. In fact, he thought of everything he could to turn his mind from thoughts of the woman who presumably stripped down to her shift in the adjoining room.

"Lawrence," came Clara's signal at length.

He hesitated long enough to frown at the untouched mugs of beer, wished for brandy, and left the mugs where they stood.

Clara was abed when he entered the room, well snuggled under the thick blankets, her gown hanging from a peg, her stockings rolled and stored in her shoes. She had no night cap to don, but she had contrived her waist-long length of blond hair into a plait. Had he known her hair reached to her waist? How intimate it seemed, to see a woman, this woman, with her hair not pinned or curled or swept up.

She gave him one long look, then turned first her head, and then her whole body, facing away from the side of the bed that remained yet unoccupied.

Lawrence took his cue, moving to the far side of the bed. There he turned his back as well and removed his cravat, boots, stockings, coat, and waistcoat. Summer weather had done away with a woolen under-vest, else he would have abandoned his shirt as well; now he pulled the shirt's length free of his breeches and let it serve as a kind of nightshirt. His breeches he left as they were.

He slid beneath the blankets, moving gingerly, unable to tell if the still figure eight inches away from his length was asleep or not.

"Lawrence," Clara said, making evident the fact she was yet awake. Curious how he had imagined a scene not unlike this many a time, but there had been some crucial differences, not least of which was Clara's desire to be there. "Lawrence, there is something that concerns me."

"What is that?" he asked, staring up toward a dark-enshrouded ceiling.

"I have been thinking about Phyllis."

The cause of all this, Lawrence thought, but did not say aloud. Instead he said, "What about Phyllis?"

"I was wondering, how are you going to kill her? For she really ought to be killed for being so much a noddy as to tell that immense lie, right there in the middle of Almack's."

Lawrence blinked, trying to make sense of the brutal words coming from Clara's soft and kissable mouth, and not quite able to reconcile the two. But then there came a half-stifled snigger from the other side of the bed, closely followed on by a giggle.

He laughed, with a big from-the-belly guffaw such as he had not had in weeks, if not months.

Clara giggled on her side of the bed, and Lawrence felt the tremors her shaking shoulders set off in the stuffed mattress, which only served to make him laugh all the more with her.

"It w-was not that f-funny," Clara said, the words broken by her laughter.

Lawrence shook his head against the pillow and grinned as he reached up to run a hand through his hair.

"Oh, how I have missed that," Clara said, a smile lingering in her voice.

"Have you?" he asked in surprise. Clara had missed their shared laughter?

"Mmmm," she said, a cautious sound, as if she had just re-membered she was not supposed to enjoy his company. There was a rustle of the bed covers, and he felt more than saw Clara turn over, so that she faced him now. There was a dim outline of gold along the curve of her brow, a result of the fireplace's dancing light behind her. "There are, what?" she asked. "Three or four more days before we arrive in Gretna Green?"

He nodded, but did not know if she could see him at all, and so he answered her aloud. "About that, yes."

"Four days in a coach," she said, her voice very low, too low to determine a tone, a connotation. "We must find a way to be . . . comfortable with one another. I was thinking that, as we drive along, we should determine how to go on about the busi-ness of living together."

"What? No more schemes to affect an escape?" he asked, hoping he had achieved his aim of making it the lightest of jests.

She chose not to let him know if he had succeeded, for she did not answer in kind. "I mean to say, there are so many mundane things to decide," she said. "Am I to have the first dance of you at any event we attend? How shall we divide our entertaining? Is it to be your friends one night, and mine the next?" Her voice came out of the dark, warm and smooth on the ear . . . except for the thin edge of sorrow that tugged at his conscience.

Once he had begun to question Clara's devotion he should have asked her for her feelings outright, or at least given her an opportunity to speak her piece. But, no, instead he had avoided being alone with her, had even begun to avoid her company in public places. If—his logic had wrongly persuaded him—he gave her no chance, then she could never dismiss him from her side.

If he had faced her flagging devotion head on, then perhaps he could have spared her this potentially scandalous elopement, this marriage that was doomed to make them both unhappy.

"Yes, we have much to settle." He gave a breathy little laugh that contained none of his prior humor. "But we are assured of plenty of time in which to discuss it."

"Exactly," she said, her voice growing sleepy.

"I do have one question to ask of you now, however."

"Yes?"

"Since we will be quit of London for at least a week, I wondered if perhaps you cared to make a kind of actual bridal journey out of this jaunt. It would look more typical if we were to linger away from the city for a few weeks or even a month or two. We could go to Brighton, or Bath if you like. Or on to Salisbury, to my estate there. I always imagined we . . . the woman I married and I would wish to go there."

"To be alone," Clara said, a statement, not a question.

"Yes. And to go on picnics together, or to walk barefoot out in the sunshine, if we liked, with not even a servant to look at us askance. To fish together in the pond . . . well, that manner of thing, I always thought," he cut off abruptly, flushing at the note of longing he had heard in his own voice.

Clara was silent for a moment, and Lawrence began to think she must have drifted off to sleep.

"You thought about such things?" she said, ending the pause, and perhaps there was a hint of wistfulness in her words. "You surprise me," she continued when he did not reply at once. "I thought city life, the gaiety, the social rounds absorbed all your attention. I had no sense of your pining for the country."

"For the life to be had there," he corrected her.

"The life? There are social calls, it is true, but country life is mostly about fields being plowed, cattle being moved from field to field, and about home, hearth, and family!"

"Yes." Just everything he wanted in this world, if a loving Clara could be willingly at his side.

"Yes?" she sounded puzzled, but then she cried, "Oh! Oh yes, I see. I see," she finished in a small voice.

Lawrence lifted up onto one elbow. "What is it? You sound hurt."

"It is just . . . ! No, I, I think I understand. You wish to be married . . . only not to me, of course. Do you . . . ? Lawrence, do you love someone else? Is that why you did not want to marry me?"

"Not—!" he choked out only the single word, unable to grasp what Clara meant, what she asked. He sat up to stare down at her, the blankets falling to his waist. Clara sat up abruptly, too, perhaps startled by his outcry or his stare, her shift faintly glowing gray-white in the firelight.

"It is all right," Clara soothed, one hand clenched unconsciously against her heart. "I knew you wanted to cry off, of course, but like the widgeon I am, I thought it was just that you had fallen out of love with me."

"Clara—!" he tried to interrupt, but the floodgates of declaration had been opened, and Clara went on, speaking rapidly, as though to get an unpleasant task behind her. "And then you would not set a date for our marriage, and when I asked you, you . . . you cried off. Now, I never, not really, for a moment

thought you could have fallen in love with that horrid Lady
Esther, but when I saw her in your arms, and how you carried
her so tenderly . . ." Her gaze fell to the covers, and her un-
clenched hand plucked at the fabric absently. "But of course it
must be that you love someone else. How tiresome and thick
you must find me! I did not think how it was that, clearly, some
other lady has captured your affections—"

"Clara!" Lawrence interrupted, this time more forcefully, even
putting his hands on her upper arms to capture fully her attention.
"What madness is this? I never wanted to end our betrothal."

Clara sat up a little straighter, stiffening under his touch. "But
of course you did! You . . . you would not set a date, and when
I pressed you for one you were vague, until you told me that
you had not cried off only because it is not considered honorable
for a man to break the engagement—"

"I never—! Well, I think perhaps I did say something very
like that, but, Clara, it is not at all what I meant," Lawrence
cried in sheer frustration.

"You—!" Clara began to say something, but stopped
abruptly, a curious mixed expression on her face, half confusion
and half something that looked almost like fear.

Lawrence stared down at her, the only sound their mutually
uneven breathing and the crackling of the fire on the grate.

"Clara," Lawrence said, feeling as if the word came from a
space very deep inside him, a space that could not pretend or
lie or fight his own emotions any longer. Enough of dread, or
vanity, or misplaced hopes! The only decent, soul-preserving
thing to do was to speak the unblemished truth, once and for
all, consequences be damned!

"Clara," he repeated, his hands sliding down to gather up
hers. "I do not know why we ceased to . . . why our affections
cooled, except I must tell you now that mine never did."

Clara gasped and stared into his face, and he hoped the fire
helped her to see his sincerity.

"I grew cold and distant in my behavior to you because it
was the only way to hide from you that my heart burned with
jealousy. Not just of the men who danced with you, promenaded

with you, and made you laugh, but that you chose to continue in such a style, choosing such light gaiety over marrying me. I thought to make you jealous in return, by dancing and playing cards and supping with other ladies, but your gaiety only increased. It became clear to me that freedom from my company was what would please you most . . ."

"Oh, Lawrence, no," Clara said, pressing his fingers with her own.

"I love you, Clara. I have for years. I never stopped." He gave a shaky smile. "I doubt I ever could stop."

Clara sucked in a sharp breath, and closed her eyes. "But," she said, not opening her eyes, "you were so eager to let me go. You offered nothing but rejection when I asked you for a marriage date. If you love me, how could that be?"

His silence forced her to open her eyes, as he wanted, because she must see his earnestness for herself.

"The only thing I was eager for was to avoid hearing you say the awful words I dreaded."

"Oh, Lawrence," Clara whispered on a sigh. "If only you had thought to ask me if I loved you."

"It was the question I most feared."

"You needn't have. I would have told you I did."

Did. He recoiled from the word, but it was too late to run from the truth.

"And now?" he asked. He would have let his hands slip from hers, but she held him tight as she gave a small laugh.

"The only way to save my reputation following Phyllis's lie was to do as everyone said I should and elope with you," she said. "But I refused you. Why would I do that, Lawrence?"

"Because you could not bear a life married to me?"

Clara blew out a breath, sounding rather like a headmaster disgusted with a slow-witted student. "I suppose I can see how you might leap to that conclusion, but, no. I refused you because I could not bear a life married to a man who did not love me, not when I was in love with him, with you, Lawrence."

She rose up on her knees, to take his face between her two

hands. "I loved you then, and I love you yet," she said straightly, directly into his eyes.

He shuddered and reached up to grasp her face even as she grasped his. "Sweet heaven, Clara, have we been two of the world's greatest fools?" he whispered.

"Have been, but need not remain so," she assured him.

"How to undo all the harm—"

She did not speak her answer to him, demonstrating it instead by pressing her mouth to his. If he had any doubts remaining, she meant to burn them away by the fire of their kiss, a kiss too long delayed, too nearly lost—only to be lost herself to the flames his touch created.

There was no talk of wounds past, nor of gentlemanly honor, nor of marital prerequisites. There was only the two of them and their newfound and nearly-missed joy, their need to touch one another and know that their deepest dreams and hopes had somehow sprung to life.

The dawning sun discovered their limbs entwined, their whispered words of love embodied, and their belated slumber granted only now that they could joyously sleep in one another's embrace.

Six

Clara sat in the coach that had pulled up before the unprepossessing entrance to Almack's. Lawrence, her husband of a little more than one month, sat opposite her. Neither one spoke, but they both waited and watched in a companionable silence as Lady Esther made her way under the arched portal that led into the interior of the most exalted assembly rooms in all London.

"I wonder she dares to come here," Lawrence said, sounding faintly sorry for the woman.

Clara nodded, having been already appraised of Lady Esther's latest escapade even though she and Lawrence had only returned from Salisbury two days ago.

"Lord Dalton threatens to shoot her on sight," Lawrence said with a twist of his lips.

Clara grinned. "Stuff!"

"I do not know about that. Lady Esther stayed at his mama's home for three weeks, and I know of no way to twist an ankle to warrant that manner of imposition. It was clearly a ploy, and equally clearly one that Lord Dalton severely resented. But, then again, who could not resent having Lady Esther at hand for three weeks?"

"Poor girl. I cannot dislike her entirely, as it was her ridiculous act that did induce us to marry at long last. Whereas without her efforts, we might have in truth become estranged from one another."

Lawrence conceded the point with a lift of his shoulders, but added a grin. "Tell me again how jealous you felt when you saw her in my arms, in that wetly diaphanous gown of hers."

Clara sniffed. "I will not. But, thinking on it, I amend my statement. I do dislike Lady Esther entirely."

Lawrence laughed and stole a kiss before climbing from the carriage to offer a hand down to his wife.

"We might be turned away, you realize, if rumors of the elopement have spread," Clara cautioned as she adjusted her shawl.

"Trouble and Bertie say they have not heard one word. But even if tales have indeed spread and we are refused entrance for being so low bred as to elope, then we will simply go find new company among the other couples who have married for love, *ton* be damned."

"Such language! You must be low bred indeed," Clara teased.

They were still smiling when they approached the Major-domo, Mr. Willis, at the bottom of the stairs. To Clara's mild surprise, Mr. Willis merely nodded at them, granting them permission to pass beyond him to the ballroom above.

"It seems we are yet acceptable to the patronesses, my dear," Lawrence noted in a whisper, then kissed her ear.

"We shall not be if they see you constantly putting your lips about my person."

"Like this?" he asked, and kissed her on the forehead and made her laugh.

They entered the ballroom in time to hear the musicians abruptly cease playing in response to a long, high wail of despair.

"Oh, dear," Clara said, and felt a touch of pity as she spied Lady Esther standing at the center of a circle of gawking faces.

Lord Dalton had plainly turned his back to the girl, but that was not the cause of Lady Esther's anguished cry. It was the sight of four other backs turned to her—those of four of the seven patronesses—that had surely caused her to wail. If Lady Esther had not understood the deeper meaning by then, the approach of a frosty-faced Lady Jersey would have served.

Lady Jersey came to Lady Esther's side. "Myself and my good friend, Lord Dalton, say good evening, Lady Esther," she said, and it was absolutely manifest in her tone that the words were not a greeting but a dismissal. A dismissal from the company at Almack's, Clara knew, was for life, with no second chances. Lady Esther would never pass through these rooms again.

Lady Jersey turned without another word, and three footmen stepped forward to surround the dismissed Lady Esther. She was escorted from the room as a murmur of gasps and whispered words followed in her wake. Clara might have found room in her heart to feel just a little sorry for the girl—if only Lady Esther had chosen to present any finer emotion than the look of petulance that filled her face as she was led away.

"I do not think Lady Esther will soon be changing her name to Lady Dalton," Lawrence said dryly.

Clara shook her head "The disgrace of being turned away from Almack's could have easily been our own," she pointed out. She caught sight of her sister-in-law, Phyllis, across the room, and tipped her fan in greeting. Even from this distance, Clara could see Phyllis's relief at seeing that her brother and his wife had been admitted this Wednesday night.

"Oh, I suppose I should have minded banishment from Almack's for a bit, but not for long," Lawrence said.

"Oh, truly?"

"Truly. There is only one thing I mind a great deal about the place."

Clara turned to look up at her beloved husband. "And what is that, pray tell?"

Lawrence caught up and lifted one of her hands, turning it over to press a warm kiss on her wrist just below her glove. His eyes glittered with laughter and a more earthy sentiment as well. "That it keeps me from being home in bed with you," he said.

"Then we are of like mind," Clara said, and knew it was only the truth.

Lady Of Intrigue

Alice Holden

One

"Is our quarry visible from here?" James Ware asked. Attired in his evening finery, he leaned forward in the straight-backed chair, his clasped hands falling between his knees.

"She is the blonde in the emerald dress," Rachel Kendall replied, as Lady Granville waltzed by in the arms of Lord Bennington, a moderately tall, haughty-faced man.

James sat up straight, slid a little forward in the small chair, and gaped unabashedly at the honey-haired beauty with the scandalously exposed bosoms. Rachel's blue eyes narrowed with a mingling of amusement and annoyance.

"Stunning," he murmured under his breath.

Throwing her eyes heavenward, Rachel said dryly, "Regardless of how prettily she is packaged, she is still a thief." Had her own heart not been encased in marble as far as men were concerned, she might have felt a little jealous, for the man sitting beside her was most attractive with a tall, lean manliness. But she was as immune to him as she was to the rest of the male species. Let him ogle if he must, it was nothing to her.

But Mr. Ware seemed unable to take his bemused eyes from his whirling visual feast. Rachel pulled a face, which he was too distracted to notice. It was time she and her fellow investigator got down to business. Removing her fan from her wrist, Rachel rapped her partner smartly with the closed fan on his nicely formed shoulders to regain his attention.

He looked at Rachel rather oddly through a pair of golden-brown eyes set in long lashes as dark as his raven hair, then gave her a sheepish grin of understanding and said, "Really, Mrs. Kendall, the lady is not in my style."

In truth, James was embarrassed to be caught by the comely widow behaving like an inexperienced callow youth. True, he had been preoccupied a little with the goddess's beauty (what virile man wouldn't be?), but he had also been considering how Lady Granville had become embroiled in the misadventure of which she was accused.

Rachel's pretty brows arched with skepticism. "You do not care for a strikingly beautiful woman?" He had not seemed immune to Lady Granville a moment ago.

James laughed at her droll expression, which he admitted was reasonable considering his suspect reply. "Well, that is, not unless she is unencumbered. I really would find no joy in pursuing another man's wife."

Not having a clever retort at hand, Rachel snapped open the ivory spokes of her fan and stirred up a breeze with rapid motions.

Since James Ware had arrived a short time ago and found Rachel waiting for him, she had assiduously avoided small talk. Now she quickly cut off what in her opinion was an unfruitful sidetrack on his part while she completely ignored her own responsibility for goading the response from him.

"You do agree that Lady Granville pilfered the jewels to pay her gambling debts?" she asked in her best no-nonsense voice to put them back on track.

"It would seem so," James said absently, his eyes fixed on Mrs. Kendall's attire. The young widow was as up to the mark as the other fashionable women here at Almack's. The décolléte of her expensively cut peach silk gown displayed the roundness of her breasts to within an inch of accepted standards. To all outward appearances, she was one with her sisters of the ton, while, in reality, her unfeminine pursuits would have had her barred forever from these hallowed rooms had the influential patronesses discovered her true vocation.

Forcing his mind back to the investigation and off Mrs. Kendall, whom he was finding more interesting than their business discussion, James said, "The problem is we have no hard evidence to prove that Lady Granville duped her husband and used the profits to cancel her obligations."

Rachel snapped her fan closed and slipped the decorative accoutrement over her slender wrist to dangle free. "No, not as yet. It will be our job to find the evidence. But consider this, in spite of several thorough investigations by the authorities, no other suspects have been unearthed. And Lord Granville, himself, suspects her."

Frowning, James looked down into Mrs. Kendall's serious dark blue eyes. "Why doesn't he just question his wife? If the lady is guilty, she will surely break down under aggressive interrogation."

"Ah," Rachel said, "there's the rub and the answer to why you and I are on this case. Lord Granville fears if he accuses his wife without solid proof, she will indignantly deny any involvement and turn against him. His greatest concern is that Lady Granville will withdraw the little regard she still has for him."

"It is astonishing what a man will put up with for a morsel of affection from a woman who takes his breath away," James observed, shaking his head.

Rachel nodded her agreement. "Lord Granville is a good thirty years older than his wife. But he worshiped the lady when he married her, and he still loves her beyond reason. Such addiction puts up with a lot. He has turned a blind eye to her indiscretions with Lord Bennington, but he cannot in good conscience watch his family treasures slip into the hands of unscrupulous moneylenders."

"Is Lady Granville Bennington's mistress?"

Rachel waved a careless hand. "Most people think so. Do you know him?"

"We were on the social scene at the same time during my salad days, however, we were never friends." James rubbed his chin. "I understand there were three separate thefts, in three disparate locations, investigated by three different local law officials with no positive results."

"Yes, that is so. The sole common denominator is Lady Granville, herself. On each occasion, she had in her possession a piece of family jewelry which Lord Granville had removed from his safe and allowed her to wear. She was the one who raised a cry and claimed each piece in turn had been stolen."

"That doesn't look good for her. It defies reason that at least one of the supposed robberies has not been solved."

"Then you agree that Lord Granville has good reason to be suspicious of his wife?" Rachel asked.

"Yes, although I doubt the jewels went to a moneylender. Moneylenders generally hold on to collateral, at least for a time, nor need they be circumspect when they decide to sell the valuables, making the transactions easy for an investigator to trace." He shifted in his chair. "I believe Lady Granville's booty was fenced for a better profit, maybe even abroad."

"Hmm," Rachel said thoughtfully, "that could make the pieces difficult to recover."

"Probably impossible," James said, arching his back. He had selected the two uncomfortable chairs pushed up against the wall in a secluded corner for their fortuitous positions. Private words could be exchanged without fear of being intercepted by curious ears. But he needed to stretch his long frame.

"Would you care to dance, Mrs. Kendall?" he asked, rising to his feet. Rachel looked up at him with unsure eyes. She had not come here tonight to engage in a pleasurable evening. Her contact with James Ware was to be all business.

"We can't sit in this spot all night without drawing undue attention to ourselves," he explained, when he saw the indecision on the oval face framed with dark curls.

Rachel shrugged, rose, and walked into his arms to the strains of a waltz already in progress. Melding in with the male patrons in their de rigueur silk breeches and elegant evening coats and the women in their sumptuous gowns, creations of the leading dressmakers of London, James swung Rachel smoothly around the dance floor.

After a few turns, during which James weighed the merits of the case, he picked up their prior conversation. "I will be honest with you, Mrs. Kendall. I do not think we have a prayer of recovering the jewels for Lord Granville. Nor are you and I, by some happenstance, going to be in the right place at the right time to catch his wife red-handed."

Rachel's face clouded. "Tell me, Mr. Ware, just why did you agree to work with me if you have such a pessimistic view of this endeavor?"

"Ah, there's the rub," he said repeating her words. "It would not speak well of my gratitude to your father for having saved my skin more than once if I were to refuse to step in and assist his daughter in performing this commission while he is laid low. Had Lord Granville, instead of your father, approached me on his own, I seriously doubt I would have given him any encouragement or agreed to take the case."

The two whirled around the dance floor in silence. Rachel knew her father respected James Ware's intelligence and investigative abilities. Sir Henry had been Mr. Ware's mentor when they were both covert agents for the Bow Street Runners, but Rachel was disturbed by her new partner's negative approach to the enterprise. The Granville case certainly had troubling aspects as Mr. Ware had pointed out, but *impossible* was not in Rachel's vocabulary. She wished her father's heart had remained strong. If he had stayed healthy, she would be working with him now instead of the bothersome Mr. Ware.

The waltz came to an end. James offered Rachel his arm and walked to the side of the dance floor with her. Peering over the top of her head, he said, "Lady Granville has just gone into the card room. How skilled is your play with cards?"

"Tolerable," she answered.

"Shall we see if we can find an opening at the table where Lady Granville is playing?"

Her skin tingled from the touch of his fingers on her back as he guided her toward the card room door. Rachel was certain the tingling sensation was caused by their finally making a positive move toward solving the case, for it would be foolish to think that Mr. Ware's impersonal touch could possibly excite her.

Rachel was the first to secure a seat when a disgruntled loser left, mumbling something about the curse of being born unlucky. She fished in her reticule for her steel-rimmed glasses, looped the spectacles over her ears, and picked up her cards. With nimble fingers, she arranged the cards by suit. James observed the play from over her shoulder. Her cards were mediocre at best, but with some skillful maneuvering and a spot of bluffing she managed to win the first hand. She gathered the cards for her deal and shuffled them deftly with expert ease. James smiled to himself in admiration. Tolerable, indeed. Mrs. Kendall was a shark.

Within minutes, James was able to ease himself into an abandoned seat next to Lady Granville. The delicate scent of her rose perfume tantalized his nostrils. She turned her head to him and smiled. He grinned back at her. The slightly slanted eyes as green as her stylish gown exuded a blatant sensuality. James could almost understand and forgive Lord Granville's foolish enslavement.

Luck was not with Lady Granville, however, but she bet conservatively and suffered only minor loses. Almack's apparently was not the place where she was accumulating the debt that would require draconian measures to raise money to repay.

After an hour's unsuccessful play, James threw his cards into the center of the table and relinquished his seat to a waiting patron. With his hands clasped behind his back, he watched as Rachel concentrated on the cards while he concentrated on observing her. She had an uncommon prettiness, even with the funny little spectacles perched on her nose. In fact, the glasses gave her the winsomeness of a youngster playing grown-up. Quite endearing. His gaze never left her face as he watched the subtle changes in her expression with the turn of each card. Reading people was his job. Under the businesslike facade he was certain she was a tender, loving woman. He wondered why she had never remarried. Not from lack of opportunity, he decided. It had to be her choice.

Rachel swept her considerable winnings toward her, scooped up the coins, and deposited them with her spectacles into her reticule and drew the strings together. She pushed back her chair, stood up, and hooked her hand through James's proffered arm.

"She is cautious because of Almack's rigid rules," Rachel said, commenting on Lady Granville's play when she and James had cleared the card room.

"I think so, too. If she is using the ill-gotten money to cancel gaming vouchers, those debts were not amassed from the sort of prudent wagering we saw here tonight."

"In time we will discover where those mounting debts occurred. Those things cannot be hidden," Rachel said with conviction.

"You are right," James agreed, but he was afraid their investigation would begin and end there. Searching for the jewels and proving the beautiful thief was the culprit would be an exercise in futility. He had voiced his realistic opinion once before tonight to Mrs. Kendall, and she had pronounced it cynicism. He would not do so again. Sir Henry had his word that he would remain on the case for a month. He had never shirked his responsibilities nor given less than his best effort to a commission while with the Runners; he would do no less on this hopeless venture.

"The supper room is open. Shall we find a table?" James asked.

Rachel knew she should refuse, leave James Ware's company, and seek out the friends to whom she had been merely nodding all evening. The dining room would be crowded and continuation of business would be impossible with the danger of eavesdroppers. Taking supper with Mr. Ware would be a social act, not business. But her success at the card table had mellowed her. She preceded him into the supper room. Not particularly hungry, she filled her plate sparingly from the buffet while James piled his plate high.

At a table with other patrons, they sat side by side. The conversation was general across and up and down the table. Rachel knew some of the people; James others. Introductions were made this one to that and chitchat was exchanged. Finally, James was able to secure his partner's attention exclusively.

Rachel sipped her punch and looked at James over the rim of her glass. Her vow to shun pleasure while in James Ware's presence had been completely forgotten with the laughter they shared with the others and his easy manner. She had relaxed and, without conscious thought, was enjoying his company enormously.

They talked about everyday events, the food and the dancing and their mutual acquaintances.

"The cards were not kind to you this evening," she said in a teasing tone, keeping up the banter that had flowed between them.

"I have been dreading since we left the card room that you would decide to point out my inadequacies," he said, grimacing.

"How much did you lose?" She tried to appear sympathetic and failed. Her lips quirked.

"Oh, less than a pound, I imagine. I did not keep track. Stop gloating, ma'am. I am aware that you came out several shillings ahead."

Rachel shook her jingling reticule before his face, her deep blue eyes dancing. "In here, sir, is your pound and quite a bit more."

"Remind me, Mrs. Kendall, never to play cards with you again."

Simultaneously, the pair smiled into each other's eyes. The jolt that went through James shocked him. He burned to snatch her into his arms and kiss her thoroughly.

Now that he had passed thirty, he found himself, at times, wondering what he had missed by not having a wife and family. Always before the adventure of a new assignment had been all he ever craved. He had thrived on danger. There had been several women over the years, but none who had made a lasting impression. Rachel Kendall eclipsed every one of them, and, at that moment, James knew he wanted her, not for tonight, but for a lifetime.

His hand covered hers while she spoke to a woman across the table who had gained her attention. He idly fondled her fingers beneath his hand.

Rachel became aware of a warm, pleasant emotion running through her breast. When she identified the source, she quickly slid her hand from under his, picked up a fork, and began to viciously fragment a piece of salmon into bits.

James cursed himself for letting his own feelings dictate his action. She obviously did not share his strong emotions, although when their eyes met, she had appeared as shaken as he.

"Do you come to Almack's often?" he asked to erase the discomfort he had caused her and restore a measure of normalcy to their discourse.

"Not often," she replied in a stark voice. "I attended occasionally for my mother's sake before my father's illness. Mama finds much pleasure in society."

"And you?"

"Not as much."

"I, myself, had a devil of a time securing a voucher for this evening," he said, his voice a tone unnatural with unease. He wanted very much to reestablish their former amiability. "I found a friend who had an invitation, only to discover the thing was not transferable."

When Rachel had met Mr. Ware in her father's study for the first time the previous day he had not had a voucher, but assured her he could secure one. She had been dubious, for one did not obtain an invitation without knowing the right people or having the right connections. Many outsiders with pretensions to acceptability aspired to vouchers to Almack's. None received them.

"I was surprised when I got your note saying we could meet here. How did you finally manage an invitation?" Rachel was too curious not to ask, but her voice had an edge to it.

"I called in a long ago favor," James said.

"Long ago favor? From whom?"

He was painfully conscious that he had not softened her. She was still starched up.

"Lady Jersey," he answered.

"Oh," Rachel said. The foremost patroness of Almack's did not give out vouchers indiscriminately. Rachel was secretly impressed that Sally Jersey was obligated to Mr. Ware, but she had no intention of letting him know. The man was too self-assured as it was. Too handsome and too . . . oh lord, she would not have it. He was awakening needs that she had dismissed as unnecessary in her life, but she would never succumb to his magnetism. Never.

For six years she had carefully avoided anything approaching an involvement with a man. She had actively discouraged suitors from murmuring compliments and dancing attendance on her. Now James Ware, with his inescapable charm, had been thrust into her life for at least a month. She would be forced to endure a close contact with him, but she was determined to keep their relationship impersonal and professional.

"I would like to go home," Rachel said, breaking into some desultory comment James was making and which she had rather rudely disregarded. "Would you please send for my carriage?"

"Why don't I dismiss your coachman and take you home myself?" James put a conciliatory hand on her arm. Rachel was keenly aware of his masculinity. It had been years since her bones had weakened at a man's touch. She panicked.

"That won't be necessary. I have been a widow for six years and am quite accustomed to go about without protective escort."

James removed his hand from her arm, stung by her waspish tone which was an affront to his intentions.

"As you will, ma'am," he said, with a cool deference.

James schooled his face into a cordial smile as he exchanged leave-taking pleasantries with the people at the table who had begun to take an interest in the proceedings between him and Rachel. Rachel, too, smiled, aware that she needed to quell any incipient gossip.

With the silence between them lengthening, the two investigators walked from the supper room without touching one another. James retrieved Rachel's evening cloak, laid the black velvet garment over her shoulders, and took his own silk hat and silver-headed cane from the attendant.

When her carriage was announced, James set his tall hat on his head, tucked his cane under one arm, and escorted Rachel to the vehicle with its coach lights dancing in wisps of fog. He helped her up into the plush interior, mumbling his adieu, and receiving an equally indistinguishable farewell from her. He shut the well-polished door firmly and stepped back as the wheels of the carriage rolled forward and the vehicle faded into the fog.

A puzzled James stood under the haze of light from a street-lamp and stared into the foggy darkness. Mrs. Kendall had taken an aversion to him. Yet before he made his admiration clear, she had given him eager smiles, her cheeks filled with vivid color, their conversation congenial, jolly, affable.

The fog swirled around James as he walked back toward the entrance of the building to seek out the doorman to send for his own carriage. In his job, at times he relied on instinct and intuition. He felt strongly there was something about Mrs. Kendall's reaction that had more to do with men in general than with him personally. But capturing her affections seemed suddenly to be on a par with solving the disappearance of Lord Granville's family treasures.

Two

Rachel rose late the next day, for she had been a long while getting to sleep after returning from Almack's, kept awake by a troubled conscience. Her shrewish behavior toward Mr. Ware had been inexcusable. Her past was laden with rejected men who had been turned off successfully without the need to resort to a viperous tongue. After all, she was a sophisticated woman who had moved with admirable ease through every imaginable social situation. Yet she had let Mr. Ware completely unnerve her.

Having dressed and breakfasted on toast with marmalade washed down with a single cup of tea, and her meager meal having been interspersed with deep penitent sighs, a chastened Rachel entered her father's study at eleven o'clock.

"Good morning, Papa," she said when she was inside the door.

Sir Henry rested the book he was reading on his lap and returned her greeting from the wheelchair where he sat wrapped in a black woolen shawl. Rachel leaned over and pressed a kiss to his forehead. She smoothed the thick brown hair that showed no signs of thinning and, were it not for the strands of gray, could have graced the head of a much younger man.

"Did you sleep well?" she asked as she did each morning.

"The same," he said, giving her his usual terse enigmatic reply.

She adjusted the black shawl more snugly around his thin

shoulders before going to the fireplace grate and poking up the fire. Her mind was on the imminent arrival of James Ware. What he must think of her! His good-looking features, tense and unsmiling when she had last seen him, haunted her mind. She felt the sharp stab of guilt again, for she had been totally responsible for the awkward moment. She had already fallen under the spell of the way he looked and the way he talked when he caressed her hand with such devastating results.

"Leave the fire alone," Sir Henry said to her back. Her uncharacteristic fidgeting led him to believe something was bothering her, and he guessed it had to do with her meeting with James Ware at Almack's.

"Come here and tell me what you thought of James Ware."

A tinge of color crept into her cheeks, verifying his supposition. Rachel stowed the fireplace poker into its holder and moved to the front of her father's desk, resting the small of her back against the wooden edge.

"He seems quite efficient," she said, divorcing her factual answer from the ones that would have more honestly revealed her disordered emotions.

"You are reluctant in your praise. What bothers you about him? And don't wrap your response in clean linen. The two of you will have to work as a team. You can't be tugging in opposite directions."

"Mr. Ware seems lukewarm about the investigation. Given his attitude, he would be doing you and me, to say nothing of poor Lord Granville, a disservice by remaining on the case."

Sir Henry made a steeple with his long, thin fingers. "I have never known James not to give his all when he takes on an assignment. Granted, this case is hardly up to his normal complex probes, but his orders with the Runners were sometimes of an unusual nature, and the Granville case could be considered in that category."

"Papa, Mr. Ware said he doubted we can recover the jewels or prove Lady Granville's guilt."

"The lad's playing devil's advocate with you. James is the most competent, resourceful, and clever agent I know. I cannot believe he has lost all those qualities in the three years since I last worked with him."

Rachel did not care to argue Mr. Ware's merits, but she would be more relaxed and feel personally safer where her emotions were concerned if he was off the case. Otherwise, she would have to spend a whole month on guard. If there was a chance she could convince her father . . .

"You know, I can handle this matter alone," she said. "I have entrance into all the functions Lady Granville is likely to attend." But Sir Henry was already shaking his head. "Papa, you refuse to even take into account that I have worked closely with you the past few years. I am quite capable of executing this commission without Mr. Ware's assistance."

"That is out of the question, Rachel," Sir Henry said. "James has the experience. The sort of thing you have done for me was legitimate work for barristers and solicitors. We have kept your activities secret even from your mother only because you would be ostracized in society for being employed in deeds that are considered highly improper for a woman. But the Granville case requires working undercover and maintaining secrecy. You can't handle that alone. Now, no more about it. The subject is closed." He picked up his book and began reading.

Rachel made to speak, thought better of it, turned to face the desk, opened a folder, and took out a sheaf of papers. Although she was disappointed at her father's intransigence, she knew better than to press the point. Sir Henry might take it into his head to remove her from the case altogether if she could not get along with Mr. Ware. Her father's consent for her to work with his former protégé had been hard won. Originally, he had planned to ask his fellow investigator to handle the case without Rachel's help, but she had worn him down with methodical pleading and cajoling.

Rachel removed her spectacles from the white cambric pocket of her navy blue dress and fixed them on her nose. She picked up the top sheet from the small stack of papers and began to review a list of the missing Granville jewels and the manner in which each piece vanished. She had perused but a few lines when the sound of carriage wheels crunching across the gravel drive outside the window alerted her to James Ware's arrival and caused a nervousness to tickle her stomach.

A minute later the door opened and the butler announced the former agent. James approached Sir Henry and shook the frail hand his former robust partner offered him, turned and bowed to Rachel, who nodded her unsmiling acknowledgement of his presence. His heart slumped to find her gaze no more forgiving than last night.

James had been mulling over his problem with Mrs. Kendall almost steadily during every waking moment since parting from her. She had been no more than seventeen or eighteen when she had been widowed, a tender age when the tragic loss of a young husband could become romanticized all out of proportion to reality. He decided that she might well have elevated her first love to a towering pedestal where no living man could displace the icon.

The other side of the coin was that the dead husband had been a brute whose callous manner had turned Mrs. Kendall into a misogamist. James hoped the second analysis was the reason for her strange behavior. While he had no desire whatsoever to do battle exorcising ghosts, he did have some confidence that over time he could convince Mrs. Kendall that he was not a beast, but a man with the attributes that made for an agreeable husband.

"I hear, James, that you do not believe there is a shred of hope that you can solve the Granville case to his lordship's satisfaction." James's eyebrows rose fractionally at Sir Henry's charge, his speculative brown eyes on Rachel. She hunched her shoulders and raised her hands in a gesture of feigned innocence, her eyes sparkling with mischief.

"Tattletale," James said, encouraged to be playful from her own reaction.

Rachel's sunny smile sent a surge of joy through James as their eyes met, promising an end to their discord and a new friendliness. Sir Henry breath a relieved sigh and moved his book from his lap to an end table.

"Sit down, James," he said. "You appear so tall hovering over me. You, too, Rachel. I don't feel at a disadvantage when everyone in the room is on my level."

Rachel tucked the paper she had been reading into the folder on the desk and moved to sit in an armchair on the opposite side of the room from where James was sinking into a man's leather chair.

"No, no," Sir Henry said. "I refuse to swivel my head back and forth between the two of you. Over there, both of you." His thin index finger was extended toward a green love seat directly in front of his wheelchair.

"I explained to Rachel that you were playing the devil's advocate with your skeptical pronouncements," he said as James seated himself next to Rachel on the settee, leaving a proper three or four inches between them.

"As a matter of fact, I wasn't," James said honestly. "I meant what I said."

Sir Henry frowned. "That does not sound like you, my boy. Weren't you the one who constantly reminded me that there is no case that can't be solved."

"I believe, Henry, it goes, every problem has a solution. We only have to find it."

"You think you can't find the solution to this case?"

"I already know what the solution is," James said, squaring his shoulders. "Catching Lady Granville in the act. What are our chances of that happening?"

"There is another road you can take. Finding the jewels and tying her in with the sale of them."

James planted his hands on his knees. "Henry, those jewels went to Germany or France or possibly Italy, or some other foreign country. The merchandise was too unique for Lady Granville to take a chance fencing them anywhere in England."

"If that is true," Rachel broke in, "then, Lady Granville must have an accomplice. I have never known her to travel abroad, and she definitely has not been out of the country in the past few months."

"Good point, Rachel," her father said, then held up a hand

to silence the conversation as a knock was heard at the door. Sir Henry answered verbally. The butler came in with a letter in his hand and handed it to his master. "This came by special messenger, Sir Henry."

"Thank you, Billings." Breaking the seal, Sir Henry read the single sheet while the butler left the room, closing the door unobtrusively.

"This is a schedule of Lady Granville's social activities for the next few days."

"I see you have Lord Granville's full cooperation," James noted.

"Yes, he thinks if he can prove his wife's guilt, he can use the knowledge as a lever to bind her to him and curb her infidelity. Love does strange things to a man. He refuses to accuse her without proof, for fear she will elope with Bennington. I hope, for his sake, it works out as he wants. The lady married him; she should have the decency to remain faithful."

Sir Henry held out the paper to Rachel. "Daughter, copy this for James."

Rachel rose from the sofa and took the sheet Sir Henry held out to her, circled her father's desk, and sat behind it. Locating paper and a pen, she first read over Lady Granville's schedule, then dipped the pen into the inkwell, and in a neat hand began to make the copy for Mr. Ware that her father had requested.

"I know the odds are long, James," Sir Henry said. "If you want out, I will understand. After all, I am the one who owes a debt to Granville for keeping my dual life a secret when he could have socially ruined me and my family."

Rachel looked up hopefully from her task.

James smiled at his former mentor. "Not on your life." With a sigh, Rachel resumed her copying. "When did I ever back out of an impossible case? I owe you, too. Remember the Blackstone caper?" Sir Henry's memory of tough cases he had worked on with James spilled from his lips with something of a fond remembrance.

James did more listening than talking. Everything had changed since he had last sat in this room two days ago and promised to take the Granville case for a month. Since then, he had fallen in love with Rachel Kendall. The investigation, which he had viewed as an obligatory inconvenience, had turned into a blessing. James's lips quirked in a contented smile, not at Sir Henry's animated tale, but because he had sneaked a quick peek at his pretty new partner and realized she would be at his side for four whole weeks.

Rachel sanded the copy of Lady Granville's schedule unaware that at that very moment she was the vision revolving in her handsome fellow investigator's head. She came from behind the desk and handed James the paper. He smiled his thanks with what seemed to Rachel a particularly smug grin. But he quickly looked over the itinerary with a serious mien before folding the paper neatly and tucking it into the pocket of his black coat.

"Tonight Lady Granville is dining at Bennington's townhouse and then going with the other guests to a gambling establishment on Curzon Street. I don't know the place," James said, the investigator's blood coming to the fore to temporarily block out his secret adoration of Mrs. Kendall.

"I believe it has been open for less than a year," Rachel told him. "From what I hear, the clientele is drawn in a large part from polite society who have abandoned the gambling hells of Pall Mall."

"This could give us the information we were unsuccessful in securing at Almack's. I think I shall drop in there tonight and see how Lady Granville fares at the gaming tables."

"I will accompany you," Rachel said.

"No!" The stern rebuff came from her father.

"That is no place for a lady," Sir Henry said. "I forbid it, Rachel."

"Papa, how can I be a part of the investigation if you deny me access to where I can gather evidence?"

"M'dear, James will share his findings with you. There are times such as this when you must rely on your male partner."

"I will come by first thing tomorrow and share my experience with you," James promised. Rachel missed the hint of regret in his voice, for she was too immersed in her own silent defiance. She had no intention of being summarily cast aside, but she would not cause her father further agitation by openly arguing with him. She looked at the clock on the mantel and said, "You will stay for luncheon, Mr. Ware?"

"Of course, he will," Sir Henry interceded. "Rachel, go see that an extra cover is laid for him."

James rose with Rachel and held the door open for her to pass through. She gave him a soft smile that brushed his heart. He reseated himself on the sofa and looked into Sir Henry's pensive face.

"I just want to say a few words about Rachel before she rejoins us. I know you are wondering, James, how I let my lovely daughter into the world of intrigue. When she was seventeen, she fell head over heels for a military type who was all flashy uniform and no substance. I heard things about him that were not to his credit. But Rachel would not listen and rushed into the marriage. Within six months, William Kendall was sent to America to fight in that skirmish Britain was involved in several years back and managed to get himself killed. I think Rachel came to her senses long before he left. She never confided in either me or her mother, but while she did not exactly withdraw from all social life, it was apparent she had no intention of remarrying. Because she was so much at loose ends, after I left the Runners, I let her become something like a female secretary to me with a little harmless investigation thrown in. Before my heart gave out, I invited Rachel to work with me on the Granville case as a boon, fully intending to keep her under my thumb. But then I became bedridden and too weak to lift even a cup."

"And when you informed her you intended turning the case over to me, Mrs. Kendall would not hear of being pushed out," James said.

Sir Henry nodded, but before he could add another word the conversation was terminated, for Rachel breezed through the door and announced, "Mama's headache vaporized when she learned Mr. Ware was remaining for luncheon. She will join us at the table."

Sir Henry laughed. "My wife is a darling woman, but she will not be completely happy until she sees Rachel wed again. Her byword is: Every woman needs a husband. Do not be surprised if she proposes to you on my daughter's behalf."

"Oh, Papa, Mr. Ware will think you are serious." She brushed her hand on James's arm, evoking a desire in him to clasp his own hand over hers.

A footman came to wheel Sir Henry into the dining room where James was introduced to Lady Henry. Rachel had inherited her mother's jet hair and blue eyes, but the older woman lacked her daughter's vitality, which had less to do with age than with personality.

When the family with their guest sat down to luncheon the footman served them poached cod with dill sauce. Lady Henry said, while she indicated the piece of fish she wished to be placed on her plate to the servant, "Rachel, dear, do take off your spectacles." She looked at James across the table. "She is so much prettier without them, don't you think, Mr. Ware?"

James drained his water glass while he thought of a diplomatic reply. "Nothing as inconsequential as spectacles could spoil Mrs. Kendall's looks," he said at last.

"Thank you, Mr. Ware, but my spectacles are not so inconsequential. I do need them to bring the world into focus." She softened the mild reproof with a faint grin.

"Posh," said her mother, as the spectacles vanished into Rachel's dress pocket. "You only need the ill-favored implements for close work." She patted her daughter's hand. "Now you look more the thing."

She turned her attention to James. "Rachel said that you were at Almack's last night, Mr. Ware. Your first visit?"

"Yes, ma'am," James answered, as he speared a broccoli floret.

"And how did you find it?"

"The rooms are elegant and spacious, but not as magnificent as I was led to believe."

"The orchestra is quite tuneful, though, don't you think?"

"Quite tuneful," James agreed.

"Mr. Ware and I played cards," Rachel interjected.

Lady Henry had drastically curtailed her social life since her husband had become ill and would not have had it any other way for she was devoted to her mate of twenty-five years, but she still liked to keep up with the doings of society and enjoyed experiencing the parties and dances vicariously.

"Who was at your table?" she asked.

Rachel named the players. When she mentioned Lady Granville's name, Lady Henry said, "Has Lord Bennington returned from Paris? The two are so much in each other's company that people talk."

James stared at Lady Henry over his lifted fork. "Lord Bennington was in Paris recently?"

"Yes, he has been going to France frequently for a half a year or more, I have heard. I suppose his trips do not sit well with Lady Granville. Paris is filled with beautiful women of loose morals and Bennington is known to be a philanderer."

Sir Henry asked his wife, "You are sure of this, my dear?"

"Oh, yes," she said, her blue eyes large and round, "the man has been a veritable rake since he was a stripling."

"No, Mama," Rachel interrupted, "the part about his going to Paris frequently."

"Yes, it is true. Lady Francis, his sister, mentioned it when she visited me just last week. Is it important?" She looked around the table puzzled at the interest she had stirred up, which reflected on the faces of her family and guest.

"No, no, dear heart, it has to do with some business of mine with Lord Bennington. Mr. Ware has kindly agreed to take over my business affairs while I make my recovery. Nothing for you to concern yourself about."

Lady Henry was accustomed to being put off with the same sort of excuse over the years by her husband and thought nothing of it. It never occurred to her to question the relevancy of Lord Bennington's journeys to Paris. After all, business was a man's dominion. As a woman, she did not expect to be able to understand that male world.

Nothing more was said on the subject. The conversation by

design of the master of the house became quite pedestrian for the rest of the meal.

When the luncheon concluded, Lady Henry reminded her husband that he must rest. "Doctor's orders," she said to James and offered her hand to him. "I will say goodbye, Mr. Ware, for I have some letters to write while Sir Henry naps. But please stay and visit with Rachel."

James bowed over her hand and thanked her for the excellent luncheon.

A short while later, Rachel and James sat once again in Sir Henry's study. "What do you make of Bennington's frequent trips to Paris?" she asked when they were seated next to one another at a large library table, her spectacles reperched on her nose.

"It seems to be in line with my theory that the jewels were sold on the Continent. It doesn't take a giant leap of faith to believe Bennington is her accomplice."

"No, it doesn't," Rachel said. "It is really quite logical." She nudged the papers spread out on the table before them. "Do you think it might be helpful to review the thefts to ascertain if the authorities might have missed some less obvious clue?"

James was willing to agree to any suggestion that would keep him in Mrs. Kendall's company, although he was certain that further examination of the manner in which the goods were stolen would yield no pertinent information.

"Yes, let's do that," he said, and moved his chair to where their heads were close together. Her hair, as dark as night, had a clean, soapy smell. He leaned back a little so that he could observe her without her noticing.

"The first occurrence was at a house party at Lord Bennington's estate," Rachel said, as she concentrated on the paper before her. "Lady Granville carelessly left a sapphire ring unsecured on the top of her dresser."

"That was seven months ago."

"Just about that," Rachel said.

"I suppose the servants were questioned and searched as

usual in such cases?" James edged a little closer to Rachel until their shoulders almost touched.

"Yes, but without success. Two months later a topaz necklace was purloined from Lady Granville's hotel room in Brighton while she was at dinner in the dining room."

"Same results on that investigation, right?" he asked casually, his mind on her. Her scent had the fragrance of a spring bouquet.

"You are correct, Mr. Ware. The necklace has an estimated monetary value of twenty-five hundred pounds, but was priceless to the family for it was a gift from the first King George."

James turned in his chair to face Rachel. Her blue eyes were luminous in her creamy complexion. "Do you think you might call me James?" he asked with a charming grin.

Rachel met his disarming gaze. His feelings were there in his sensual brown eyes. His look was causing a tug at her heart again. Rachel picked up a paper from the table. William had looked at her in much the same manner before their marriage turned unhappy. But she would not make the mistake of over-reacting again to Mr. Ware's simple request as she had at Almack's the previous night when he had asked to drive her home.

"Of course," she said, "and you must call me Rachel." She pushed her spectacles more firmly onto her nose. To show him she was quite amiable, she used his given name. "You see, James, that the necklace's history makes it irreplaceable."

James moved his head to a position where Rachel's soft hair enticingly brushed his cheek. While drifting into a delicious reverie of what might yet be between him and Rachel, he pretended interest in the sketch of the antique necklace that George the First had bestowed on the Granville clan.

"The last bogus theft was during a houseparty at the Granvilles' own country estate," Rachel continued, unmindful that her words were falling on flagging ears. "Lady Granville lost a ruby brooch. The usual suspects were questioned and the house was turned upside down, but without results."

"Three pieces of jewelry that Lord Granville will never see again," James murmured, speaking without considering what he was saying. Rachel looked up at him fretfully over her spectacles.

"I do wish you would not persist in throwing cold water on the case. Miracles do happen," she said curtly.

Her tone cured James's inattention. "Ah, yes, I suppose my years in detection have made me a realist, but, believe me, I am not a defeatist. You, dear Rachel, shall inspire me to seek a miracle."

Rachel shook her head and affected a resigned expression. "Go home, James. I think we have quite exhausted our powers of detection for today."

James was nonplussed for a moment at the abrupt dismissal, but he put on a congenial smile, pushed his chair back, and rose with her. She stood close to him. If he wrapped his arms around her, the top of her head would just clear his shoulders. James moved back out of her sphere before he committed a social blunder and kissed the unwilling lady.

"I shall see you tomorrow when I call with news of my investigation at the Curzon Street gambling house," he said.

Rachel nodded and went to the wall to ring for the butler to show James out. When he had cleared the room, she said to herself, "Or perhaps sooner than tomorrow, my dear James."

Three

Very late that same night, Billings flagged down a hackney cab in front of Sir Henry's townhouse. Rachel came down the front steps at a signal from the butler. Both her parents were long asleep.

Billings was accustomed to Mrs. Kendall coming back well after midnight from a party or ball, but this was the first time he recalled her going out at an unseemly hour. He had offered himself as an escort, but had been turned down. Moreover, it was a mystery to him why she chose public transportation over her own comfortable conveyance. But a servant was not in a position to question his employer's grown daughter.

Billings considered informing Sir Henry of Mrs. Kendall's irregular behavior, but the master's fragile heart might cease to function if he became unduly aggravated. The butler shuddered at the thought of being the instrument of Sir Henry's demise. Worried for the young widow's safety, but impotent to launch a successful challenge to her obstinate independence, he could do nothing but watch the cab until it vanished into the next street.

Through the trap door, Rachel gave the driver the address of the fashionable gaming establishment on Curzon Street. She fluttered a scented handkerchief in the air to ameliorate the pungent odor of the hack before putting the bit of lace back into her reticule, resigned to tolerate the malodorous stale air for the relatively short ride.

Pulling a black mask with silver sequins from the pocket of her long cloak, Rachel fitted the disguise over her face. She tied the black ribbons at the back of her head, only to become annoyed to find that the narrow eye slits seriously impaired her vision.

The clerk in the shop where she had gone late that afternoon to buy the mask had assured her it was the latest disguise for a woman of unblemished character who wished to retain her reputation in ticklish situations. Grimacing, Rachel lifted the mask and tucked the domino up onto her forehead. No sense in being discomforted before necessary.

The hack creaked to a halt before a house, which from the outside was indistinguishable from the other respectable-looking residences on the block.

"Are you sure this is the right place?" Rachel asked the driver, as he reached into the cab through the trap door for his fare.

"It's the address you give me, missus," he said. "But if you're asking if it's the gaming house, it is."

"Thank you," Rachel said and paid him. Out on the sidewalk, she remembered the mask and pulled it down to hide the upper part of her face before she climbed the front steps and rang the bell.

Rachel was admitted into a well-lit vestibule by a giant attendant who looked capable of culling the undesirables from the worthy and dispatching the unwanted expeditiously, which she was certain was his purpose in manning the door. He politely volunteered to see to her wraps. She handed over her cloak and walked to the public rooms in the direction he had pointed.

The card room, which was just off the entrance hall, was relatively quiet. She squinted through the slit in her mask at the customers, searching for Lady Granville and promptly bumped into a table. The two men playing piquet scowled at her and muttered words she wished she had not heard. Feeling her way, rather than actually seeing where she was going, she yearned to tear the hampering disguise from her face. Besides restricting her visual ability, the thing was uncomfortably scratchy and warm.

Rachel raised the mask off her eyes and peered from under it around the room of tables filled with card players. She saw a scattering of women whom she identified from their outré ensembles as of the Fashionable Impures seated among the men, but Lady Granville was not among them.

From an adjoining room she heard a croupier cry, "The point is six." Replacing the mask, Rachel followed the sound into a much larger room of the casino crowded with gamers. The level of noise from the clinking chips and a mangle of gentlemen's voices was considerably louder than in the card room. From a silver tray, a waiter in a blue and gold uniform offered Rachel a selection of glasses of wine and brandy, which she refused with a polite, "No, thank you."

Rachel lifted the encumbering mask for several seconds to inspect her immediate surroundings, before dropping it back into place. She was adjacent to the hazard table where a shooter was just casting the dice against the side of the table. The black dotted ivory squares bounced back and came to rest on the green surface to a chorus of groans from several spectators grouped around the gambler who missed the point. Rachel leaned in for a closer look when she felt an unwelcome arm snake around her waist. She froze as she found herself pulled against a hard male body.

"Lovely lady, would you like to place a bet?"

The very idea of such indelicacy sent a spurt of anger through Rachel. She forcefully removed the bold hand and spun around with her palm raised to slap her accoster's brash face. But her wrist was captured in a strong grip as she squinted into James Ware's merry eyes.

"Lud, sir, you startled me," she said, half in relief and half in irritation.

"I did not mean to. I thought you would recognize my voice immediately." He put a comforting hand on her shoulder. "Forgive me," he said with that endearing grin of his, which she could not seem to resist.

"It was a corkbrained joke," she said, compelled to rip up at him just a little.

"It was," he freely admitted.

"Well, since you acknowledge it, I guess, I must forgive you," she said, not sounding totally forgiving.

"Thank you," he said, in turn, not sounding as contrite as Rachel felt the offense warranted. She lifted her mask to get a clearer view of him.

"That mask is not going to be very effective if you keep lifting it up as you have been doing since you arrived."

"I cannot see awfully well with it on," she confessed.

"Take it off, then, and put on your spectacles. No one is going to pay attention to you here. These men are too busy gambling."

That James had not shown displeasure to find her in a place where her father had forbidden her to go, surprised her. She had expected at least a senseless lecture from him.

"You are not going to berate me for coming here against my father's wishes?" she said, as she rummaged in her reticule for her spectacles.

"No, I'm not." His voice was soft and rimmed with sympathy. "Rachel, I wanted you with me tonight, but once Sir Henry gave his very definite order, it would have been rag-mannered of me to try to override his decision."

Rachel felt a glow of good feeling toward James at the admission. She became acutely aware of how close they stood, forced together by the spectators pushing to get close to the hazard table. And those irresponsible sensual stirrings were rising in her body again.

"Have you seen Lady Granville?" Rachel asked, hoping that directing the conversation back to business would wipe clean her unwanted emotions.

"Yes, over there at the faro table." He pointed across the room. With her spectacles on and the hindering mask removed, the details of the room came clear to Rachel. Every conceivable gambling activity was represented at the crowded tables.

None of the women she saw, and a good number of them were perfectly respectable ladies, wore masks. She wished she had not listened to the unknowledgeable clerk. James must think her the worst sort of gudgeon.

Lady Granville was sitting next to Lord Bennington at a table covered with a green baize cloth enameled with card suits.

"Come on," James said enclosing Rachel's hand in his. He wedged his tall form past several gaming tables to the far side of the room and wormed them into a position where both he and Rachel had a clear view of the faro table.

Lady Granville whooped as the dealer lifted a card from the

box in front of him and exposed a ten. "I win again," she cried. Lord Bennington, who was not betting, smiled at her.

"You are exceptionally lucky this evening, m'dear. Don't stop now," he said.

Noting the sizeable pile of tokens in front of the beauty, Rachel whispered to James, "She has won a great deal of money."

"For now," James said, his mouth close to her ear. "I'd bet a pony it won't last."

Attracted by Lady Granville's fantastic string of consecutive wins, a sizeable crowd had gathered to cheer her on. But within minutes Rachel saw the beginnings of the fulfillment of James's prediction, as Lady Granville sustained three straight losses.

The disillusioned spectators began to drift away as the croupier raked in more and more of her unsuccessful wagers. Rachel noted a frantic determination replacing the former euphoria on the beauty's face. Lord Bennington assumed a sympathetic mien, but urged, "Don't give up now, m'dear, your luck is bound to return," and Lady Granville seemed to take heart from her lover's assertion. Her face reflected a new confidence that her prosperity would recommence.

Rachel spoke over her shoulder to James. "She is foolishly increasing her wagers."

"Yes, with disastrous results." The croupier was again raking in a substantial wager.

James motioned Rachel to come away from the table where Lady Granville had diminished her previous winnings to no more than a handful of chips.

As he came to the roulette wheel, James stopped, took a couple of tokens from his pocket, leaned over and piled them on the line between the twenty-nine and thirty-two.

"No more bets," the croupier called as the wheel slowed to a stop. The ivory ball came to rest on the twenty-nine.

James picked up the considerable winnings the croupier pushed toward him.

Rachel snatched his arm and turned him to her with widened eyes. "How did you do that?"

He grinned. "Intuition," he said smugly.

"Indeed!" Rachel shook her head in disbelief.

James reached over and with his index finger gently pushed Rachel's spectacles, which had slid to the end of her nose, back into place.

Rachel was not immune to the gentle affection in his eyes, but love was dangerously deceptive. She knew to her sorrow that a man could be a consummate actor and feign admiration to get exactly what he wanted, only later to turn into an insensitive brute. She had learned her lesson and would not be taken in again.

"Lord Bennington appeared to goad Lady Granville into wagering imprudently," Rachel said, concentrating on their enterprise. "Why would he do that? It was as if he had an interest in seeing that she lost. It somehow just doesn't make sense."

James seemed deep in thought, his unfocused eyes looking toward the floor. "Rachel, do you know who owns this casino?" he asked, returning his eyes to her face.

"No, I suppose it must be some syndicate. These operations are rarely in the hands of one man."

"That's true. However, it is not unusual for members of the aristocracy to buy an interest in a profitable gaming establishment."

"You suspect that Lord Bennington owns a part of this house?" Rachel said, reading his thoughts.

"It is possible. I think I saw someone here tonight who might supply the answer." He offered Rachel his arm. To an onlooker their ambling might appear aimless, but she knew James was seeking the unnamed man he had mentioned.

"Over here, m'dear," he said, when they entered the card room. He led her to a balding middle-aged man with dark bushy brows who sat alone with a hand of patience laid out on the table before him. He had just placed a red queen over his black king.

"May I have a word with you, Willoughby?" James said to him.

"How do, Ware." The man half rose from his chair until James introduced Rachel. Then he stood up. He was plump and not much taller than she.

He smiled at her, but the toothy grin disappeared when James asked him bluntly, "Willoughby, who are the owners of this casino?"

Mr. Willoughby rolled his eyes and muttered under his breath. "This have to do with the Runners? Cause if it does, I ain't saying."

"No," James told him, "it has nothing to do with the Runners."

"You ain't ever lied to me, James." Mr. Willoughby searched the former agent's face.

"And I am not doing so now, Harry. This is a personal matter."

Mr. Willoughby's jelly jowls quivered as he worked his mouth and considered whether or not to answer. "All right. But I ain't the one who told you, James, if you're asked. Lord Bennington owns the building and gets the top cut of the substantial profits. There are five or six others with lesser shares, but his lordship has the controlling interest."

"Thanks, Harry." James dribbled his winnings from the roulette wheel onto the table beside Mr. Willoughby's unplayed hand. "For your trouble . . ."

Harry Willoughby's pudgy mouth spread into a smile.

"If I knowed the information was that important to you, I would have set a price of my own."

"I would not have paid it," James said. He placed his hand on Rachel's back and guided her toward the door.

In the vestibule he said, "May I call for your carriage?" The giant who had admitted Rachel appeared with James's hat and cane and her cloak. James popped the tall silk hat onto his head and pressed a shilling into the burly man's outstretched hand.

"I came by hackney," Rachel said.

"Then, by all means, allow me to see you home. A public cab is not the safest form of transportation for a lady alone at night." He paused a moment. "That is, if I am not insulting your independent sensibilities by offering my escort," he added through quirking lips.

Rachel grimaced. "I deserved that. I would be honored to take advantage of your gallant offer."

"A most sensible decision," James said with a grin and helped her into her cloak, which the giant doorman handed him. The burly man waited with an inscrutable face to give James his cane, then held the front door open for his two departing patrons to step into the clear, cool night.

When Rachel, her spectacles safely tucked in her reticule, was settled opposite James in his well-sprung carriage that had been parked nearby, she said, "Would you have turned him down?"

"Who?" James asked puzzled at the non sequitur, for they had been commenting on the lack of fog and the brightness of the half moon while they descended the gaming house stairs and walked the few steps to the luxury coach.

"Mr. Willoughby. You said you would not have paid him."

James laughed. "Oh that. Yes, I meant it. I could have gotten the information from a dozen different informants, but Harry was at hand. In spite of what he said, all he deserved or expected was a gratuity, which I gave him. He saved us some time by telling us Bennington has control of the establishment, that's all." He rested his folded hands over the silver head of his cane, which he balanced on the floor of the carriage.

"I have a new sympathy for Lady Granville," Rachel said.

"How so?" James asked.

"Lord Bennington is not only prodding her into increasing her gambling debts for his own gain, but the despicable man is profiting from the sale of the pilfered jewels."

"And she doesn't even know it."

"No, of course she doesn't. She is probably grateful to him for putting his own reputation in jeopardy by disposing of the jewels for her."

James wondered, "Why doesn't Lady Granville confess all to her husband? If the man is as besotted as Sir Henry claims, would he not be willing to pay off her gaming vouchers to get rid of Bennington?"

"I think there is a good reason why she doesn't do that," Rachel said. "Lord Granville informed his wife an age ago that she must curtail her gaming or he would be ruined. His country estate is mortgaged to the hilt and the townhouse entailed to a first cousin who is ten years his lordship's junior. Lady Granville promised her husband she would live within her allowance and apparently kept her word for a time, but seven or eight months ago she became thick with Bennington. It is easier for her to steal the jewelry than face the idea of financial ruin. After all, she would suffer too if Lord Granville became destitute."

"What a bumble broth," James said, laying the cane across his lap. "Lady Granville feels it would be useless to confess to her husband because she thinks he will be ruined if he bails her out. Lord Granville's conscience, on the other hand, won't let him ignore the sale of the family treasures. He thinks the only way to keep both his wife and the jewels is to prove her perfidy beyond a shadow of a doubt and, thus, coerce her into remaining with him instead of running off with her lover. And Lord Bennington is laughing up his sleeve at both of them."

"Exactly," Rachel said.

James could not see Rachel's face clearly in the deep night shadows of the coach, but he suspected her expression mirrored his own disdain for Lord Bennington. They had fitted together the pieces of the puzzle concerning Lady Granville's gambling and her tawdry relationship with Bennington. But the information was meaningless. For indisputable proof, he and Rachel would have to snare Lady Granville while she carried out her swindle, a highly unlikely phenomenon.

The carriage stopped before Sir Henry's townhouse. James hopped down and reached an assisting hand to Rachel. At the door, she handed him a large brass key she had pulled from her reticule. James fitted the key into the lock, pushed open the door for her, and returned the key to her.

Rachel offered James her gloved hand. He clasped it between his own and looked down at her. The moon shined brightly in the sky above them.

"Thank you for seeing me home," Rachel said graciously, tipping her head up to meet his eyes.

"My pleasure," James replied. He found his heart beating unnaturally fast. Before he could act on his need to pull her into his arms, she disengaged her hands from his, slipped through the door, and closed it against the night and him. He heard the key turn in the inside lock as, frustrated, he walked down the stone steps to his carriage.

When Rachel was tucked beneath the covers, she thought about Lady Granville. The idea of going to the lady and explaining the situation to her came to Rachel. Once Lady Granville heard of her lover's perfidy, surely she would recognize the wisdom of throwing herself on her husband's mercy. Facing Lord Granville's wrath had to be less daunting than continuing to be forced to steal from her own husband to line Bennington's pockets. If the unhappy Granvilles were candid with each other, they could find an equitable solution to their dilemma and force Lord Bennington out of their lives.

Rachel's compassion for Lady Granville was strong and real. Visions of her own days in despair still haunted her. She, too, had been subjected to humiliation by a man whose character she had sadly misjudged.

But what if Lady Granville failed to see the truth? Rachel, herself, had refused to listen to anything said against William, even from her own father, whom she had trusted implicitly since she was a small girl. In her naiveté she had imagined that she could never have fallen so much in love with a devious man.

If Lady Granville should doubt Rachel, the beauty would alert Lord Bennington. Her and James's cover would be pierced and the investigation would collapse. The risk was too great. James could be put in danger, for Bennington was known to be a vindictive man. James. She was not unaffected by his charisma, nor could she seem to dismiss him as effortlessly as she had her previous admirers. She did have a real fondness for her investigative partner. She enjoyed his company and his conversation. But she was determined not to fall in love a second time.

Rachel turned over onto her side and snuggled her head deeper into her feather pillow. She had had six years of delicious liberty and intended to remain in an independent state forever. But she had a strong premonition that someday when James Ware walked out of her life, he would still remain quite unforgettable.

Four

James stood in front of a wall of paintings at the Royal Academy. Religious pictures, portraits, a landscape, and a sea battle, probably Admiral Nelson's death aboard the *Victory* at Trafalgar, James decided, but the rendition was placed too high for him to identify the hero with any certainty. But, in any case, he was not interested in that particular painting. He was completely absorbed in examining the Constable landscape of the Suffolk countryside, which providentially had been hung at his eye level.

Rachel was a little apart from him, not looking at the paintings but scrutinizing the spotty number of spectators spread along the gallery.

"They must have changed their plans," she remarked.

"Probably," James said, not removing his fascinated eyes from the painting.

"James, attend to business," Rachel said, nettled at his disregard for the purpose of their visit to the art exhibit. "We are here to shadow Lady Granville and Lord Bennington."

"But the beauty and her villain are not here," James pointed out sensibly. "Enjoy the paintings, Rachel. Just look at this landscape. Have you ever seen such visual beauty captured on canvas?"

To James, trailing Bennington and his mistress to the Royal Academy was a bootless business. They could learn nothing to advance their investigation by spying on the two in this public place. But when he saw a tentative visit to the Academy written in on Lady Granville's schedule, he shamelessly used their quarries' possible presence at the Academy as a ploy to entice Rachel into spending a pleasant afternoon with him. He wanted to be alone with her and to share with her his passion for art. He had not seen her for two days and found he had missed her companionship.

Rachel, unaware of her handsome escort's true agenda, had been anticipating the arrival of their prey and had not been attending to the paintings with the deliberate concentration that James had been giving them. She glanced at the summer landscape.

"Landscapes are not fashionable," she said without thinking.

"Rubbish," James retorted. "Don't believe such idiotic prejudice. Serious collectors have validated their importance. Look at Mr. Constable's work and judge for yourself. Note his superlative execution of reflections on the water." He punctuated the air with a pointed finger. "In that patch of blue, right there in the corner, he has captured the early summer sky to perfection. And there, look, you can almost see the clouds moving."

Rachel pushed her glasses more firmly up on her nose with a single finger and squinted unnecessarily at the landscape. "Yes, I guess I see what you mean. There is definitely a sensitivity in the artist's brushstrokes. I must admit, that foliage in full leaf is true in color and texture. Yes, one can see that the artist has studied nature."

Pleased with her assessment, James said, "If the canvas is for sale, I intend to purchase it."

"Today?" Her mind was still engaged with the Granville case. She was not pleased with the possibility that James would abandon their watch too soon, for she had hoped that their investigation would take a dramatic turn.

"No, I can't buy it today. But Mr. Constable has a studio here in London and once I get his direction, I can write to him and seek an appointment." He stepped back from the painting to gain a new perspective, clasped his hands behind his back, and studied the work in the manner of a connoisseur. He could envision the picture hanging in a prominent location in the library of the townhouse he had just inherited from a distant uncle.

Rachel tilted her head to the side and gazed at the Constable landscape critically for a long time. The artist had executed the work with admirable skill. "I like it, James," she said at last.

Satisfied with her receptiveness to his attempt at art education, he decided to humor her. "Come, Rachel, we will spend another half an hour here. Maybe Bennington and Lady Granville were detained." She was pleased that he had not dismissed the possibility that the objects of their chase would materialize.

James guided Rachel to a marble bench from which they could peruse the viewers taking in the exhibit. Any late arrivals would pass by their station on the way to the main gallery.

Directly opposite them on the wall was an enormous canvas depicting a battle scene between the British and French armies. The artist had captured the horrors of war in graphic detail. Bayoneted corpses sprawled on the ground, their arms flung in grotesque caricatures of living men. One could almost hear the neighing of the wounded horses thrashing on the earth where fresh blood ran.

"What do you think of this?" he said.

Rachel shuddered. "Horrible."

"Gad, Rachel, I am sorry," James said, as he realized his inadvertent insensibility. "I forgot that your husband was killed in a battle. Come, we shall find another place to wait."

He was getting up from the bench, but she stopped him with a hand on his arm. "Sit down, James. I cannot be shielded from battle scenes for the rest of my life."

James sank back onto the hard bench. "Your husband was killed in America, your father said."

"Yes, a place called Chippewa."

"The name sounds Indian."

"I suppose it is."

"Did you love him very much?" He wanted to bite his tongue at the rather improper question that had slipped past his lips because it was so much in his mind. "I should not have asked that."

"It's all right," Rachel said. She ignored the battle scene which covered half the wall and stared at her hands tightly clasped in her lap.

"I did love him at first. I was just out of school and inexperienced. He was dashing and older and the kind of man who had a disturbing effect on female hearts. But he was not honorable. The marriage I begged my father to consent to against his wishes turned out to have nothing to do with love. William needed money and my dowry was supremely generous."

James yearned to slip a comforting arm around her shoulders, but he knew that she would not welcome his touch.

"It took me less than a month to realize I had committed a dreadful error." Rachel couldn't speak for a moment. The ache of that first disastrous encounter with love, which she had thought could no longer pain her, brimmed up inside her. She had never discussed the matter with anyone and did not examine why she was now confiding in James.

"Had William simply neglected me, he would have done me a kindness, but I was subjected daily to his sharp critical words edged with anger. He voiced unfounded suspicions of my relationships with other men while it was he who humiliated me with his bold warm attentions to loose women."

James cupped his hand protectively over hers where they lay on her lap. His throat was tight. Rachel lifted her woeful face and looked up at him with misted blue eyes. Her distress filled him with an almost unbearable tenderness.

Rachel slipped off her spectacles and dabbed her eyes with a wisp of a handkerchief.

"I know the thought was ignoble, but when I learned he had fallen in battle, I was glad I would never have to see him again." She felt as if she had broken down a wall within herself with the admission.

James ached to kiss the tremor from her soft lips and wrap her in sheltering arms. "My dear girl, under the circumstances, your reaction was perfectly normal," he assured her. His unqualified support touched her. She bit her lip and forced a wan smile.

For several seconds neither of them said a word. Then, James smiled at Rachel and pulled her up beside him. "Do you have any other pressing engagements this afternoon?" he said.

"Neither pressing nor otherwise," Rachel said, giving her wet

eyes one last dab before she pushed her spectacles and the handkerchief into her reticule.

"Can I kidnap you then for another hour or so?"

"You sound mysterious. Dare I ask what you intend?"

He squeezed her hand. "Would you let me show you my
house?"

His query was casual, but his golden-brown eyes reflected a
keen desire for an affirmative answer. Her assent, she could see,
was important to him.

"It's not quite the thing to visit a bachelor's abode, but I think
my consequence will not suffer unduly if you have servants
about."

"I have a very proper housekeeper and an eagle-eyed butler.
The two are a married couple. You may choose either one or both
to dog our steps as we tour the house."

Rachel smiled. "I think not. I feel quite safe with you."

James grinned wickedly and winked at her. "Keep thinking
that way, my lovely."

Rachel's smile broadened as she appreciated his obvious attempt to erase her heartache by making her laugh.

When James opened the front door of his townhouse and stood
aside for Rachel to pass through, she came face to face with the
butler. "Harrison, Mrs. Kendall and I will be touring the house.
Would you have Mrs. Harrison prepare tea to be served in the
library in fifteen minutes."

"Very good, Mr. Ware," the rotund, florid-faced man said, his
sleepy orbs anything but eagle-eyed, and waddled off toward the
back of the house.

James placed his hat and cane on a hall table.

"Let me take your pelisse and bonnet," he said.

"Thank you." Rachel shrugged off her gloves after James hung
up the coat he had helped her remove. She patted her hair in
place before a hall mirror while he set her bonnet and gloves on
a settle.

"Most of the furniture in the rooms are under Holland covers," he said. "I think I should explain. A distant uncle passed away two months ago and left me this townhouse and a country estate."

"I am not sure whether to felicitate you or offer my condolences," Rachel said, her mouth curled up at the corners.

"Certainly not condolences," he said. "Benedict Ware and I, while not unknown to each other, were never close. I have not seen him these ten years or more."

"Nevertheless, he must have had some feeling for you." Rachel waved a hand to encompass the house, the rooms.

"No, he did not. The properties came to me through entailment. It seems all of my lesser relatives fell prey to accidents, disease, or advanced age, and I won by default." He motioned toward the staircase.

"Let me show you the upstairs first." They left the large Italian tiled entrance hall and climbed toward the second level. The wooden banister was dull with built up wax, and the faded blue carpet treads were worn bare in spots.

On the first floor was a spacious drawing room cast in Stygian gloom by the rich, red velvet drapes, which had seen better days, drawn across the windows. Leaving Rachel at the door, James threaded his way among the furniture and pulled open the drapes. Dust particles danced in the sunlight, which streamed through the grimy panes.

"You can see for yourself, the refurbishing of this place is going to cost me a small fortune," James said.

Rachel was peeking under the Holland covers. "But James, you have some splendid pieces of furniture here."

"Do you think so? I don't know a great deal about furniture."

Rachel uncovered a lady's desk from the Queen Anne period. "What a treasure," she cried. "James, the furniture in this room is wonderful. With a little elbow grease and polish and some selective upholstering, it could be restored to its original beauty."

The two remaining rooms on the floor were a large bedroom and a small adjacent sitting room. In both chambers the parquet floors had been swept, the furniture dusted, and the windows cleaned. Rachel surmised from the bits and pieces of male accoutrements placed here and there on the bureau and tabletops that James was using the bedroom. The headboard of the massive walnut bed was deeply carved in a rose and leaf pattern.

Both James and I together would be lost in that bed, Rachel thought. Her cheeks became warm as she wondered what brought such an improper idea into her mind. She pulled her eyes from the bed and examined the other fine pieces of furniture, murmuring her approval to James.

The next floor contained four small guest rooms also under Holland covers. Rachel determined from a quick perusal beneath the fabric shields that the furniture was mostly crafted by Chippendale and Hepplewhite.

The top floor was divided between attic space and six sleeping alcoves for the personal servants of visiting guests.

Back down on the street floor, James said, "The kitchen and servants' quarters are down there," pointing in the direction the butler had gone earlier.

"This is the dining room." He opened a door on their left. The Ware ancestor who had bought the cherrywood table must have entertained a great deal, for there was seating for twenty guests.

The tea things were set out on a table before a worn settee in the library, where James led Rachel after he had shown her the tarnished silver crammed into the drawers and onto the shelves of a large cupboard in the dining room.

The wall above the brick fireplace in the library was bare, but a large square of a lighter color than the surrounding paint showed that a picture had hung there until recently.

"Is that where you plan to display your Constable?" Rachel asked.

"Yes," James said. "Look at the former occupant of the space." He pointed to a picture on the floor that leaned against the wall.

Rachel tilted the picture forward to expose the portrait. "Uncle Benedict, do you suppose?"

"More likely his papa from the style of the clothes," James said.

"He looks nothing like you. What a fierce expression." Rachel replaced the portrait against the wall, sat down on the settee, and volunteered to pour their tea. James sat in a faded red chintz-covered armchair near the cold fireplace, his long legs crossed one over the other.

"Should I keep the house?" he asked when Rachel had handed him his teacup.

"That is not for me to say, James." His expression begged an answer, so she added, "Were it mine, yes, I would delight in bringing it to rights again. It has so little bad, and so much good in it. The woodwork needs a coat of paint, and the walls some decent wallpaper. The rugs and drapes must be replaced, of course, but I would retain most of the furniture."

Just looking at her sent James's pulse racing. He could easily imagine Rachel as his wife making a real home of this impaired house.

"That settles it then," he said. "I keep the house. But the portrait of Uncle Benedict's papa shall be banished to the attic."

Rachel laughed and gave a decisive nod. "Most definitely. I wish to be here when you hang the Constable in its place."

Conscious of an odd pluck to his heart, James said, "I promise you, my dear, the landscape shall not be hung unless you are here."

Rachel replaced her teacup in its saucer. His statement was the kind of meaningless promise that one makes on the whim of the moment, but she sensed James meant it and even something deeper which eluded her. He, too, put his cup down and leaned forward in his chair.

"Let me tell you about the country estate my uncle left me."

Rachel had an irrational feeling that James was about to make a revelation that in some fashion was about to alter her life.

"I visited Acrefaire only two or three times when I was just a boy," he said. "I remember it as having rich soil and a rambling old manor house with a thriving kitchen garden and productive fruit trees. Off at a distance from the main house were great barns and stables. My youthful memories are pleasant ones. Yet when my late uncle's man of business turned over the keys to me at the reading of the will, his descriptions of how the property has fared in the ensuing years were less than glowing."

James took up his tea cup, drained it, and placed his cup neatly in its saucer.

"It seems I shall have to tidy up the place," he said in an understatement. "The buildings, from his accounts, will need extensive repairs. The land has not been used wisely, it seems. I know nothing of the tenants, but I want to. I want to know them as living men and women with individual personalities, not just as faceless names on an estate roster. I want to live there, Rachel, with a wife, the two of us working together, as partners, making decisions in concert for the betterment of the property, raising children . . ."

As soon as the words were out, James found them utterly inadequate as a proposal of marriage and too specific if Rachel was not ready for his declaration. Still, to say more without knowing her mind . . . there was one bold step he could take to discover her willingness to have him. His heart beat a little faster at the thought.

Rachel glanced at the clock on the mantel. "Oh, dear, look at the time, I really should start home." She slowly lifted herself from the settee.

James rose with her and moved to her side. The second she looked into his face, she knew what he intended. A quiver of expectation fluttered in her breast. His arms came around her and his lips brushed hers, deliberately keeping the kiss gentle and undemanding. Her lips softened, molding themselves to fit against his and one arm moved to the back of his neck. A delicious desire she had never experienced before licked through Rachel's body. James's kiss was so warm and so tender and so different from William's hard hurtful embraces that she wanted to prolong the pleasure.

James lifted his lips from hers and gave her a long sensual look from under his lids. Rachel averted her eyes. He had nearly made her cast aside her normal caution. If he had pressed on . . .

"I really must go now, James. Mama will wonder what has become of me."

His arms dropped from her slender waist. "Let me get your things, and I will see you home," he said, moving toward the door. He had felt her passion. She had not been anything like indifferent to his kiss, but neither was she completely ready to give herself to him. Her unhappy marriage had left a scar that made her leery of love. He wanted her to come to him without reservations. For now, this small victory would have to do.

Perched on the seat of the high phaeton, on any other pleasant, sunny, warm afternoon such as this one, Rachel would have enjoyed the ride, but she was still shaken by James's kiss and her own self-doubts. James had shared his innermost thoughts with her and had all but proposed to her. But a man said one thing and acted in one manner when he desired a woman and often quite another way entirely after he was wed to her. Conventional dogma held that there was no worse misfortune for a woman than to remain unmarried, but she knew from her own experience that the belief was a falsehood, a fiction foisted upon naive young females by misguided mothers. But, then again, James was not William. He was a man of honor. She had trusted him, even to baring the secrets about William's treatment of her, which she had not even revealed to her own parents. There was no doubt James was making inroads into breaking her will to remain independent. But it was still not too late. She must decide if she really wanted to be answerable to any man.

James was glad the press of traffic gave him an excuse to remain silent and pretend to concentrate on his driving. He wanted to think. His adventures with the Runners had been heady, but he was prepared to settle into a more normal life with Rachel as his wife and love. His disposition was at odds with simply becoming a man-of-leisure. However, if he actively ran Acrefaire and, also, became involved in his business interests here in London, the two occupations should keep him from going to seed. With Rachel at his side, the life he sketched out for himself could prove to be most satisfying.

James parked the phaeton at the curb before Sir Henry's house. "The next event on Lady Granville's schedule that will involve you and me is at Lady Mouton's," James said. The Duchess of Mouton was holding a soiree in five days' time to which Rachel and James had been invited independently. "I have some estate business to attend to at Acrefaire and will not see you before then. If you are agreeable, Rachel, I will take you up in my coach the night of the soiree, and we can drive to the duchess's together."

Rachel agreed and the two settled on a time. A footman came from the house and helped Rachel down from the high seat of the sporty carriage. She welcomed the five days' reprieve James offered her. She feared another kiss would melt her resolve before she had time to know her own mind. At least at Lady Mouton's soiree, she and James would be back on task again. With Lady Granville there, the investigation would proceed and the danger from James's advances would be minimized.

Rachel lifted her gloved hand in a brief wave and returned James's farewell smile, before he turned the phaeton in the street and headed in the direction from which he had come.

Five

On a rainy afternoon five days later, James took an agitated turn around his library for the tenth time, eroding the frayed blue carpet further into tatters. At Acrefaire he had ridden every day with the resident bailiff inspecting the property and meeting his tenants. He had been relieved to find that the necessary renovations to make the manor house livable and improve the outbuildings would not deplete his pocketbook more than his bank account could bear. Rachel had been constantly in his thoughts. He did not make a single decision concerning the rehabilitation of the house without considering if the renewal would please her. His determination to ask her to be his wife was as strong as ever, but he had decided to forestall his actual proposal until either the Granville case was settled satisfactorily or his verbal contract with Sir Henry ran out. Of course, he thought with some trepidation, his happiness depended on a change in Rachel's attitude toward marriage. She might have decided that she did not care for him sufficiently to forgo her independence. Lord, he wasn't even certain that she loved him.

The faded flowered drapes were open, offering a watery view of the small overgrown garden through a window with raindrops trickling down the pane like miniature rivers. A fire crackled and blazed brightly in the brick fireplace giving the room a cozy ambiance. But James's restive mood was incompatible with his surroundings.

He turned from the window, paced over to the fireplace, and

stared for a moment at the unadorned wall above the mahogany mantelpiece. Late yesterday afternoon he had kept an appointment with John Constable and negotiated successfully with the artist for the landscape on display at the Academy. The painting would be delivered to him at the end of the month when the current exhibit closed.

Not a man accustomed to idleness, James dropped into the chintz-covered chair and picked up the latest issue of the *Edinburgh Review.* The periodical usually held his interest, but today his mind insisted on conjuring up images of Rachel's splendid little figure and lovely face to the exclusion of all else. Her luscious curves, her alluring dark blue eyes, her hair black and curling, her enticing lips, relentlessly invaded his receptive mind. Damn, but he was smitten. A small wave of panic raced through him. Suppose she was to reject him? The possibility was too painful to entertain. This was not some light romance that would easily be pushed from his mind. Because love had struck at a moment's notice, it did not mean it would be any less enduring. Rachel had become his life and, he was convinced, would remain so forever. She hadn't been indifferent. He could not believe she had been indifferent.

James flung the magazine aside. He glanced at the mantel clock. A mere five minutes had elapsed since he had last checked the time. Five hours and twenty-two minutes were yet to be borne before he took Rachel up in his carriage to escort her to the Duchess of Mouton's soiree.

If he remained cooped up in this room thinking about her, he would certainly go mad. He walked to the bell pull, summoned Harrison, and ordered the butler to have his carriage made ready and sent around. He would spend the afternoon at White's. At the club he would be with male companions with whom he could talk about horse races and politics and non-feminine subjects, which he hoped would divert his mind from Rachel.

During the time that James agonized over her in his library, Rachel had gone to the drawing room window that faced the street, where a stream of water ran along the curb, so often that Lady Henry, who was embroidering a tapestry near the fire, chided her for showing unmannerly restlessness.

"I know the rain is depressing, dear," Lady Henry said, "but one must find an occupation to keep the day from dragging."

"Yes, Mama," Rachel said dutifully and sat down at a small desk in the corner. She took a sheet of writing paper from a cubby hole, adjusted her spectacles, uncorked an ink bottle, and dipped a sharpened quill into the black ink.

On the blank sheet Rachel wrote the heading, *Evidence*. When she had listed all the bits and pieces of information she and James had gathered on the Granville case, she printed his name on two full lines in large block letters.

James's kiss the other day had invaded her from head to toe with a sweet sensation of blissful pleasure, leaving her wanting more. His tenderness had made her realize that she hungered for the love she had dismissed as unwelcome in her life. The very thought of his warm lips on hers made her ache to once again be in his arms. The last few days she had hardly been able to put two thoughts together without James's face intruding.

"Dear, you really should take a rest or you will be all fagged out at the duchess's soiree this evening," Lady Henry said.

"I will later, Mama," Rachel promised.

"Mr. James Ware is such a nice man." Rachel's heart raced at the sound of his name. "You really should put forth more effort. I am certain he is taken with you and could easily be brought up to scratch."

"Yes, Mama," Rachel said mechanically, unwilling to discuss James with her mother.

"Widowhood is all well and good for a time, but you, my dear, have quite exceeded a decent mourning period by a number of years. The aim of any young woman of breeding, and at four and twenty you are still a young woman, is to find herself a suitable husband. You must agree that Mr. Ware is an eminently suitable prospect."

"Eminently suitable," Rachel echoed.

Lady Henry looked over her shoulder toward the corner

where Rachel sat at the desk. "You are playing with me, daughter. You are not even thinking of Mr. Ware, are you?"

"Oh, but I am thinking about him, Mama," she said truthfully, but her expression, manner, and tone of voice suggested the opposite.

Lady Henry pulled a face and flapped a dismissive hand in Rachel's direction. "Your obstinate refusal to consider remarrying quite surpasses my understanding, especially when you could attract any number of eligible men with a mere crook of your finger." She tucked her embroidery into a basket, got up, and smoothed her skirt. "I must see if Papa has risen from his nap."

Alone in the room, Rachel traced a heart around James's name like a besotted school girl misusing her copybook. She had finally admitted to herself two days ago that she loved him. He had all but offered her a marriage that was an independent minded woman's dream. ". . . Working together as partners," he had said. ". . . Making decisions in concert." James would not always act on her opinions, but she was certain he would always respect them.

His love for her was in his smile, the compassion she had seen in his eyes when she told him about William, and in his kiss. He was a confident man who would never need to control or dominate the woman he loved to prove his masculinity.

She smiled to herself. And, beside all that, oh, lud, no man had a right to be so outstandingly handsome.

Rachel gave a contented sigh and looked down at the evidence she had written out on the letter paper. As she read over the locations of the bogus thefts in a cursory manner, her mind was still filled with James. But as she studied the sites more carefully, it came to her that Lady Mouton's house was an excellent venue for Lady Granville's trickery. She would disclose her discovery to James and explain to him that in light of her suspicion it would behoove them to be especially vigilant tonight and keep a close eye on Lady Granville

Rachel wadded up the private notes and tossed them into the fire, making certain the confidential writing had been burned to ashes. The thought that she would be seeing James in just a few hours caused a warm excitement in her breast and brought a smile to her face. He would soon be here to fill the void that had caused the restlessness she had felt ever since he left her five days ago.

James walked into the drawing room that evening to find Rachel waiting for him. She came forward to greet him in a rustle of French blue silk, hands extended, and lips smiling. James gave her an ardent grin and clasped both her hands firmly in his. He had acquired a lightly bronzed countenance while in the country, which, Rachel thought, made him better looking than ever.

James gazed with unabashed desire into Rachel's eyes. "You are so lovely," he said, lifting her hand to his warm lips. Her own clear look of pure affection carried straight to his heart. He vowed to keep that shining look on her face forever. Their eyes locked, their hearts touched, and James's head moved down toward her lips, but Lady Henry came into the room just then. Rachel reluctantly disengaged her hands from James's in the interest of propriety. His touch and the unmistakable look of devotion in his eyes had sent sweet tendrils of love through her.

Mother, daughter, and suitor stood together for a few moments while James inquired after Sir Henry's health.

"He is doing better," his wife said. "My husband keeps early hours these days, or I know he would have been pleased to see you. He has said to me that he feels much more the thing since he turned over his business affairs to you. I have no head for such matters being a mere female, but I am grateful, Mr. Ware, that you have eased his mind."

James inclined his head. "A mere trifle, my lady, but I shall call on Sir Henry, if I may, in the next day or two. I have been away from the city on personal business these five days."

After a few more exchanges of inconsequential chitchat, Rachel and James were able to extricate themselves from Lady Henry's hold, get Rachel into her wrap, and themselves out the door to James's waiting coach.

In the carriage, the two sat close together with James holding

Rachel's hand in a proprietary manner while he filled her in on his sojourn to his estate and his acquisition of the Constable painting. In the way of lovers, he frequently lifted her hand to his lips, and she tipped her head into his shoulder with the need to bring herself ever closer to him.

The elegant reception room in the countess's mansion that Rachel and James entered ten minutes later was buzzing with pleasant conversation from Lady Mouton's guests who were gathered in this room to greet one another and their hostess. Fresh colorful blooms decorated niches and tables, while from above, the candlelight of the great chandeliers played across the green of the potted palms and tropical plants that had been brought in from the conservatory.

James circled Rachel's narrow waist and guided her through the impeccably attired crowd to Lady Mouton's side. Twenty years had passed since the duchess had made her debut. She had never been a beauty, but she had a pleasing face and a natural friendliness.

"Mrs. Kendall and Mr. Ware," she said, one eyebrow arched for a second in speculation as if to say, "Have I somehow missed the latest on-dit about you two?" The Duchess of Mouton was not so ill-bred that she would have asked such an impertinent question aloud from the parties involved, but she made a mental note to query either one of his friends or one of Rachel's about the couple's relationship.

Rachel, James, and the duchess exchanged a few trivialities and the customary, "Thank you for inviting me" and "Glad you could come," before the two investigators moved on and another guest took their place.

Uniformed waiters passed among the guests dispensing glasses of port, Madeira, and lemon punch, and a various array of delectable tidbits. With wineglasses in hand, Rachel and James circulated, stopping here and there to speak with friends and acquaintances.

With a hand on the sleeve of James's dark evening coat, Rachel stopped their aimless wandering before a potted schefflera. Speaking so low that he had to bend down to catch her words, she said, "We just passed within a few feet of Lady Granville. Lord Bennington is not with her. This is a perfect opportunity for you, James. There is no telling what clues you might pick up if you get her in private."

James was in no mood to spend the evening playacting as he pretended a fondness for Lady Granville.

"I think not, Rachel."

With pleading eyes, she said, "James, has it not struck you that Lady Mouton's soiree would be just the sort of place Lady Granville might misplace her jewelry? It has been two months since the last incident. I have a strong inkling that we shall be successful tonight. Please speak with her."

He shook his head. "Even if those are her intentions, she is not going to bare her soul to me."

"No, but she may inadvertently drop a clue. We need to make some headway in this case." Rachel studied his scowling face. "Don't frown, James, Can't you admit I might be right?"

"Very well, I admit this house could be the site of the next bogus robbery. But I think Lady Granville is too clever to accidentally reveal the manner in which she will create a phony theft."

"My father once said that someone told him that a successful criminal is often caught because he becomes complacent and careless as a result of his triumphs."

James grinned in spite of himself as he heard one of his oft quoted maxims tossed at him. "As you say, partner. And what will you be doing while I interrogate the beauty?"

"I will cover the room. There are any number of people in attendance who know Lady Granville and Lord Bennington intimately. A chance remark here or there could stand us in good stead."

"All right, my sweet," James said, surrendering. "I shall court the beauty with a plethora of male sensuality and charm her until she falls into my arms and confesses all."

Rachel made a face. "Don't overdo it, James, or you might find yourself with an unwanted mistress."

"Unwanted?" James waggled his brow and moved quickly

to avoid the blow Rachel was about to deliver to his person with the closed fan dangling from her wrist.

Rachel's mouth quirked into an affectionate smile and remained so until James was lost to her view in the crowded room. Gad, the man was irresistible. She gave an exaggerated sigh and moved into the press of people to seek out a likely guest to engage in a conversation that might produce results.

She was speaking unproductively with Lady Granville's aunt when her heart lurched. Lord Bennington stood at the door with his jeweled quizzing glass raised ostentatiously, scanning the room, Rachel was certain, for Lady Granville.

Having excused herself to her recent companion and added her empty wineglass to the collection being gathered by a passing waiter, Rachel drifted to Lord Bennington's side, she hoped in a manner that would suggest an accidental encounter. The set of the earl's thin lips made him seem to have a perpetual sneer, and his usual mantle of haughty boredom made him a daunting figure for a chance acquaintance to approach.

"Good evening, Lord Bennington," Rachel said, her heart beating faster than normal. She affected a dazzling smile.

He looked her up and down through his quizzing glass. Rachel felt herself being assessed and measured for worthiness of attention.

"Mrs. Kendall, isn't it?"

"That is correct, my lord." The odious creature, Rachel thought.

"I know your father. How does Sir Henry go on? I heard he is incapacitated by a weak heart."

To keep Bennington trapped, Rachel was inspired to launch into a long dissertation on the doctor's diagnosis of her father's illness. She could see Bennington's eyes glazing over, but she boldly went on for much too long. Finally, having run out of credible material she was forced to finish with, "But he seems to be improving."

"Glad to hear it. Give him my regards," his lordship said, and took a step forward, effectively dismissing her.

Rachel repositioned herself in front of him. "Excuse me, my lord, but would you have a moment to answer a question?"

A flicker of annoyance touched his face. "Go ahead, ask it."

"You have lately traveled much to France, I hear. Now that the war with Bonaparte is over, I have been thinking of making a trip to the Continent. Could you suggest some places of interest?"

"Who told you I traveled to France?" Lord Bennington stared at Rachel with chilling gray eyes.

"Why, Mama mentioned it the other day," Rachel said smoothly, although her hands were trembling.

Lord Bennington tapped his quizzing glass against his upper lip and looked down his long nose at her for a long moment. Then, a sudden look of amusement came into his gray eyes and his expression became almost pleasant. Rachel felt a blush creep onto her cheeks. His altered face had the look of a man who suspected she was trying to fix her interest with him. The wretch must think that she and her mother had been discussing him as an eligible parti. Rachel was mortified.

"France would suit you, Mrs. Kendall," he said in a congenial tone. "There is the countryside, the cathedrals and, of course, every lady finds the shops of Paris fascinating. Now, madam, you must excuse me, for I have not yet paid my respects to our hostess."

Rachel felt humiliated to be brushed aside by this detestable villain, who actually thought she was seeking his attentions. However, she recovered her aplomb in a minute, only to have a nervous tremor shoot into her chest when she became afraid that Lord Bennington would find James with Lady Granville and cause a scene. At the moment, Bennington was speaking with Lady Mouton, but he would not remain with her for long. She must find James and Lady Granville before Lord Bennington did.

Rachel noticed a balcony that ran the width of one side of the room. From there, guests gazed down at the festivities below and promenaded along a gallery, which displayed portraits of former Mouton dukes and duchesses.

Rachel pushed through the crush of people toward the staircase leading to the gallery. More and more guests had arrived as the evening progressed and open spaces on the floor were at a premium. She reached the staircase and mounted the stairs. Securing her spectacles into place, Rachel leaned over the carved marble balustrade to peer down into the room she had just vacated.

People were drifting toward the ballroom where an orchestra had begun to play a lively country tune. But although Rachel meticulously examined each head individually twice over from her upper vantage point, she could find neither James nor Lady Granville in the crowd.

Where could James have taken the beauty? She regretted having urged him to become cozy with the lady. If Bennington found James and Lady Granville with their heads together, things might get nasty.

The balcony was cooler and less packed than the floor below. Noticing another descending flight of stairs at the opposite end from where she stood, Rachel walked toward them to investigate their terminus. She found that the stairs led down to a glassed passage that connected the main house with a conservatory. The conservatory would be a perfect trysting place for lovers or two people who wanted to engage in a private conversation.

Rachel walked down to the passage and through it to the door of the large unlit greenhouse. The rain had stopped earlier, leaving a clear night bathed in moonlight. She opened the conservatory door and stepped in among the tropical plants. Ferns and orchids hung from baskets above her head. She moved around a stand of bamboo and listened for the sound of whispering voices. The air was silent.

Outside on the walk, she heard the unmistakable tread of male footwear rapidly coming down the flagstone of the passage. Rachel peeked from between a palm and a ficus. The door opened to reveal the shadowy silhouette of a large male. She crept behind a sago palm planted in a great pot, squeezed her eyes closed, and hunched her shoulders as though the ineffective movements would somehow save her from being discovered. Her heart was tattooing in her chest.

Rachel forced her eyes open and leaned forward a little to where she had a clear view of the door. It was closed. She had not heard receding footsteps. She cocked her head and listened tensely. Nothing. Her stalker, for that is how she had begun to think of him, could be waiting for her to move and reveal her position. Wild thoughts flew through her brain. She pictured an evil-faced man watching her descend the stairs from the gallery and following her to this secluded place. His intention was to ravish her in this isolated building where her screams for help would be obscured by the noisy revelry in the main house. No one would hear her or come to her rescue. A shiver of ice crawled along her spine.

Rachel clutched her breast to muffle the raucous beat of her heart. She strained to hear any untoward sound. Hearing nothing, she screwed up her courage and decided not to be a victim. As she searched in her immediate vicinity for a rake or hoe as a weapon with which to bash the scoundrel over the head, a faint rustle of leaves unnatural in this sterile environment caught her attention. Her head snapped around in the direction of the sound just as a voice whispered close to her ear, "Rachel?" She shrieked. Her chest heaved alarmingly as she struggled to control her breathing.

"Hush, sweetheart, hush," James soothed as he pulled her into the circle of his arms. "It's all right."

"James!" Rachel's tense body went limp with relief. "Oh, you gave me a fright." His arms tightened protectively. He rubbed his hands up and down her slender back with comforting, calming strokes and emitted soothing incoherent murmurs of endearment.

Rachel pushed James from her with a sudden strength that surprised him. "Must you make a practice of startling me out of my wits? What do you mean skulking about like that? Why did you not identify yourself?"

"Why didn't you?" he countered.

Her eyes behind her spectacles glared at him. "Are you saying this is my fault?"

He shrugged. "Why would you come into a conservatory at night?"

"Not to smell the flowers. I was searching for you, if you must know."

"In here?" His voice was incredulous.

"Yes, in here," she said a bit snidely. "What brought you here?"

"I noticed you hanging over the balcony, but by the time I worked my way through the mob and up the stairs, you had disappeared. Then, I noticed the conservatory and decided to have a look. When I opened the door, I thought I heard breathing. Afraid I might embarrass a pair of lovers, I moved stealthily until I saw you clearly in the glow of the moon."

"My heart was in my throat as I imagined the worst when I noticed a man at the door."

James could appreciate her sense of vulnerability at the appearance of an unknown male in this remote part of the house.

"It was my fault," he said with a sudden magnanimity. "I should have called out when I came in. Caution has become such an ingrained habit with me, I acted from instinct."

"You are always frightening me! First at the gaming house, pretending to be a bounder, and now this!"

"I admit that the incident at the casino was a sorry joke. I have apologized for that, sweetheart, and taken the blame for tonight. What more can I do?"

"I know; I know. You're right, of course," she capitulated. "I suppose I should not have come here unescorted."

Moonlight streamed into the greenhouse. The residue of raindrops glistened like crystal on the glass panes.

James ran a finger down Rachel's cheek. "Then you forgive me?" His voice had turned low and husky.

"Yes," she said, meeting his eyes, golden-brown in the moonlight. His long, slow, sensual gaze sent a delicious shiver down her back.

James removed her spectacles and slipped them into his pocket. His large hands took her face between his palms.

His lips settled over hers with the same sweet gentleness she remembered. But, then, his mouth began to move with a new urgency as he pulled her to him. She responded with unrestrained fervor, her own arms enclosing his neck, delving in his hair. The kiss unleashed her years of suppressed emotions. She passionately gave him back kiss for kiss. His murmur of her name over and over mixed with the wildness and fire.

Every rational thought was blocked from Rachel's mind. Only the tumultuous madness that seemed unable to be satisfied was real or important. James lifted his lips from hers.

"James!" she cried. "I never dreamed it could be like this."

Rachel cupped his head and brought his lips back to her mouth and moaned. The small sound brought a measure of sanity to James. With a monumental effort of self-discipline, he broke the kiss and held her from him.

He gave her a melancholy smile and brushed a silky strand of hair from her cheek with a gentle finger. "If we keep on, neither of us will be able to go back into the house without being gawped at by the assemblage who are always ready to invent scandal."

"I know," Rachel said. She sighed deeply. "I guess we had better go back inside now."

James gave her a quick hug, then put his arm around her shoulders and moved her toward the door.

"Would you take me home now, James," she said, "that is, unless you think we should continue our surveillance."

"No need. Lady Granville left with Bennington just before I came looking for you. He arrived a little while ago to escort her to a late dinner with the Prince Regent."

"Goodness, I had no idea they traveled in such elite circles," Rachel said. "Did you gather any clues from her?"

James held the conservatory door open for Rachel. As they walked through the glass enclosed passage, he answered her.

"No, we engaged in gossip and useless exchanges about the card game at Almack's since that was the one place we had been in each other's company."

"I was concerned when I could not locate you and Lady Granville," Rachel told him.

James grinned. "But, dear heart, it was never pleasure I sought from the lady, only information."

"Fool." Rachel walked up the steps to the house. "I was not worried about your honor, only your neck. I saw his lordship when he came in." James opened the glass door and stepped into the gallery after her. He held out his arm to Rachel. She linked her own arm through his.

"I attempted to detain Lord Bennington by engaging him in a protracted conversation, but he soon shook me off. I guess you were never in danger."

"Hardly, my sweet, but your concern does wonderful things to my heart." His fingers tightened momentarily over hers. "I simply took the lady for a very public turn around the premises, which eventually led us into the ballroom where Bennington found us. I bowed the lady over to him and made a hasty exit from their presence. That is when I spied you looking over the balcony railing."

James was busy collecting her evening cape, his things, and sending a footman for his coach after he and Rachel reached the reception room. It was not until the two were once again sitting beside one another in the carriage rolling toward Rachel's home that she continued the conversation.

"Somehow I missed seeing you when I scanned the room from the gallery, although I did have my spectacles on."

James dug into his pocket. "Which reminds me, I believe I took these from you earlier." He handed Rachel her glasses.

She tucked them into her reticule without a word. Her romantic feelings were dampened. She was disappointed that Lady Granville had not made a decisive move. It was beginning to seem to her that James's pessimism about the case was justified.

"You would not consider foregoing Almack's tomorrow for a night at the opera, would you? I have a friend who would lend me his private box," he said. "There would just be the two of us."

She shook her head.

"I thought not," James said, with a faint grin.

"Lady Granville will be at Almack's," Rachel said.

"I know, but the lady is not going to do anything so ramshackle as to cut up at Almack's," James pointed out. "It will be a wasted evening."

"Nevertheless, it is our duty to be there. And I do think, James, that we should not stay in each other's pocket. We must dance with other people."

"Since Almack's does not have a conservatory, I suppose I can manage to exhibit my terpsichorean splendor to the polite world, although my true talents are better unfurled in private among the plants."

Rachel chuckled. "I can vouch for that," she said daringly, and promptly received a toe-tingling kiss for her impudence.

Six

"Remember, my love," James said, his eyes glistening impishly, "if I find you enjoying yourself while dancing with another man, I shall be forced to intercede and damn the consequences."

Rachel's eyes, radiating an angelic innocence, swam up to meet his. "I had no idea, James, of the depth of your emotions, but being warned, I shall do my utmost to force myself to be thoroughly bored with every gentleman who dances with me."

Having just arrived at Almack's, they were preparing to circulate and converse with friends and acquaintances. They smiled at each other, enjoying their own silly banter, their hearts in their eyes. The wooden dance floor shook beneath their feet from the vibrations set off by dozens of energetic dancers engaged in a lively country dance.

"Shall we promenade," James asked, holding out his arm to her. Linking hers with his the two began to skirt the dance floor. They paid their respects to the patronesses, traded a word or two with the master of ceremonies, and spoke briefly with the other promenaders they met on their rounds.

Rachel was soon claimed for a mazurka by a married friend, Tom Masterson. His easy familiarity and ready congeniality made her forget her mission until Lady Granville crossed her view. Her letdown at guessing wrong as to the beauty's intentions the previous night still bothered Rachel. Even now, she felt a residue of discouragement that she and James had been unable to come up with the proof to connect Lady Granville and Lord Bennington with the thefts. More and more she was beginning to think that there might be some real merit in James's gloomy predictions that it was highly improbable that they would be able to catch Lady Granville filching a piece of jewelry.

The dance came to an end and Rachel moved with Tom to his wife's side. While she listened to the latest news about their son who was at Eton, she admired the easy grace with which James was moving across the floor toward her.

When he took her into his arms for a waltz, Rachel said, "We did promise we would dance with other people, and here we are back together."

"We did dance with other people. You danced with Tom, and I danced with Frannie Whetstone."

"Frannie is such a sweet woman. I could strangle those insensitive clods who saddled her with that deplorable epithet of Antidote," Rachel said.

"Yes, it's a shame. She is a really nice girl," James agreed.

"I saw her sitting with the dowagers looking incredibly unwanted. It was kind of you to ask her to dance. You are most considerate, James."

James looked embarrassed. "Don't refine on it, Rachel. Frannie happens to be an excellent dancer."

But his ability to look beyond Frannie Whetstone's outward appearance reinforced Rachel's conviction that she had been right to put behind her William's legacy of mistrust. James was nothing like her former husband. He had depths of character that had been sadly lacking in William.

"I see Lady Granville is without Bennington again this evening," James said.

"He might appear later as he did at Lady Mouton's last night."

Without missing a step, James drew Rachel close to him, his brown eyes dancing. "Must I still stand up with other women?"

"Yes, certainly," she said.

James groaned.

"All but the waltz," she amended. "I shall reserve all the waltzes for you." Her eyes twinkled.

"At least I need not suffer the pangs of envy at seeing you in another man's arms." He whirled her about with admirable ease, never taking his eyes from her face until she was dizzy not from the dance but from his sensual gaze.

"We could be cuddling in a box at the opera this very minute," James said with a wistful sigh.

"I don't know how you ever solved a case with the Runners when your mind is so much occupied with prurient notions."

James laughed. "I never had a partner before who knocked all proper thoughts from my head."

Rachel smirked. She would have liked to have flung her arms about him and given him a warm kiss.

When the waltz ended, Rachel was taken from James's side to dance the boulanger with a man of her father's generation. The portly Mr. Whiggs did more grunting than speaking and was an indifferent dancer, but Rachel plodded through the set in good-humor.

When the older gentleman excused her after the dance, Rachel saw James near a potted palm in what appeared to be a spirited, but friendly, discussion with a contemporary. The man whom Rachel knew by sight, but not name, had an arm on James's shoulder and was waving a warning finger before his face. James was throwing his head back, laughing heartily.

With her fellow investigator occupied, Rachel decided to freshen up and made her way to the private room set aside especially for the ladies. She entered the brightly illuminated room, nodding to the half-dozen ladies present. She slid into a vanity chair before a mirror and tucked the hairs that had strayed from their appointed places back to where they belonged. In the mirror she saw the reflection of Lady Granville who, on entering, beckoned immediately to an attendant. It struck Rachel with a jolt that she had once again temporarily forgotten the beauty. Scolding herself, she vowed to get back to business and follow Lady Granville when she quit the ladies' room.

Sitting next to Rachel was Mrs. Bradshaw, a friend of her mother's. Rachel answered the polite inquiries about her father's health and promised to convey Mrs. Bradshaw's regards to both her parents. Mrs. Bradshaw talked on, giving Rachel news of her married daughter, a schoolgirl friend of Rachel's.

"Susan is expecting her third child in October," the woman was saying, when Lady Granville's shrill voice interrupted their chat. Both Rachel and Mrs. Bradshaw looked in the direction where the beauty was chastising the maid.

"The clasp is loose, you idiot. Get away! Get away! I cannot abide incompetence."

Necks craned and women stood for a better view. Lady Granville quickly acquired an audience of curious women who watched with interest as the haughty beauty lost her temper at the expense of the trembling young attendant.

"You ought to be turned off without a character, you clumsy dimwit!"

"It fastened perfectly when I placed it on your wrist, my lady," the maid said, near to tears, her voice quivering. "I did not break it." She retreated into a corner quaking with fear that she would lose her position.

Lady Granville played with the bracelet's clasp, while a number of ladies offered advice and related their own experiences with faulty fasteners both to her and each other.

With the flair of an accomplished actress, Lady Granville stood in the midst of her bewitched audience and raised her shapely hand high above her head. The lamplight gleamed on the diamonds and highlighted the green luminescence of the ancient emeralds as the careless hand swept through the air. A collective gasp rose from the spellbound spectators as the bracelet soared in a high arc from Lady Granville's exquisite wrist and landed with a soft thud on the rug at her feet. No one budged.

"Dear Mrs. Bradshaw," Lady Granville said to the woman who had moved from Rachel's side for a better view of the proceedings, "would you kindly retrieve the bracelet for me and fasten it onto my wrist. I am sure you can do better than that twit."

Mrs. Bradshaw glowed at being singled out by a personage with Lady Granville's credentials. She picked up the fallen object and with undue care affixed the jeweled band to the lady's wrist. "There, my lady, that seems to be solid," Mrs. Bradshaw said, patting the beauty's wrist.

"Thank you, my dear, it does feel more secure. I shall send the bracelet to my jeweler tomorrow and let him examine it." Several women concurred orally with her wise decision and others nodded their agreement.

Rachel's heart tripped over. The theatrics executed to perfection by Lady Granville lacked an air of verisimilitude. Her artlessness seemed too precisely calculated. The antics were a planned performance for a receptive audience who would recall vividly the antique bracelet with the defective catch when it turned up missing.

Rachel knew she must find James immediately. She slipped unnoticed from the ladies' room and walked purposefully to the ballroom. A dance with an array of intricate movements was being executed on the floor.

Rachel searched the room for James's tall figure. From habit, she reached for her glasses, but retied the strings of her reticule without removing her spectacles when she easily discerned his dark head above the other dancers' heads.

Rachel situated herself on the edge of the dance floor in a spot where she would be directly in James's line of vision when he made his next turn. Smiling down at his middle-aged partner, he waited for the plump lady to pass under his raised arm. To Rachel's chagrin, he was totally immersed in the progression of the dance and failed to look toward her. She rejected a number of ticklish ploys that flitted through her mind, including shouting, waving, or dashing to his side, which would have gained James's attention, but which would have had her barred from Almack's for life.

Rachel sent a slew of rapid prayers up to heaven. Some angel must have heard her, for James's eyes met hers.

He missed a step and apologized to his dance partner. He could see that Rachel was anxious to speak to him, but he was not free to leave Mrs. Grady in a lurch and pitch the set into an incurable tangle. She would just have to wait.

The music went on and on. Rachel's eyes darted toward the

hall leading to the ladies' room. Lady Granville would soon emerge. Sometime this evening, Rachel was certain, Lord Granville would once again lose a priceless piece of his family's history unless she and James could uncover the lady's ruse. Why didn't the orchestra stop playing and release James to come to her? She needed him.

Rachel glanced again in the direction of the ladies' room. She winced, for Lady Granville was walking toward her. The beauty's eyes were fixed intently on the entrance to the ballroom as she passed within inches of Rachel.

Giving up on securing James's help, Rachel turned and marched after Lady Granville. At that moment, she saw Lord Bennington lounging near the door. Rachel kept pace with her quarry.

She stood a little off from Lady Granville and Lord Bennington when the two came together, smiled at each other, and began to converse. With a magician's sleight of hand, Lord Bennington whisked the diamond bracelet from his mistress's wrist and deposited the band into the pocket of his coat. Rachel's eyes widened at the sorcery she had witnessed. Had she been less vigilant or had she looked away for even a split second, she would have missed the lightning exchange.

Rachel stood mesmerized, uncertain of what she could do at this point, if anything. Lord Bennington was speaking to Lady Granville. He bent his head to kiss the hand she offered to him, turned on his heels, and strode toward the exit.

Rachel froze, irresolute. Her breath caught in her throat. She was unaware the music had stopped until James suddenly appeared at her side. Her eyes flew to his and her constricted throat unfettered. "Bennington has the bracelet in his pocket. He's leaving. Go, James!" she cried, pushing him after their escaping target.

Without hesitation James rushed toward the door.

Rachel looked around for Lady Granville among the throng waiting for the musicians to finish replacing the sheets on the music stands and to begin the next dance tune. A loud scream stopped all conversation in mid-sentence and sent heads swerving in the direction of the card room.

Patrons left the floor en masse to investigate the source of the commotion. Rachel trailed right behind Lady Jersey for whom a path parted in the crowd of curious. Inside the card room, Lady Granville was draped in a chair clutching her throat with one hand and pressing her forehead with the other in a fair imitation of Sarah Siddons.

"It is gone; gone," she moaned over and over.

"What is gone?" Lady Jersey asked with uncommon calm. She had an aversion to hysterical women.

"Lord Granville's grandmama's diamond bracelet. Oh, dear, oh, dear, how can I face his lordship?"

Lady Jersey sat down in the empty chair beside Lady Granville. "Are you saying it was stolen? Here at Almack's?" Her look of utter disbelief clearly questioned Lady Granville's sanity in making such an outrageous charge.

The beauty emitted a hesitant, "I don't know." Her awe of Lady Jersey had tempered her answer. She collected herself, and as if reciting from a playbook declaimed, "No, the clasp apparently was unsound, for, I must admit, I did have trouble with the catch earlier this evening. But, I had thought it was tight when I left the ladies' room, but it seems that it was not." She had miraculously recovered completely from her hysteria.

"You should not have worn it then," Lady Jersey sniffed. "But I shall order the premises searched at once. Surely, if the bauble slipped from your wrist, it is even now lying undiscovered embedded in a carpet or reposing under a chair or table."

"Thank you, my lady," Lady Granville said, but the gratitude did not reach her cold eyes.

Rachel watched the interplay between the two women in disgust. To think she had nearly championed Lady Granville in a weak moment of misplaced sympathy. She had actually wanted to protect the beauty from her deceitful lover. Rachel could not forget the distress of the poor vulnerable ladies' room attendant whom Lady Granville cruelly used while she wove her web of

lies. The beauty was as designing, avaricious, and unscrupulous
as her male partner in crime.

Rachel's heart skipped a beat. She had temporarily forgotten
about James during the stir Lady Granville had caused. Bennington was an unprincipled villain and would be a dangerous
adversary. Concern for James flooded her being.

Rachel pushed past a clique of stimulated patrons, abuzz with
assumptions about the fate of the missing bracelet. The dancing
had been temporarily suspended while the servants scoured
each inch of the assembly rooms. Rachel was sure the ogling
patrons were storing up impressions to recite in embellished
versions to the unfortunate who had been absent on this his-
torical, never to be rivaled night, at Almack's. She walked on
past the gawkers and went to retrieve her evening cloak and
James's hat and cane.

When James burst onto the pavement in front of the assembly
rooms, Lord Bennington's carriage with the elaborate crest on
the door was parked in the fog at the curb. Bennington was
grasping the door handle, preparing to enter. That the arrogant
lord had not waited for his footman to open the door for him,
spoke volumes of Bennington's haste to distance himself from
the scene of the crime. James flew across the space between
them, seized his prey's shoulders, and spun the villain hard
against the carriage.

With one scoop, James lifted the bracelet from a shallow
pocket of Bennington's fashionable coat and stashed the antique
jewel into his own pocket.

"Very bad ton," James said, "to take things that don't belong
to you." His unappreciated sally was met with a string of vit-
riolic oaths.

"Damn you, Ware, hand that back. Lady Granville entrusted
her bracelet to me since the clasp is broken."

"That won't wash," James said. He could be in deep trouble
if Bennington was telling the truth, but his intuition told him
Bennington was dissembling.

"I will have you arrested," Lord Bennington said, but his voice lacked conviction. James noticed that his lordship had paled and had not called for help from his own coachman or the other drivers who were huddled around the entrance gossiping with the doorman.

James went with his instinct and seized the advantage.

"Right now inside Almack's Lady Granville has issued a cry for her stolen bangle," he guessed. Looking into Bennington's apprehensive face verified that he had hit the mark. "The two stories won't jibe. Methinks Lady Granville will save herself and name you as the thief with a quickly concocted explanation of how you might have noticed the dropped bracelet and made off with it."

To James's surprise, Lord Bennington crumpled visibly, shoulders sagging. The pompous facade had been replaced by that of a trembling craven.

"Are you working for the Runners, Ware?" he asked in a choked voice. He had heard such a rumor but until this moment had discounted it.

James shook his head. "Fortunately for you, I am working solely for Lord Granville on this. In order to avoid a scandal, he will not prosecute, but he insists that you clear Lady Granville's debts from the books at your Curzon Street gaming palace, return the money from the sale of the jewels, and cut off all personal contact with her."

Lord Bennington had seen flashes of Newgate in his future until James revealed the name of his current employer. Emboldened by the alleviation of his worst dread, Bennington revived enough to affect a sneer, but wisely said, "As you will," complying with James's terms.

"Incidentally, my lord, send a list of the Paris jewelers to whom you sold Granville's treasures around to my residence by tomorrow afternoon," James demanded. He heard an affirmative grunt before the door of the splendid coach was slammed shut by the aristocratic occupant. The coachman clicked the horses into motion and the coach moved out of sight into the dense night fog.

James turned from the street as Rachel walked up to him. She reached up and popped his silk hat onto his head and pressed his silver-headed cane into his hand. With the other hand, James adjusted his hat.

"I thought I best bring your hat and cane," she said, "for it is too late in the evening to gain entrance again."

"Thank you, my love," he said. He pulled her into his arms and gave her a strong hug. He signaled over his shoulder for the doorman to send for his carriage.

The fog closed around them. "Did he get away?" Rachel asked.

"Not before I collected the merchandise," he said.

Rachel took a deep breath. "I was so afraid."

"That we would fail?" James asked.

"No, that you might be hurt."

James put his palm against her cheek. "Don't you know, my sweet, that I'm indestructible. What happened inside?"

Rachel related the events that had taken place in the ladies' room, which led to her deduction that Lady Granville would engage in the unlawful escapade this evening.

"James, you would not believe how clever Lord Bennington is in prestidigitation. I would never play cards with the man. The bracelet disappeared from Lady Granville's wrist into his pocket in the wink of an eye. And as for her, she should go on the stage, such machinations."

Rachel went on to describe the scene in the card room. "I wish we could reveal the truth to Lady Jersey. The woman will be beside herself if scandalous rumors fly around concerning Almack's."

"We can have Lord Granville send around an apology to Sally, explaining that the bracelet was caught in the hem of Lady Granville's gown. Sally can scotch any bad publicity with that version." Rachel nodded her approval.

"Ah, here's my coach," James said.

He opened the carriage door, boosted Rachel up inside, and swung himself aboard. Sitting opposite her, he tapped the roof with his cane to set the carriage in motion.

James reached into his pocket, pulled out the bracelet, and dangled it before Rachel's eyes. She took the bangle into her hand. Even in the poor coach light, the diamonds and emeralds gave off a marvelous glitter. "It's a magnificent piece," Rachel said, handing the bracelet back to James.

He told her of the demands he had made on Bennington. "I deliberately gammoned him, since I did not have Lord Granville's instructions as to the terms he wished to impose on Bennington. But I am certain Granville can have no objections. He might even be able to retrieve his lost jewels, using the names of the Paris shops Bennington will supply me."

"I hope Lord Granville has sense enough to place his wife on a short leash," Rachel said.

"I think he has. He holds the upper hand and can dictate the particulars for her future conduct."

James set his hat and cane on the seat beside him, reached over, and pulled Rachel onto his lap.

"Bravo, my love," he said, "without your superior detection, those two would have flimflammed us for certain."

Rachel burrowed her head against his neck. "But I needed you. I could never have run after Bennington and confronted him. He would have flicked me off like a pesky flea."

"We make a good team," James said, "wouldn't you say?"

"I would," she agreed. "Darling, please stop procrastinating. I want you to ask me to be your wife."

James laughed. "Brazen hussy," he said lovingly. "Lord, Rachel, I do love you so." He claimed her lips in a long kiss.

When he lifted his lips, he said, "Will you marry me, sweetheart?"

"Oh, James, I love you, too, and yes, I will marry you."

"Partners for life," James said.

"Partners for life," Rachel echoed and raised her head for his magical kiss that would seal their promise for all eternity.

A Last Waltz

Isobel Linton

One

It might have been due to the flattering effect of the soft, flickering candlelight thrown off by so many crystal chandeliers, or it might have been due to a surfeit of Lady Ramsay's truly excellent claret, but Lord Denton felt certain that the young lady who stood before him was the most beautiful creature he had ever before beheld.

Miss Somerville's hair was ebony black; she wore it upswept, with a fringe of small curls that hung in ringlets about her face. Her eyes were large, dark, and very fine, framed by thick ebony lashes. On that particular Wednesday evening, she had chosen, as she usually did, to dress very demurely, as befitted her maiden status; she wore no ornaments beyond a small golden heart on a red satin ribbon tied round her neck and a pair of small gold circles on her shell-like ears.

Her skin was an almost radiant white, and her cheeks were naturally rosy. Her lips were a deep rose-color as well and were slightly upturned. She had a small chin and a round, sweet face, with a charming dimple that appeared upon her right cheek when she smiled, which she did very often. She was petite and witty and gay; her manner was fresh, unspoiled, and completely delightful.

Lord Denton was of the opinion that, of all the many young ladies who appeared to great advantage that evening at Almack's Assembly Rooms, Miss Somerville was by far the most lovely, and the most charming.

Her abigail had selected for her mistress a gown of sheer muslin that was simplicity itself, its lines were low and flowing and showed off her fine figure very well. Its bodice had been cut in a line that was flattering without being overly revealing; the gown had small, puffed sleeves, and a square neckline. She wore tiny white satin slippers, white gloves, and she carried a pretty beribboned posy of fresh flowers sent to her by one of her many admirers.

Seeing so near to him such a perfect figure of maidenly beauty, the impetuous Earl of Denton felt himself enchanted beyond all endurance—even though he was, come to think of it, just as good as betrothed to another.

But the spontaneity of romantic enchantment meant everything to young Lord Denton, and when he felt that singular emotion arising within himself, he felt urgently driven by an old and powerful force beyond reason to take action, in order to try to secure the lovely Miss Somerville as his very own.

Casting all caution to the winds, Denton felt impelled to let Miss Somerville know that he loved her deeply, beyond all things.

The Earl of Denton, with all the confidence instilled in him by his great wealth and nobility, then did just as he was inclined to do—he seized her tiny hand and attempted to bring it to his lips.

"No!" cried the young lady, wresting her hand away from the amorous earl, and tapping his hand sharply with the pretty ivory fan that her chaperone had loaned her for her first London Season. "Lord Denton, *please* stop kissing my hand like that! Everyone will be watching us! Whatever can you be thinking of? You must not do that, certainly not here at Almack's, of all places!"

"I must not?" the earl said blankly. "Then tell me, Miss Somerville—where *may* I kiss you?"

Miss Somerville shot him an exasperated glance.

"Nowhere, Lord Denton! Do be reasonable!" replied Philippa in an urgent whisper, putting up her fan as if trying to hide her reddened countenance from the rest of the guests in the crowded ballroom. "Can't you see that Lady Castlereagh is standing not so very far behind you? She is speaking to Lady Jersey! We must not attract their attention, at all costs! It would be fatal to my chances!"

The Earl of Denton still had sufficient grasp of his wits to stop what he was doing, turn around toward the Patronesses, and to take a rational measure of the whole situation and its social risks.

Having done so, he turned back toward Miss Somerville and replied in a reassuring tone, "Do not be alarmed, Miss Somerville. The Castlereagh isn't looking at us, she's looking at Sir Guy Trent, and he's looking at Sally Jersey. Silence appears to be favoring them both with one of her interminable speeches, all the while cutting some poor lady to shreds, no doubt. They're not concerned at all with us."

"But I *am* alarmed! How can you be so sure that it's *not* us that they're discussing?" said Miss Somerville with asperity. "Furthermore, should you insist on continuing to harass me in such a place as Mr. Willis's rooms, it is only a matter of time before they *will* be discussing us, Lord Denton. Oh, dear: *do* go away, won't you? Please consider my reputation, if you won't consider your own!"

"My reputation? What has that to say to anything? I'm sure I have enough credit with society to carry off makin' love to a lady, even at Almack's!" said Lord Denton defensively. "I'm from an old family. I have a noble title. I'm just as rich as Golden Ball. Why shouldn't I do just what I like? I wear the right clothes; I move in the best circles. Why, I can even kiss you here, if I wish, and no one will think the worse of me. I promise you!"

"But they *will* think the worse of *me!*" whispered Miss Somerville, who was beginning to lose all patience with her all-too-intrepid admirer. "Please, I mustn't do anything that would put my reputation at risk, Lord Denton. You know that! It was everything that Lady Bergeron could do to arrange for my presentation at Court, and then she had the most dreadful time talking Lady Sefton into giving her vouchers to bring me in here even as a guest!"

"Did she have a dreadful time getting your ticket? How very odd. Maria Sefton is the soft-hearted one among them, as a general rule. There should have been little problem, for, though Almack's is even more exclusive than the Queen's Drawing Rooms, I see no reason for Lady Sefton to have hesitated about your admission at all! Your family is very old, though not noble.

Why, if I had known you *then*—which of course I did not, nor could not—I wish you would have asked *me,* Miss Somerville! Would've been happy to obtain some vouchers for you. M' mother's very well connected with *all* the Patronesses, y'know."

"That must be very gratifying for you, I'm sure," she said rather wearily. "Though how I could possibly have asked you for help in gaining tickets *to* Almack's, before having met you here *at* Almack's, I cannot conceive."

"There is that," Lord Denton admitted.

"But, see here, sir, you really must leave me alone now, and go away. Please, Lord Denton, do go away."

"No, I shan't," he replied with finality. "Don't have to. Not going to."

Philippa nearly stamped her small, white satin-clad foot, and said, looking around helplessly, "Oh, where *is* Lady Bergeron?"

"I don't know, I'm sure. Glad she's gone away. Now, see here, Miss Somerville, I'll take you away from Almack's, that's what I'll do. Will you come outside with me? I have a very nice house back in Grosvenor. Find your chaperone and bring her along, if you wish. There is a very pretty little garden out in the back. Lady Bergeron could sit out there, and so could we, at a small distance, so we might talk there together, privately. I have so very much to say to you, Miss Somerville," said the earl feelingly. "Oh, and by the way, speaking of which, may I call you Philippa?"

"No!" she cried, unsure whether to laugh or weep. "Certainly not! Do keep your voice down, Lord Denton! Really, this display of sensibility is most inconvenient!"

"My dear Miss Somerville! Are you quite sure you do not wish to come outside with me?" he asked, trying to take hold of her hand, while the young lady just as quickly withdrew it, and hid it behind her back. "The room is so hot and so crowded. You are quite right, of course, we cannot be private here, and I must speak to you in private. Wouldn't want to break my heart, now, would you, dear Miss Somerville? You cannot be unaware of the deep and warm feelings you have inspired in me. You must pay the piper now, for, you know, my love for you is all your doing! You must allow me fully to express my profound feelings for you!"

"I believe you have just done so, Lord Denton, and with great eloquence," said Miss Somerville firmly and candidly, stepping to the left, and deftly avoiding the arm he was attempting to place round her small waist. "There is no need to explain your feelings any further, and certainly no need for us to go outside, or anywhere. I fear it is you who must leave me, and do so now, if you would be so kind."

"If you won't go with me now, Miss Somerville, may I call on you tomorrow? Would you care to take a drive with me about the park?" he asked in a desperate tone, looking for all the world as if he were about publicly to burst into tears. "Please, Miss Somerville, you must believe me! I am very deeply in love with you, and I will not be cast aside!"

Is there no one here to help me? Where can Lady Bergeron have gone? wondered Philippa unhappily. *Why must she wander off and leave me to try to escape from these suitors all on my own!*

Miss Philippa Somerville could only wish, with not little exasperation, that her mother's dear friend would take more seriously her duties as a chaperone! Lady Bergeron kept disappearing from sight, on one pretext or another, either to speak with her friends, or to hunt down another glass of orgeat.

Much as she felt genuinely obliged to her hostess and benefactress, who had, after all, done her the great favor to bring her down to London, bear the expenses for her come-out, and take her about in high society, Philippa was beginning to believe Lady Bergeron was more than a bit bird-witted, if not downright eccentric, for she seemed forever to be floating off in one direction or another, as fickle as a summer wind.

Rather than faithfully standing guard over her young charge as all the other chaperones did, she would stand around the floor for a few minutes, then seem to lose interest and drift away, and it was just this benign neglect that made possible embarrassing little scenes such as this one with Lord Denton.

The thing that was most irksome to Miss Somerville this evening was that the Earl of Denton was carrying on his silly little scene not four yards away from Lady Castlereagh and

Lady Jersey, two of the most top-lofty guardians of Almack's
Assembly Rooms. If her star was to fall with them, if she were
to lose their favor, it would be the end of all her hopes, and
upon her hopes lay the hopes for the other girls in her family.

She could only trust that neither lady was yet aware of her
ongoing *contretemps* with ardent Lord Denton.

Alas, Miss Philippa Somerville's hopes were in vain.

In fact, there were three persons who were powers in the world
of fashion who were close enough to notice Miss Somerville's
predicament, and the first to notice was the celebrated Sir Guy
Trent. Known widely as perhaps the most fashionable gentleman
in London, Sir Guy was an astonishingly imposing figure, very
tall, very lean, and very broad-shouldered. From his black hair,
brushed back in a deliberately tousled fashion, to his shining
polished black evening slippers, he was the perfect pattern-card
of what a gentleman ought to be.

Sir Guy Trent was in all respects immaculate: his black coat
had been cut to perfection by Weston, greatest tailor of his time,
and Weston's remarkable close-cutting served to show off the baronet's powerful build. His shirt and cravat were a dazzling white,
ironed and starched to a crisp. He wore his tie in the notorious
waterfall, a devilish hard knot, and one to which most hopeful
Pinks of the Ton could only aspire. On his left hand he wore his
only ornament: a massive golden signet ring, whose large center
stone was a great Thai sapphire, and had belonged to his late father.

Following the established custom of Almack's, Sir Guy wore
the old fashion of evening wear: he was dressed in the requisite
black knee-breeches with white silk hose. To wear trousers to
Almack's would have meant refusal of admittance by the top-
lofty Mr. Willis.

Sir Guy's eyes were large, dark, and very penetrating. It was
obvious to anyone that there would be nothing that would easily
escape the notice of such a gentleman, nor did it: he had been
listening politely to a long speech by Lady Jersey, when some
small, unusual commotion off to his side attracted his attention.

Sir Guy Trent turned his head slightly, toward the sound, and raised his quizzing glass to his eye, trying to make out the sound's source and significance.

The tall baronet had to lean down a bit in order to reach her ladyship's ear and whispered in it, "I say, Sally, what *is* young Denton doing?"

Lady Jersey at once turned to look across the room, and she had to squint, as she was a bit shortsighted, trying to see to what Sir Guy referred.

After a few moments of study, she replied, "I should say that Lord Denton appears to be making a cake of himself over Lady Bergeron's little *protégé*, Miss Somerville. If he keeps it up, Cynthia Protherow will be all over him in a minute's time. What a tiresome, silly boy, to display such poor judgment in front of everyone!"

This pronouncement in turn attracted the attention of Lady Castlereagh, who began to study the event herself, and proffer her opinion.

"I fear Lady Cynthia has seen them already. Look at her— and her mother—they both look fit to be tied!" pointed out Lady Castlereagh. "Should I go over there and tell her she must disguise her feelings with more adroitness? It certainly does the girl no good in terms of looks—Cynthia's face has gone all red and unattractive!"

"Denton's conduct is really very bad, but I do hope that Lady Cynthia is not going to make a fuss about it! It would be *so* weary-making: I vow, it would be intolerable! Guy, my love, *do* be a dear and go over and make that silly boy leave poor little Miss Somerville alone! I cannot endure the thought of Cynthia making a scene at Almack's. I will surely get the headache, and I have left my vinaigrette at home!"

"Alas, I hardly know young Denton's character, as he is from, shall we say, somewhat of a later generation?" demurred Sir Guy.

"Oh, stop trying to make yourself out as an ancient, Guy," said Lady Castlereagh. "It won't fadge with us!"

"And, of course, there is the simple fact that Miss Somerville and I are not properly acquainted," added the baronet.

"That's because you've come to Town so late this season,

you naughty man! Well, please, I beg you for once not to stand on ceremony, Guy! I call upon your sense of honor! Can't you see that the poor girl's chaperone is not in attendance upon her? And that she is having no luck at all trying to rid herself of Lord Denton on her own? I vow, Lady Bergeron has no more sense than a goose! What did she think would happen to such a pretty thing as Philippa Somerville if left to her own devices in a crowded ballroom, unaccompanied by family or friends?"

"I quite agree," said Lady Castlereagh. "I do not consider it at all the girl's fault—it's Lady Bergeron's! So shatterbrained of her to go away and leave a diamond of the first water all alone!"

Sally Jersey made her voice warm and ingratiating, and she squeezed her friend's arm as she said, "Do be a good fellow, Guy, and go over and give Denton a little word to the wise, won't you? Make him behave like a gentleman, and rescue the little Somerville girl away from him."

Sir Guy Trent, rather against his better judgment, bowed to the ladies and then headed across the room in order to comply with this request.

At nearly the same moment, on another side of the ballroom, Lady Cynthia Protherow, dressed in a frilled gown of pale pink silk, was having her ears soundly boxed by her mother, the Dowager Duchess of Harwich.

"Ow!" she cried, putting her hand to her ear. "Mother, do stop! People will see!"

"People will see nothing at all, except they will see me remonstrating with my foolish daughter, and then they will think nothing more about it!" hissed her grace, in an irrational fury. "What can you be thinking of, now? Look over there, Cynthia! Look at what has become of Denton! He is all over the Somerville chit and has no time left for you, it seems! How can you have let him slip through your fingers like this? Why doesn't he come over and dance with you again?"

"He can't dance more than two dances with me in an evening, after all, Mama. By custom, he *has* to dance with someone else, does he not?" whined Lady Cynthia, rubbing her reddened ear. "He may just as well ask Philippa Somerville as anyone else."

"He's not simply asking Miss Somerville to grant him a dance, young lady!" replied her grace sarcastically. "If you will just open your eyes for once and attend, you will see that he keeps trying to take her hand and kiss it! He's trying to make love to her, don't you see? And the worst part of it is that he is making a fool of himself over that girl in full view of the ton! Why don't you go over and put an end to it? Don't you feel mortified by his behavior?"

"Yes, Mama, as it happens, I do! That being the case, I wish you will lower your voice! I'm sure we don't want to attract any more attention to his behavior, or to ours," she said feelingly, *sotto voce*.

The Duchess of Harwich looked nervously around the room, trying to make out how many among the ton had become aware of Lord Denton's conduct.

"I can't think what could have gone wrong!" said her grace crossly. "I'm sure that it is all your fault. You must have said something, or done something, that put him off."

"I did no such thing, mother," snapped Lady Cynthia, tired of being the cause of all misfortune. "Don't make such a fuss!"

"Don't speak to me in such a way! Kindly explain to me what has happened! You told me things between Denton and you were just as good as settled already!"

"They *were* as good as settled," said Lady Cynthia with a resentful little pout, "at least until *that* girl came along."

The Duchess's eyes darkened in a frightening fashion, and her brows drew together in a frown as she snapped, "Why did God give me such a nodcock for a daughter? I'm sure I never did anything to deserve such a fate! You just do not seem to recognize the importance of retaining your hold on Denton, do you?"

"Yes, I do, Mama, and I've done everything you told me, just as I ought!" whined Lady Cynthia.

"Then why is Lord Denton, *your* Lord Denton, over there by the window, making such a fuss about that pretty little vicar's daughter, in the very shadow of two Patronesses, I might add?

Do you think that just because she is poor, he will not choose to offer for her? Denton has enough money to marry a million penniless wenches."

"I *know* that, Mother."

"The penniless wench he must marry is you, Cynthia! You know very well that your brother and I are depending on you to make sure this connexion is made! You do not seem to regard this situation in a serious light! Recall, if you please, that we may very well lose Berleigh Court if you do not marry Denton!"

"Yes, Mother, I know all about losing Berleigh Court if I do not marry well; you and Stanley have told me so a hundred times," she replied wearily.

"Then, do something about it! Go over there, and *say* something to him, I don't know what, go beguile him again, but for heaven's sake, don't just *stand* here, fretting me to death! Oh, no, what's this? Sir Guy Trent is going over there to intervene with Denton! What has *he* to do with this?" wailed her mother miserably. "All we have worked for, coming to nothing! Everyone is going to know our sad business now!"

"Stop it, Mother, right now! Turn around and look away, or I'll box *your* ears for making such a fuss and ruining my chances!" said Lady Cynthia with sudden bravery, as a determined look appeared upon her countenance. "I know my duty to my family. I'll find some way to make things right with Denton before the night is out, I promise you. I won't give Denton up without a fight!"

"See that you do not, Cynthia. See that you do not!" hissed her mother.

The two ladies turned away from the scene, as if to give less import and credence to it. They walked away in the opposite direction, mother and daughter, arm in arm, smiling and nodding to their acquaintances, just as if nothing of terrible significance to the family fortunes were happening on the other side of the ballroom.

Two

Lady Cynthia Protherow was the only daughter of the late Duke of Harwich. The young lady in question was eighteen years of age, very tall, very blonde, and an acknowledged diamond of the first water. She had been well-educated and was always well-spoken. She had a definite elegance of style and a commanding address that bespoke the natural sense of superiority characteristic of those to the manor born.

For all the advantages she had been blessed with, however, her circumstances were not universally excellent: due to the unfortunate profligacy of the late Duke, her father, and due to the spendthrift nature of her younger brother, Stanley, who had inherited his dignities much too young, the family's financial situation was undesirable, to say the least. Everything that the young Duke could mortgage, he had mortgaged, and he spent a great deal of time moving from Seat to Seat, trying to outrun his father's many creditors.

In fact, all things duly considered, the Protherow family had now become almost as poor as church mice, although they had taken great pains to insure that this fact was not generally known amongst the *haut ton*. To admit poverty would be fatal; one's creditor's would take the opportunity to swoop in and tear one to shreds.

Things being at such a turn, the Dowager Duchess of Harwich's life work was to ensure that her beautiful only daughter would, this very season, be wed in such a way as to repair the family fortunes, and save the ducal estate from final ruin.

Which made it very understandable that her grace had taken it so badly when it seemed that the affections of the fabulously wealthy Earl of Denton had somehow been transferred from her daughter to a mere nobody, a vicar's daughter.

It was not to be countenanced. After all, what would a vicar's daughter know to do with all that wealth and splendor?

The Duchess knew how to spend money, and upon what it should be spent. Her son knew. Her daughter knew.

But little Miss Somerville from Shropshire? She couldn't be expected to know how to spend *half* of Denton's monthly income!

Raised with her fond family in the quiet hamlet of Penbury, it had been a great surprise of all society when Miss Philippa Somerville had so unexpectedly taken the ton by storm. When she learned, soon after her arrival in London, that she was being deemed one of the Beauties of the Season, it had come as quite a shock, both to Philippa herself, and to her more established rivals on the Marriage Mart, like Lady Cynthia Protherow.

Philippa had simply wished to come to London to marry, and to marry well. Her London season was a serious business, an obligation she wished to meet well. There were the twins, after all, to be considered. Miranda and Ellen were turning fifteen; they desperately needed a married sister who was firmly established in society, could help them with their own come-outs, and could make the connexions necessary to establish themselves in respectable marriages.

Notoriety was completely beside the point. Notoriety based upon mere physical beauty was nothing desirable to Miss Philippa Somerville: in fact, it was a distraction from her main task of husband-hunting, for it insured that silly little scenes such as that with Lord Denton were occurring with boring regularity.

Almost from the moment she arrived in town, pretty little Miss Somerville had been singled out for admiration by those of the opposite sex. Poems were written to celebrate the magical enchantment of her upturned nose. Handwritten notes indicating longing attachment were secretly thrust into her hands by admirers when, in the dark of a performance of *Richard III* at the Drury Lane, they passed by her box.

As Pink after Pink after Pink of the Ton recklessly cast himself at Miss Somerville's tiny feet, her life was transformed into a whirlwind of gay activities. Myriad posies arrived daily at her door and were received by Jarvis, Lady Bergeron's butler, with stony silence that belied his perception of them as a dreadful nuisance. Her social schedule was full to overflowing, and the flurry of note-cards and calling cards that obscured Lady Bergeron's mantel stood as proof of the power of her sudden popularity.

Happily, Miss Philippa Somerville had always been a reasonable, intelligent girl with a strong sense of appreciation for the ridiculous. Her father and mother had instilled in her, as they had in all their children, a very proper recognition of the order and importance of things, so that none of this immoderate adulation went to her head, as it no doubt would have in another girl less intelligent and less carefully raised.

Miss Somerville thought the whole fuss a silly joke, really; only the matter of her trying to contract as good a marriage for herself as she possibly could was of any real concern to her. The thing was, for all her apparent success in London society, she was making no progress in achieving her main aim. Lady Bergeron was at a loss to explain this, and Miss Somerville herself found the situation oddly perplexing.

Not that she had been at a loss for offers for her hand—far from it!

Less than one week into the current Season, Viscount Copley had asked her to marry him. However, although the man was titled and very rich, Philippa felt she had to refuse him. It was not precisely that Miss Somerville was of a romantic disposition, for she swore that she was not, but she found it very off-putting that Lord Copley was nearing sixty years of age and had three grown daughters and three grown sons! Although he seemed a sensible and pleasant man, a match with him seemed neither pleasant nor sensible to Miss Somerville, and so, with some reluctance (but not a great deal), she broke his heart and sent him packing.

Not too long afterward, while on an excursion to Richmond

Hill, young Lord Kinney had asked her to marry him. He was a handsome, personable young man of five and twenty, with a dashing manner, and excellent taste. She thought over his offer for two whole days before crushing his hopes, telling him that his Irish property was much too far from her family to be comfortable for her. She never told him that she had been made aware of his own situation, and that she knew his mother expected him to marry to add more money to the Kinney family's coffers. Although his lordship, in the normal run of things, was well able to marry a girl without a dowry, she felt that a poor wife would surely bear the brunt of Lady Kinney's wrath for all her married life. Miss Somerville then broke Lord Kinney's heart and sent him packing, too.

As the season continued, the number of her rejected suitors mounted vastly, and Miss Somerville's reputation as a pearl beyond price escalated accordingly.

Mr. Frederick Parkhurst, heir to a great estate in Derby, had tried to single her out for his attentions, but she didn't like the way he kept his whiskers, or the way he refused to look directly at her when they spoke, and so managed to keep him dangling in such a way that he was never even given the opportunity to try to offer for her.

The incident that crowned her glorious legend as an unattainable paragon was when she refused, out of hand, the handsome, wealthy heir to the Duke of Bewley.

David Brinton had first spotted Miss Somerville at Lady Hensley's rout and had pursued her with all imaginable vigor. Even though his was the highest title ever offered her, and his estates were essentially limitless, she could not like him, much less consent to marry him. The man had rusty hair, which she had always disliked, but beyond that, the fact that he had absolutely no sense of humor whatsoever made him, in Miss Somerville's sapient eyes, completely unacceptable. Still, she was very flattered and very sensible of the honor he had done her, and was rather irrationally pleased to think that she had *almost* been a duchess, and so she refused Lord Brinton in the most gracious possible way.

Miss Somerville's refusal of the wealthy heir to an eminent Duchy only added to the legend of her consequence.

Philippa found the whole thing lowering and weary-making. Often, she would come home after a long night, weary as could be after attending party after party, her feet red, swollen, and aching from dancing quadrille after quadrille. She wondered what was the point of it all, and she began to wonder where it would all end. How many more men would she have to attract and to refuse, before she would find an eligible gentleman whom she could grow fond of?

By that particular night in May at Almack's Assembly Rooms, Miss Somerville had really begun to lose hope. She had started to consider giving the whole project up to go back home to Mama and Papa and the twins and little Harry.

But the expense of it! To repay Lady Bergeron's generosity by going home husbandless! It really would not do!

On the other hand, how long could she expect her mother's dear friend to put up with her? Lady Bergeron had been kindness itself when it had come to paying Philippa's expenses for her walking dresses, and riding dresses, and morning dresses, and evening dresses, and for the old-fashioned but splendid panniered silk gown in which she had been presented at Court. But Philippa was not sure how deep were her financial resources, nor how long she was prepared to undertake the wearying job of attending party after party, on such a busy schedule as a London debut entailed.

That being the case, Philippa had been becoming increasingly more anxious that her future be settled once and for all, as soon as it might be arranged. Her heart was certainly in the right place: she knew what had to be done and was committed to so doing.

However, the great problem was that none of her many admirers, even the ones whom she had captivated enough to make actual offers for her hand, seemed, not to put too fine a point on it, at all worth marrying!

All the gentlemen concerned were very rich—wealth was a definite prerequisite, since Philippa, to her credit, had made no bones about the fact that she had no dowry to speak of. Most of

her suitors were titled. But none of them had captured Philippa's
attention, much less her heart, and it simply did not seem right
to marry any gentleman one could just as easily live without!

It was in that frame of mind that, once again, she had allowed
her abigail to dress her, and to do her hair, and deck her out for
another Wednesday appearance at Almack's, hoping against
hope that a suitable gentleman would appear and sweep her off
her feet. However, the only gentleman who tried to sweep her
off her feet was the over-ardent Lord Denton.

Three

Really, thought Philippa, *his behavior is absolutely the out-side of enough! Is Lord Denton deaf? Is he merely headstrong? Is he a rogue, or merely a buffle-head?*

Though Miss Somerville strongly wished him at Jericho, the earl simply would not take no for an answer, and would not leave her be.

Lord Denton, who was slight but strong, had by now put his hand around Philippa's waist, which she thought completely insupportable. He was pulling her forcefully toward him, as he prattled on about the strength of his feelings, and the deep tenderness of his affections. Miss Somerville was afraid she was going to become physically ill if she heard one more stupid word from him about love, or esteem, or attachment.

She pushed him away from her just as hard as she could, which was, unfortunately, not hard enough. She was terribly frightened that Lord Denton's impetuous stubbornness, now being enacted at Almack's for all to see, would swiftly put a period to her hopes for a successful end to her London Season and for making the eligible match that would mean everything to her family.

"Lord Denton!" cried Philippa, loudly now, and rather desperately. "Unhand me, sir, at once!"

"My feelings are far too strong to be denied!" replied Lord Denton, refusing to let her go. He pulled at her hand, trod on her gown, and ripped its hem, as he pulled her within his embrace, saying, "See here, Philippa! You must and you shall be mine!"

Suddenly a tall gentleman appeared with whom Miss

Somerville was not previously acquainted. He picked up Lord
Denton bodily in a single powerful motion, taking hold of the
scruff of his coat, and let the earl's polished pumps dangle
briefly in the air, before turning the earl around, shoving his
backside roughly, and depositing him in a far corner of the
room, where he slipped to the floor, astonished.

"Your attentions are unwanted, Denton," said Sir Guy Trent
very softly, dusting any lint that might have been on Denton's
coat off his hands. "Leave the young lady alone."

Lord Denton blushed a fiery red and looked around at the
company, whose attention had now been turned toward him. He
got up, brushed himself off, and backed away, bowing as best
he could, apologizing furiously for his incomprehensible lapse
in conduct.

"F-forgive me, Miss S-somerville," said the earl, suddenly
brought to rude awareness. "Don't know what came over me.
Inexcusable conduct. Most sorry, I'm sure. B-best wishes to
you. Y'won't take it amiss, Trent, now, will you? B-best wishes,
ma'am."

Miss Somerville dismissed him with an exasperated wave of
her hand and allowed herself to be led away to the safety of the
far side of the room by the tall gentleman.

"Are you perfectly well, I hope?" he asked smoothly.

"Yes, save that I am a bit ruffled, and I am certainly annoyed.
I can't think what came over Lord Denton. He is usually perfectly well-behaved. Perhaps he was foxed," she said. "Do you
think that might account for it?"

"It is possible," Sir Guy admitted. "He was certainly in love."

"Pooh! Was that love?" Philippa asked crossly. "I do not
think so."

"Love can do strange things," pointed out Sir Guy. "Or so
it is said."

"Yes, I have read all about *that,* and I can tell you, I have no
opinion of it, nor of such conduct as Lord Denton displayed
tonight," the young lady said unsentimentally. "That was not
love; it was just more of Lord Denton's lecturing! He didn't for

one moment listen to a word I said! It was his own sheer bombast; it was conceit!"

This frank comment brought a warm smile to the tall gentleman's face.

Sir Guy bowed to the young lady, and said, "Perhaps I should present myself to you, if you will permit me. Or is there anyone else about who might perform the office?"

Miss Somerville, rather embarrassed, sighed and shook her head, and poured her troubles out in a sudden stream, saying, "There is my chaperone, Lady Bergeron, who of course *ought* to be with me, but she is always otherwhere! I have lived with her while I have been staying in Town. Whenever she and I go out, whether to the theater or a private ball, or even here, she never can stay in one place, by my side, as she ought to, but she keeps forever disappearing, going off to take some refreshment, or speaking to some acquaintance! I am not at all used to London ways, of course, and it has been very difficult for me, for I can't quite take care of myself here. When she leaves me to myself, it becomes possible for things to get so very awkward and out of hand!"

The man smiled his amused smile again, and said, "Do such scenes as that with young Denton happen to you very often, then?"

Miss Somerville's attractively dark eyes widened.

"Yes, indeed, they do! All the time! It is the strangest thing!" said Miss Somerville, in a tone of pure exasperation. "This business with Lord Denton tonight was by far the worst of it, but if you can credit it (which, personally, I cannot), ever since I came to London I have had to fend off not only numerous unwanted admirers, who plagued me not unlike Lord Denton, as you yourself have seen, but I have to fight off, single-handedly, at least four firm offers of marriage!"

"None of them were to your liking?" inquired the man, diverted by such ingenuous candor.

"No, not even close! It was so very lowering!" said Miss Somerville, very glad to have a sympathetic listener upon whom she might unburden herself of her cares. "I come from Shropshire, from a family that is not very well-off, you see, for my father is a vicar, and very early on, from at least when I was six, I had the notion that, to help my sisters and my family, I should come to London and make a great marriage!"

"I see," said Sir Guy, nodding his head, and trying to keep a serious look upon his face. "So you wish to make a great marriage, do you?"

"Yes! I do! When I was eighteen, my mother's old friend Lady Bergeron came out to Hadley Vicarage to visit us, and when we were walking down the lane one day, I happened to mention my desire to marry well and advance the interests of my family."

"You sound very dutiful and disinterested," Sir Guy remarked. "In your quest to marry well, I mean."

"Well, it is perfectly true! I have always been known as a sensible girl, and upon reflection, I decided that this was the most beneficial course to take. At any rate, Lady Bergeron said she thought it a splendid plan, and she even offered to pay my expenses and bring me to London and take me about in society."

"That was kind of her."

"She was as good as her word, for I came this Season, and I was presented at a Drawing-Room, and I had my come-out. The funny thing was that I took very well, though I'm sure I can't imagine why I should have. It was most flattering, and I was introduced to many eligible gentlemen. Really, it should all have been settled and over, for I can tell you that all four offers of marriage that were made to me were most suitable from a financial point of view!" she said simply.

"Then what, may I ask, was the difficulty?" asked the gentleman, thoroughly captivated by the maiden's tale.

"I couldn't bear any one of them past ten minutes!" she explained candidly, which brought an unexpected chuckle from her listener. "Not any one of them!"

"Even though they were very rich, as you had hoped?" inquired Sir Guy, who has having increasing difficulty keeping his countenance.

"Yes, each one of them was enormously wealthy, but what has that to say to anything? I mean, to dance with a wealthy gentleman, one time, even several times, for half an hour or so, that is one thing, but to link one's life, forever, with a man who cares for nothing beyond the cut of his waistcoat? Impossible!"

"You found it difficult to be truly mercenary, then, when the time came?" Sir Guy inquired lightly.

"Mercenary?" cried Philippa, frowning a little. "What a lowering thought! Well, I shouldn't have called my plan *mercenary*, precisely, though I suppose it depends upon the way one looks at it. I thought I was being practical and dutiful to my family! To think of myself as being mercenary seems more than a little shameful, for I had really thought that I was a better person than that."

"I am sure you are, my dear," said Sir Guy, in an amused and reassuring voice. "I am sure you are."

"Dear me, I suppose it is very odd of me to be running on like this, and I really shouldn't be saying anything at all. I beg your forgiveness. I have always been a terrible gabbler; it is my besetting fault. It is very stupid of me, for I have learned since I have come to London that it is terribly unfashionable to reveal one's thoughts and feelings, and I have just been chattering away recklessly, for which I do beg your pardon, for it is inexcusable, and I must be boring you to death, and it was really most silly of me since we don't even know one another!" said Miss Somerville in a long, wild-rushing explanation.

Sir Guy raised one eyebrow and studied the girl intently, not quite sure that he believed her apparently ingenuous admission. It was one thing to be from Shropshire, it was quite another never to have seen or heard of Sir Guy Trent, the Beau's Beau, who was used to marriage-minded girls setting their caps at him.

"No, ma'am, at present we are not acquainted," he replied smoothly. "But as I said before, that can easily be remedied, even in the absence of your chaperone. I am Sir Guy Trent, at your service. May I be permitted to know your name?"

The young lady curtseyed to him at once, saying, "Sir Guy Trent! Of course! I *have* heard of you, for you are very famous! I am Miss Somerville. Thank you so much for coming to my rescue; I know it must have been very distasteful to you."

"Not at all, Miss Somerville," said Sir Guy. "I was happy to be at your service."

"It certainly was distasteful to me, I can tell you! Why, I think I shall never speak to Lord Denton again! Speaking of which, oh dear! He's come back again! *Where* can I hide?" she cried, trying to conceal herself behind Sir Guy.

Lord Denton, looking rather the worse for wear, stepped straight up to Sir Guy Trent, and his eyes came up to the baronet's broad shoulders.

"Step aside, Trent," said Lord Denton, with a loud hiccup. "Shouldn't've interfered in my affairs. Got some things to say to the young lady. Can't stop me, so away with you."

Sir Guy perceived at once that Denton was not only angry, but dangerously deep in his cups, and might at any instant disrupt the dignity of the gathering.

He said, politely, "No, I think not, Denton."

Sir Guy again firmly grasped the Earl of Denton's coat, picked him up, and propelled him away.

"I'm afraid I must be off again, Miss Somerville," said the tall gentleman, as he began to steer him out of the ballroom. "I think I shall convey our over-impetuous lover to his lodgings. Do not refine too much upon this evening, I beg you. These things happen with boring regularity, even in the best of circles, believe me. Good evening. It was a pleasure to meet you, and I hope we shall meet again, very soon."

As she watched him removing the offending earl from her sight, Miss Somerville felt very grateful to her new acquaintance; she vowed that she would not talk Sir Guy's ear off the next time they met.

Four

"Lady Bergeron! There you are at last!" cried Philippa, as she saw her chaperone, a thin woman with a worn, faraway look, threading her way toward her through the crowd, smiling and nodding her head to her various acquaintances in her dreamlike manner. "Where have you been?"

"Oh, here and there," she said vaguely, making an airy gesture with her hand. "Why, Philippa? Is there something amiss?"

"Yes, it was really very awkward," said her charge. "Lord Denton was with me, and he kept trying to kiss my hand, and told me he loved me, and I couldn't make him stop."

Lady Bergeron gave a small shudder, and said, "How tedious for you, my dear Philippa! I do wish I had been here in order to shoo him away!"

Philippa looked at her benefactress quizzically for a moment, and then struck up the courage to inquire, "Why were you not here?"

Lady Bergeron took in a deep breath and exhaled with a rather helpless sigh.

"Well, my dear Philippa, that is the strange thing about all of this. I knew quite well what I was undertaking when I agreed to sponsor you, as it were, amongst the ton, and I thought it a terribly good idea at the time . . ."

Her voice trailed off, and her eyes seemed to mist over. She almost had to shake herself awake, and went on, "The thing of it is, I found that as soon as we began going here and there together, it was very . . . oh, I don't know how to express it, really. Here at Almack's it is the very worst. There is just a sort of . . ."

She stopped speaking, paused, and then began again, saying, "Everywhere we went, you see, was someplace I had been before."

"Yes, of course, you had been there before," said Philippa almost brusquely. "I don't precisely understand what you mean."

"Well, you see, neither do I, my dear," admitted Lady Bergeron. "When I say 'before,' you see, I meant when I was young. And Almack's is the very worst venue of all, for it makes me think of long ago, when I was very young . . . before I married. All the young people were in London then, and it was very gay . . . I fear I am not making any sense. Oh, dear . . ."

Her voice trailed off again, and she dropped her reticule.

"Oh, dear, what have I done? Is it time to go home, do you think, Philippa?"

Philippa shook her head, unable to understand what was ailing her chaperone. It was clear that there was something more than a little odd about her mother's old friend, though she had always appeared perfectly pleasant when she had come to the vicarage to visit. It was as if there was something in the very act of chaperoning itself that plagued her; perhaps something had happened that Lady Bergeron did not care to recall. Philippa wished Lady Bergeron would be more like her old, sensible self, but really didn't know what to do.

Near the Doric columns upholding the circular musicians' balcony at the side of the dancing-hall, Lady Cynthia Protherow was talking in an animated way to her younger brother, now the fourth Duke of Harwich.

"It's all those violins above us, Cynthia," her brother replied. "I can't make out a word of what you're saying."

"Come closer to me, then," she said as loudly as she dared. "I have something I want you to do for me, and I don't want anyone to overhear."

"You always want me to be doing something for you," said the Duke crossly. "What is it this time?"

"You needn't be so snippy about it, Stanley. If my marriage to Lord Denton falls through because of that pretty little black-haired chit, you'll be out on the street as well, along with Mother, and your costly stable of horses. It's all very well to have a title, and have everyone bow down to the great grand Duke, but if your grace hasn't a feather to fly with, it's just a bad joke, isn't it?"

The Duke favored his sister with a glare, with one hand flicked open a fine gilt box, and took a pinch of snuff. He dusted the snuff off his fingertips, sneezed, and remarked, "You know, if you don't stop being such a crosspatch, Cynthia, no one will marry you!"

"I am your elder, Stanley, and don't you forget it!" cried Lady Cynthia. "Don't you dare be disrespectful to me!"

"Ouch! Cynthia! Don't box my ear!" cried the Duke, trying to duck another blow. "What a termagant you are!"

"I learned *that* from our mother! She gave me one nice hit earlier, and I thought I'd just pass it on to you!"

"What a way to behave at Almack's! Who do you think you are, Cynthia?" he said crossly, rubbing his reddening ear. "I hope you don't treat your husband like that."

"I'll treat him just as I see fit, and so I promise!" said Lady Cynthia, a furious look on her face.

"Poor Denton!" said the Duke feelingly. "I wonder if I should warn him?"

Lady Cynthia rapped her brother on the shoulder with her ivory fan, and said, "Enough! Listen to me, Stanley, this is important. I want you to go over right now to that young lady over there, the little pretty dark one standing next to Lady Bergeron, and chat her up a little."

"Am I acquainted with her?"

"She is Miss Somerville. I daresay you've seen her before."

"I remember now. Yes, we have been introduced. Why do you want me to go over to her?" asked her brother.

"I want you to ask her for the waltz," said Lady Cynthia.

The Duke shot his sister an incredulous look, and said, "Oh, I can't do that, can I?"

"Of course you can," said Lady Cynthia impatiently. "Why can't you?"

"Don't know if she's gotten permission from a Patroness, for one thing! Wouldn't do to ask her, and dance with her, and find out afterwards that it was her first time. They'd be furious. Might cut her. Or worse! You know how they can be, the seven dragons. No, not dragons—basilisks! Worse!" the Duke said with a shiver.

"Why did God give me such a nodcock for my brother?" hissed Lady Cynthia, throwing up her arms in despair. "Don't you understand? That's the whole point! I *know* that they haven't given her their permission!"

"See? Then I can't do it!" replied the Duke sensibly.

"Yes, you can! You must!" Lady Cynthia said with exasperation. "Don't be such a chaw-bacon!"

"Don't call me that, Cynthia! It's disrespectful! Really, sometimes you act as if you had been brought up in a slum!" snapped the Duke.

"Go now, Stanley, and ask her for the waltz!" she said insistently.

"Why?" he retorted.

"Because Denton is mad for her!" explained Lady Cynthia. "That is why!"

"What, *your* Denton?"

"Yes, my Lord Denton! *Our* Denton!" she cried, almost in a state of despair. "The one who is going to marry me, and pay all of your bills at Tattersall's, and at White's, and all of your bills at your tailor's, and your bills at your bootmaker's, and your bills at Rundell and Bridge's for all the wretched jewelry you waste on purchasing the good-will of your wretched ladybirds! The one who can redeem all your vowels! That Denton!"

"Oh," said the Duke, suddenly brought to his senses. *"That* Denton."

"I must get rid of her, don't you see? As long as Denton sees Miss Somerville around town, he'll continue to be infatuated

with her—I know how he can be. However, if I can find a way
to mortify her sufficiently so that she stays in, or, better yet,
that she gives up for the whole Season, and goes with her tail
between her legs back to Hampshire, or Shropshire, or Mop-
shire, or whatever sniveling little village she hails from, I am
sure I can win Denton back in a heartbeat. But if he goes on
seeing her in society, here and there, I shall lose him. *We* shall
lose him!"

"You don't have to be so unpleasant about it. I can't think
what has come over you lately, Cynthia. These days you are as
ill-tempered as a bee!"

"I am a desperate woman, Stanley! My future happiness depends upon my marrying Denton. This Somerville chit is an
obstacle in my way, and that obstacle *must* be removed. It must
be removed at once!"

"Oh, all right, all right," he said, miffed.

"So, Stanley? Will you ask her to dance now?" demanded
Lady Cynthia.

"Now that you put the thing in *that* light," replied the Duke.
"Yes, I will."

His grace adopted a thoughtful look, and added, "What if
she refuses?"

"Then I will just have to think of something else," snapped
Lady Cynthia. "Why, I'd poison the girl if I had to!"

"Yes, my dear sister," replied the Duke smoothly, "I am beginning to believe that you would."

Five

Lady Cynthia's plan worked out to perfection. In the end, her brother, the Duke, dutifully did as he was asked: the next time the musicians struck up a waltz, he crossed over to the other side of the ballroom, presented himself, and sought Miss Somerville's hand for the next waltz.

Philippa's putative chaperone was sitting in her usual state of distraction on a thin golden chair, gazing in the opposite direction, apparently enchanted by a silver sconce. That lady recognized the Duke, nodded to him in an otherworldly way, and returned her attention elsewhere; she did not listen to the details of the Duke's invitation, her mind being otherwise occupied.

Lacking any counsel from her chaperone, Philippa eagerly accepted the Duke's invitation to waltz, hoping she would remember the steps she had practiced long ago in the schoolroom at Hadley Vicarage. She took her place on the dance floor, thinking nothing of it; she allowed her partner to take hold of her right hand and place his right at her small waist; the music began, and the various elegant couples began to whirl around the floor. Philippa was concentrating very hard on following the steps of the music precisely, and *not* to be stepping on the Duke's toes.

Poor little Miss Somerville was so country-bred that she did not even notice when Mrs. Drummond Burrell glared straight at her, then stalked over to Silence and Lady Castlereagh, and pointed out to her fellow Patronesses the young lady's fatal *faux pas*.

"What is the chit thinking of, to accept a waltz before receiving our permission! What audacity! What want of manners! How dare the ungrateful girl behave in such a way!" cried Mrs. Drummond Burrell. "Lady Bergeron was standing right *next* to them when the girl accepted! How shocking!"

"I can see I was quite wrong about Miss Somerville," said Lady Jersey, fanning herself with great energy. "She doesn't belong here at Almack's! She belongs back at some, some little village assembly, rubbing shoulders with the local squire's son, or perhaps dancing with the son of an attorney! No, I was quite wrong: I should have insisted that Maria Sefton *not* let the girl in! Maria is too soft, too soft by far."

"I quite agree. Lady Bergeron would of *course* have acquainted Miss Somerville with *all* the rules proper to the ton," pointed out Lady Castlereagh. "One cannot blame such a breach on innocent ignorance! If Miss Somerville is dancing the waltz here without our permission, she is deliberately baiting us and flouting convention! Her behavior is the outside of enough."

"The Duke, of course, did not know she lacked permission," remarked Mrs. Dummond Burrell, her eyes flashing. "His grace, of course assumed that any well-bred young lady would act with the innate sense of social propriety that is expected of her. His grace would assume that if a girl lacked our imprimatur, she would inform him, upon his seeking out her hand, that she had not had our blessing."

"Certainly so," agreed Sally Jersey. "It was not the young Duke's fault, not at all. How could it have been? He is London bred; he would know better than to act in a care-for-nothing manner that might offend us. It was *her* fault entirely."

"Yes, it was her fault," chimed in little Mrs. Harold Braithwaite, who knew nothing at all about the matter, but happened to be standing within earshot, and who very much liked to avail herself of any opportunity to agree with a Patroness.

"Miss Somerville will pay for her little bit of insolence," said Mrs. Drummond-Burrell mercilessly. "I promise you, she will pay."

"It is necessary that she pay," said Lady Castlereagh. "Otherwise, what meaning can there be in the rules of society, if they can be broken as easily as a China cup? No, the girl must be chastised, I quite agree."

"So do I," chirped little Mrs. Braithwaite.

Primarily by means of the agreeable Mrs. Braithwaite, who was thrilled to be the first to receive and pass on any juicy bit of gossip, news of Philippa's scandalous conduct was passed round and round, from lady to lady, and lord to lord.

In less time than it took for one of the musicians to retune his violin, the word of Miss Somerville's unforgivable transgression swept all round the Assembly Room at Almack's; by the next day, detailed knowledge of the fall of the fair Miss Somerville had swept around all the most important of London's Upper Ten Thousand.

As for Philippa, herself, she remained for some time blithely unaware of the calamity that had fallen upon her. Having stood too long in a draft with only the sheerest of wraps, the poor girl contracted rather a bad case of the sniffles, was laid abed on Thursday and Friday, and was unable to attend any social engagements.

While complete ignorance of her situation was, in a sense, bliss, it was also unfortunate; while her three day absence from good society made it impossible for her to be acquainted with her downfall, it also made it impossible for her, or Lady Bergeron, or any of her friends to offer any defense for her behavior, and only gave rise to much negative speculation as to her motives for disobeying the rules laid down by the Patronesses.

By the third day, which happened to be Saturday, no one who was anyone would even *think* of speaking to the despicably wayward Miss Somerville of Shropshire, nor would they even *think* of acknowledging her on the street, nor would they hereafter send her any social invitation, nor, they swore, would they pay her a call or return a call she had made.

Even those young ladies of quality who had previously been on good terms with her, such as Miss Minter or Lady Susan

Darnell, dared not call upon her; all they could do when listening to others who roundly disparaged Miss Somerville, was to solemnly refrain from adding any of their own insults to increase her injury.

The invitation cards that had arrived at Lady Bergeron's townhouse each day with portentous regularity, soon ceased to arrive in any fashion.

Miss Philippa Somerville, the dark-haired beauty who had once been the toast of the town, was now officially *persona non grata;* she who had only recently been pursued and acclaimed was now despised and avoided.

All it had taken was one false move, one innocent misjudgment, one waltz.

On Sunday afternoon, whilst out driving in the park, Countess Lieven, who had not even been in attendance on that fatal Wednesday last, gave Miss Somerville the cut direct, and did so in a manner that even dreamy Lady Bergeron noticed. That august and eminent lady encountered Lady Bergeron and Miss Somerville on the Serpentine Road, and when their carriages met, the Countess briefly favored both ladies, one after the other, with the very coldest of glances, so frigid as to indicate that neither one of them possessed human existence. Then, raising her nose high in the air, Countess Lieven turned away from them, and passed them by, a slight, contemptuous smile playing on her lips.

"Good heavens! What was *that* all about?" cried Lady Bergeron. "Philippa, is there something wrong?"

"There must be," cried Philippa, mortified. "But I cannot imagine what is the matter."

"Nor can I, but we must try to keep calm. You mustn't make a spectacle of yourself, not here in the park, where everyone can see you! Take my handkerchief, blow your nose, and pull your bonnet down to cover your face. Hold your head up high, like this, and smile."

Philippa did just as she was told. Two or three carriages

passed theirs; Philippa and Lady Bergeron smiled and nodded, but the occupants of the other carriages stared right through them.

"They are cutting us! They are deliberately cutting us!" said Lady Bergeron with wonder. "What can have happened? Philippa, do you know?"

Just then Lord Denton's new barouche swung into view; in it was his lordship as well as Lady Cynthia Protherow. Philippa stared at them, embarrassed to see Lord Denton for the first time since that night at Almack's. Lady Cynthia gave Philippa a particularly malicious look, while Lord Denton did not acknowledge Philippa at all, but raised his nose high into the air, and turned away from her, giving Lady Cynthia a fond pat on the hand.

"What is wrong with everyone?" exclaimed Lady Bergeron.

"I don't know, Aunt Bergeron. Ever since last Wednesday, people have been being very uncivil to me!"

Lady Bergeron sighed, and said, "Oh, dear. You must have done something!"

"I didn't do anything, I assure you!"

"Oh, don't mistake my meaning. I don't really mean that you have actually *done* something offensive, it's just that all these silly people are so quick to *take offense,* which is quite another matter, isn't it? They have such peculiar tonnish customs, and somehow you, or perhaps we, have offended someone, and now the news has spread all over town. Offend one, you offend them all. The so-called *haut ton* is nothing better than a large flock of ducks. One stone thrown into the middle of them, and they *all* start squawking and fly off."

Lady Bergeron whispered to the coachman, "See here, John! Turn us round at once! We are going back to Brook Street! At once!"

Lady Bergeron removed her gloves and her bonnet, set them on a side table, and rang for tea. When it arrived, she told the housemaid that she would pour out herself, that Miss

Somerville and she should not be disturbed for any reason until she rang again.

Her ladyship seated herself at a round table and motioned for Philippa to join her.

"Sit down, my dear, and I beg you will tell me everything. I have been preoccupied with my own thoughts since you came to town and have not properly attended you. I had not thought it necessary that . . . well, I thought it all would be simple enough, that I need not shepherd you closely. I can see that I was wrong."

Immensely relieved that her troubles had finally caught her chaperone's full attention, Philippa poured out her heart to Lady Bergeron, telling in detail everything that had happened to her since she came to London, including the difficulty with Lord Denton, her rescue by Sir Guy Trent, and even her one waltz with the Duke of Harwich. Lady Bergeron listened intently to all of it, and then remained silent for some time.

At last she said, "It is my fault, you know. It is all my fault. I have not served you as I should have, and it is all because of these fatal memories I have of my own first Season, and I beg your pardon. I did not realize that going to Almack's would so affect me, watching the young girls waiting for their beaux to ask them to dance, so young and so full of hope, as I once was . . . that in seeing them, I would see again my past. I have been lost in another world of my own painful memories, Philippa, and because of that, I fear I have done you an injustice. I am sorry."

"What do you mean, Aunt Bergeron?" asked Philippa.

"It is no matter; we can talk of it another day. For now, we must solve your problem, and seek if we can reclaim your position in society, and your good name. It was the waltz that was the problem, Philippa. I cannot fathom why Harwich asked you, but accepting to dance the waltz with him was what you did wrong."

"But that's—silly," pointed out Philippa sensibly. "Why should anyone care if I dance a waltz or not?"

"It is a very good question. There is no particular reason they should care a jot; it is just the custom at Almack's for young ladies to seek the permission of one of the Patronesses before they may accept an offer to do the waltz."

"But I had no idea!" cried Philippa.

"Of course not. How could you? I, as the lady entrusted with shepherding you through the ton, was supposed to inform you of such things beforehand, or else I should have prevented you from so doing on the spot, when you were first approached by Harwich. That was my duty, and I was derelict," sighed Lady Bergeron. "I feel very desolate about it."

"Oh, I don't know, Aunt Bergeron. Why would anyone get so angry at breaking a silly rule that they would cast me into the outer darkness for what was no more than an innocent mistake?" she asked rather crossly.

"From the lofty viewpoint of the high-sticklers of the ton, Philippa," explained Lady Bergeron, "I'm afraid that no mistake is ever regarded as 'innocent.' "

Six

In the days that followed Philippa's *faux pas* at Almack's and her subsequent sudden fall from grace, Sir Guy Trent occupied himself with his usual pursuits, which happened to occur at his country seat, Buckley Court, in Kent. One of his favorite mares, Lightning, was about to foal, and as Sir Guy was an avid breeder, he preferred to be in attendance, watching the mystery of the entrance of a living being into the world, seeing that the foal take its first tottering steps on spindly legs, and being present to judge its conformation and its potential, from the very beginning.

Consequently, he heard nothing of the rumors about Miss Somerville and was unacquainted with her social mortification.

He did not drive back to town until Wednesday afternoon and spent the night quietly at home, reading, rather than going to his club, as he usually did, to discuss politics or economics or other affairs of the day. He dined in his room, and then, rather on a whim, suddenly decided he would go about in society.

Sir Guy rang for his man, Tupper, and had himself redressed in the elegant but rather old fashioned togs necessary to gain admittance to Almack's. After he had dressed, which took Tupper and his master a good two hours to accomplish, he looked splendid as ever.

To see Sir Guy Trent, dressed in severe yet elegant black against white, his chapeau bras tucked under his arm, was to be able to appreciate his every feature as being that of the quintessential gentleman of fashion.

Just in time, just before eleven o'clock, the door was opened to him, and Sir Guy Trent was admitted into Almack's.

He did not himself know why he had gone there.

As Sir Guy surveyed the ballroom, he eyed his various acquaintances, and nodded to them, or smiled at them, and realized, to his own amazement, that he was looking for someone in particular, who happened to be the raven-haired beauty he had rescued from Lord Denton.

Where was she?

Not finding her at once, he decided to take a turn around the room, and the longer he sought her out, the more unsettled he appeared.

To an impartial observer, it was almost as if he had come to Almack's room precisely in order to see Philippa again, but that could not be true, for Sir Guy Trent (a famous, settled bachelor, if not quite a confirmed one) would never do such a thing as seek out a young lady, much less so young and green a young lady as Miss Somerville of Hadley Vicarage, Penbury, Shropshire.

A complete circuit of the scene, though crowded with persons wearing the silks and satins and heirloom pearls of the high-born, who were graced with the pretension of the mighty, convinced him that the young lady he sought was not in attendance.

Sir Guy was devilishly disappointed, even uncharacteristically annoyed.

How could the chit do such a thing? Where was she? What was she doing? In whose arms was she being held? Suddenly, Sir Guy felt he must know the answers to all these questions.

At a pillar near the musicians' balcony, Sir Guy spotted Lord Denton and Lady Cynthia Protherow. She was dressed in a very ornate peach-colored gown and was hanging on his lordship's arm, hanging upon his every word, smiling and blushing, and tapping him coyly with her fan. They were clearly a couple smelling of April and May.

What a fickle young man! Sir Guy thought to himself, as he watched the couple flirting. *Denton seems to have overcome his passion for Miss Somerville entirely, and it was only a week*

*ago he was throwing himself at her feet, begging for her hand
in marriage.*

In his inspection, Sir Guy happened to catch Lord Denton's
eye, and when he did so, Denton blushed a fiery red and turned
away, obviously embarrassed to have been caught in such a
contradiction.

Sir Guy merely nodded toward Denton with a vague, almost
chilly politeness, wondering if a wish to avoid Lord Denton
accounted for the absence from Almack's of the lovely, viva-
cious Miss Somerville.

Where was she? Suddenly, the debonair Sir Guy Trent wanted
very much to know. It was easy enough for a gentleman in his
position to make inquiries.

Sir Guy Trent walked over to Sally Jersey, bowed to her, and
gave her a smile that always made her ladyship's heart race.

He brought her hand to his lips, and said, in his soft, deep
voice, "Sally, my dear, you look ravishing, as always."

"Guy!" she said, blushing like a schoolgirl. "Where have
you been? We have missed you around town! However could
you abandon us?"

"I had some business at Buckley, so I drove out for a few
days."

" 'Business'!" she replied. "You gentlemen are always involved in 'business,' and it always means we women must be
sadly deprived of your company!"

The two friends chattered on about general topics, such as
the weather, and the latest political scandals, until, at length,
Sir Guy thought the time right to bring up the subject in which
he was most interested, inquiring, "Sally, my dear, I was trying
to find a Miss Somerville, I believe her name is. Has she been
here, do you know? She came last week, but I have been unable
to find her this week."

"She? I am sure she is not here! I should think she would
not dare show her face here, ever again!" sniffed Lady Jersey.
"You have been out in the country, or you would already have
been informed of *that* particular young lady's situation."

A look of puzzlement crossed Sir Guy's face.

"What happened? Denton is not bothering the girl, is he?"

"Denton? No, no, Denton has just the other day offered for Cynthia Protherow! You are sadly behind the times, Guy! You shouldn't rusticate yourself so long, or you will be completely behind-hand. However, I'm surprised that the word about the shocking Miss Somerville hadn't at least spread as far as Kent!"

"What has happened to her?" he asked, concerned.

Lady Jersey motioned to him with her fan to come closer, and when he did so, she whispered to him in a voice that could still carry across the floor, "Well, you see, at last Wednesday's assembly, Miss Somerville accepted a waltz and danced it without our permission!"

Sir Guy nodded, saying, "I see. That is unusual and goes against the grain of things. And who was her partner?"

Lady Jersey looked a bit insulted and replied with a frown, "What has that to say to anything? I think it was . . . why I think it was Harwich. You know, the young Duke, Stanley Protherow's son. The one who's all to pieces and trying to pretend he isn't. The Protherows have always been that way, poor unfortunate family."

Sir Guy made no comment, but his silence was enough that Lady Jersey moved to fill it, rattling happily on.

"A good match his sister made, though, isn't it? I bet Lucy Protherow is home writing long lists of all the baubles and bangles she will be buying with her daughter's settlement money," said Lady Jersey, laughing. "One cannot blame her, of course. Poverty is an intolerable condition. I'd sell my daughter to the highest bidder, too, if I were in her position. Cynthia is lucky that the thing is finally settled and done. I think Lucy and Cynthia were both afraid that Lord Denton was backing off from it, for just last week, he was hanging about another girl entirely. Come to think on it, it was that Somerville girl, wasn't it?"

"Yes, it was. I recall that you asked me to put a stop to it, and so I did."

"That's true. I had forgotten. Oh, look! Here comes Lady Beaucastle! I can't say her gown becomes her, do you? That color is not very flattering to her face, poor dear. Her husband is so stingy with her pin-money, you know! There is a reason for his miserliness, of course, because when they were first wed, he would give her everything she ever wanted! But, now, I understand that she has taken Mr. Joffrey-Smith as her gallant, and her husband knows all about it!"

Lady Jersey chattered on at length, giving all the details of the affair, outlining its entire history and probably future. Sir Guy Trent listened politely for a few minutes that seemed like centuries, and then left, his mind embroiled for the second time in trying to figure out how he might rescue Miss Somerville from calamity.

Seven

Sir Guy Trent, looking as elegantly handsome as his reputation implied, called upon Miss Somerville and Lady Bergeron the very next day and was received by them in the front parlor of Lady Bergeron's home on Brook Street. Philippa was very pleased to see the kind gentleman who had saved her from Lord Denton, but was very nervous that he must have heard of her wretched *faux pas,* and might now think less of her because of it.

The three chatted away politely enough for a few minutes about the weather and about the whereabouts of a few mutual acquaintances. At length, a footman appeared at the door with an urgent summons for Lady Bergeron, who excused herself for a moment, and said she would return presently.

There was a moment of silence in the room before Philippa, unable to contain herself, blurted out, "Sir Guy, have you heard how I have disgraced myself?"

Surprised by Miss Somerville's frankness, Sir Guy tried to temporize, saying, "I would not call it disgrace, precisely. I, ah, I heard you had committed a minor *faux pas.*"

Miss Somerville blushed mightily, and explained, "It was my understanding, Sir Guy, that my misstep is far from minor! I suspect you must be trying to be diplomatic, and I thank you for it from the bottom of my heart. In fact, I'm surprised you would come and call upon me. No one else will."

The young girl sighed slightly, shook her head, and looked down in the vicinity of the Aubusson rug.

"It is my pleasure to see you once again, I assure you," said Sir Guy reassuringly.

Miss Somerville appeared unmoved, and said, rather formally, "It is very kind of you, I'm sure. You were good enough to save me from Lord Denton, but alas, you could not save me from myself!"

"My dear Miss Somerville, it was not at all your fault," said Sir Guy. "In time, once the Patronesses come down from their high horse, and think about the matter just a bit, they will realize that your chaperone, or some elder or better-informed person, should have warned you about the rules at Almack's. You should not be held accountable, by any means."

"Poor Lady Bergeron is mortified she had not warned me. She does not know what to do with me now. I might have to go back to Shropshire," said Miss Somerville despondently.

"All that way? I hope that won't be necessary."

"I hope so, too. Mama and Papa had such hopes for me. I hate to have let them down by having such poor conduct."

"As I said, the fault was not yours. The Duke of Harwich is to blame more than anybody. He surely knew that you must obtain permission before dancing the waltz. He should have approached one of the Patronesses and asked if she would present him to you as a very desirable partner. That is how it is done, and he knows it perfectly well."

"Then why did he act as he did?" asked Miss Somerville, looking puzzled.

"I shall strive to find that out. At any rate, if you will be good enough to allow me to carry it out, I have made up a plan that may serve to reacquire that splendid reputation of yours, which once had all the young men of London at your feet."

Miss Somerville clapped her hands. "Oh, Sir Guy, do you really think that there is anything you could do to help me? It's not for myself, precisely, it's just as I explained to you before. It will benefit my family very much if I can contrive to marry well, and it will harm them quite a lot if I do not. As it is, I cannot even go around town any more, because anyone who is anyone has stopped sending invitations."

A tear which Sir Guy Trent found remarkably becoming, slid down Miss Somerville's pert upturned nose; she deftly wiped it away and tried to put on a brave smile.

"How unfortunate!" said Sir Guy, shaking his head in disbelief. "People can be cruel and prejudiced."

He waited for just a moment, then said to her, "See here, Miss Somerville, will you permit me to drive you in the park tomorrow?"

"Would you really do that for me? Oh, it would be so kind of you, and it would be delightful!" cried Philippa, a bright smile on her face for the first time in days. "Why, I would like it above all things!"

The next afternoon, which proved a particularly pleasant summer day, Sir Guy Trent drove up to Lady Bergeron's small townhouse in his phaeton, just as he had promised Philippa he would.

He was ushered into the parlor at first, where he once again made the requisite small talk with her ladyship and Miss Somerville for the requisite twenty minutes or so. He then called for his hat, and Philippa for her bonnet, and he escorted her to the street. He then handed Philippa, wearing a modish beige carriage-dress, up into the seat of his elegant high-perch phaeton.

Once Sir Guy had taken the reins from his tiger (who was so tiny he had been hard put to keep Sir Guy's pair of spirited matched bays from bolting while he was walking them), he signaled to the tiger to mount up in back, for propriety's sake, and the boy did so. Sir Guy took up the reins, and they were off in a trice.

"Can you tell me what the plan is?" asked Miss Somerville, pulling her gloves a little tighter, and adjusting her bonnet nervously, as the phaeton jostled through the crowded street. "I have been up all night, wondering what precisely you might have in mind."

"You will see, Miss Somerville," he said with a soft smile. "You shall soon see."

Philippa was excited just to be riding in Sir Guy's phaeton, for she had heard he was a very notable whip. It took all her training in ladylike deportment not to *beg* him to race his vehicle for just a short while; however, though she did not ask him to race, and he did not do so, he kept his horses moving forward at such a spanking pace that she was able to enjoy the feel of the wind through her hair, and didn't mind a bit that she had to take hold tightly of her new bonnet with one hand, while with the other she was trying hard to hang onto her parasol.

"I wish I might someday learn to drive like you do!" said Philippa smiling, her cheeks blazing with color. "I do find driving prime bits o' blood very exciting!"

"I approve of your excitement—but I do *not* approve of your vocabulary. 'Prime bits o' blood,' indeed! A young lady should not speak using the cant of young men!"

"There. You see? I am impossible!" she replied, suddenly downcast. "I simply do not fit in this town! I should just give it all up and go back to Shropshire!"

"Nonsense! Don't be so dramatic, my dear. Nothing of this is as yet written in stone," said Sir Guy. "Look, here comes the first of our tests. It is Mrs. Braithwaite. Tell me, do you think she will acknowledge us?"

Mrs. Braithwaite, walking in the park with two of her most fubsy-faced daughters, was approaching the carriage lane from a side path and sending greetings to those she knew who were walking or driving on the way.

Miss Somerville looked at Mrs. Braithwaite with some alarm, saying, "Oh, no, I don't think she would dare to acknowledge us. Aunt Bergeron told me that it was she who first passed around the tale of what I had done. She cannot acknowledge me."

"That is quite true. But," he pointed out feelingly, "if she fails to acknowledge you, that means that she fails to acknowledge *me.*"

A dawning light passed over Philippa's face, and she clapped her hands in her endearing way and cried out, "Oh, I see your plan! Sir Guy, you are a genius!"

"Thank you for your compliment," he said decidedly.

"It is a most wonderful idea! You who have such credit

amongst the ton, I, as your guest, must needs be made more credible merely by virtue of appearing by your side! I don't think Mrs. Braithwaite can do anything except be polite to you—for if she slights *me*, she will slight *you!*"

"Precisely," agreed Sir Guy, smiling again, a flash of challenge in his eye.

"It is a wicked scheme, and I am most obliged to you for it!" cried Philippa. "As you know, I am most concerned to be accepted back into polite society, for I am very desperate to marry, as you might imagine."

"If you are so desperate to marry," said Sir Guy carefully, "perhaps something can be done to, how shall I put it? Something might be done to hasten your success in your search?"

"Oh, do you think so?" she said lightly. "For, even before this happened, I really hadn't been doing very well on my own, despite having had so many offers—that is, before my Downfall. Do you have anyone in mind?"

"I might," suggested Sir Guy, playing his cards close to his chest.

Mrs. Braithwaite turned off onto another path before Sir Guy's theory could be put to the test. However, it was not long before a large, venerable, burnished vehicle appeared carrying a very elegant and haughty lady, who barely acknowledged the various glances of those persons beneath her, as everyone around her clearly was.

"Oh, look! There comes Mrs. Drummond Burrell! What a harridan she is! Please excuse me saying so, Sir Guy, for she might be a dear friend of yours for all I know, but *I* think she is a harridan, for it was she who gave Aunt Bergeron and I the most shocking cut on Saturday last! It was a basilisk glare, and I shook from the cold of it for nearly an hour. Will you smile and wave to her? I cannot wait to see what she will do! It must be wonderful to be absolutely the most *fashionable* of fashionable persons, having such credit that even the haughty Patronesses of Almack's must fall to their knees before you!"

"The Thames will freeze full over before Clementina

Drummond Burrell falls on her knees before anyone!" pointed out Sir Guy Trent.

Miss Somerville considered this for a moment, and then said, "But, Sir Guy, the Thames has but last winter frozen over!"

"You are correct, and that is my point, exactly," said Sir Guy, laughing. "That being the case, we may be about to see the top-lofty Mrs. Dummond Burrell doing things she never dreamt of doing!"

"I pray you are correct!" said Philippa gaily.

"We shall soon see if the sauce for Mrs. Braithwaite is the sauce for Mrs. Dummond Burrell!"

Sir Guy Trent pulled back his pair from a trot into a walk. Slowly, dramatically, inexorably the two carriages approached one another; they were on a slight curve protected by spring-leafed chestnut trees to either side of the row.

Sir Guy Trent slowly, elegantly, lifted up his tall curly beaver hat and made a great show of greeting Mrs. Drummond Burrell in a friendly and intimate way. Miss Somerville was seated on the far side of the high-perch phaeton, on the side farthest away from Mrs. Drummond Burrell, and in a position where Miss Somerville was hidden from sight behind Sir Guy's left shoulder.

Elegant Mrs. Drummond Burrell first favored Sir Guy with a brilliant and welcoming smile, and then, when the carriage positions shifted a little, the lady's smile froze as she made out the identity of Sir Guy's young companion.

It was a horrible sight to see. Mrs. Drummond Burrell's very lips quivered and shook, not knowing whether they must turn down or turn up again. The great lady could not take back the smile she had already conferred upon Sir Guy, but neither could she dare to deal the cut direct to any young lady so highly favored as to have been taken up in his carriage by the divine Sir Guy Trent.

In the end, Sir Guy's campaign won the day. Mrs. Drummond Burrell's frozen smile transformed into a sort of a choking cough, and then into a hacking cough and a sneeze, accompanied by a weak smile and a limp, vague waving of her fingers, as she was forced publicly to acknowledge Sir Guy—*and* his guest, Miss Somerville.

The great lady passed on by, utterly stunned and perplexed, while Sir Guy and Philippa tried desperately to contain their strong mutual desire to emit loud celebratory whoops of laughter.

"If I live to be a hundred, I will never see a more diverting sight than Mrs. Drummond Burrell trying to decide which way the wind was blowing!" said Philippa, beside herself with laughter.

She looked into Sir Guy's eyes, and she saw in them a firm and deep affection that made her feel safe and warm and wonderfully fortunate.

Eight

Word of the amazing adoption of the miscreant Miss Somerville by dashing Sir Guy Trent (of all people!) spread through Town like the Great Fire of London. The outcome was a foregone conclusion: no one, not even His Royal Highness the Prince of Wales himself, had more weight in society than Sir Guy Trent. Even if all seven Patronesses were to line up against him, their power was outweighed by that of the handsome baronet.

In the days after their momentous carriage-ride in Hyde Park, Sir Guy squired Miss Philippa Somerville to the Royal Italian Opera House for a performance of Gluck's *Orphee et Eurydice;* he was seen riding with her in the park, actually letting her ride on one of his favorite, home-bred mares. He took her to see the Elgin Marbles, and even went so far as to take her to see all the London sights, the Tower of London, and all the rest. He made himself the young lady's constant companion, and society might snub them, but would do so at society's peril.

The Patronesses, caught by surprise by Sir Guy's unanticipated championship of Miss Somerville, finally gathered at the home of Lady Castlereagh in order to discuss strategies for the future, for it was clear they were going to be forced to recant.

They admitted they had been vanquished by Sir Guy Trent's superior strategy, and it was clear they were going to have to accept the girl into the society of the *haut ton* again: but, they wondered, how was this to be accomplished without losing face?

It took them a good three hours' worth of deep discussion

and argument over scones and scandal-broth, but in the end, they decided to put about a version that would exculpate both themselves and Miss Somerville.

To wit, they would endorse the story that on the night at Almack's when the incident occurred, Miss Somerville's chaperone, Lady Bergeron, had had a sick headache. Thus she had been completely indisposed at the time the Duke of Harwich approached her protégée. Their second point was to assert that the young Duke of Harwich had been accidentally misled as to his having seen the young lady in question already dancing the waltz previously, and so he mistakenly assumed that everything was already in order.

These two coinciding circumstances made it possible for the *faux pas* to occur. The Patronesses, noting Miss Somerville's lapse in conduct, rightly punished her. However, once the magnanimous Patronesses learned the true details of the mishap, they of course had to forgive the child, for it was not at all her fault.

Such a complete and rapid reversal of judgment did not sit well with any one of the Patronesses, but it was either that or have Sir Guy's championship of the chit rubbed in their faces till the end of time itself. Knowing in advance who would win and who would lose, the great ladies relented.

His plan having accomplished all that he could have wished for Miss Somerville, the baronet's victory was complete.

Thanks to the tall, distinguished gentleman from Kent, everything was once again going splendidly for the small, ebony-haired beauty from Hadley Vicarage.

Invitations inscribed to Miss Somerville and Lady Bergeron came first in a trickle, and then in a torrent. If anything, her popularity after her fortnight of scandal was even greater than it had been to begin with.

When Miss Somerville reappeared at Almack's on the arm of the great Sir Guy Trent, the reversal of her fortune was as complete as it was sweet. She was welcomed back with open arms: Lady Jersey gave her a hug and kissed her on both cheeks, saying how pretty she looked. Maria Sefton pronounced her a very fine gal. Lady Castlereagh took her aside and gave her advice on some new fashions that had come over from France. Mrs. Drummond Burrell favored her with a half-smile and even a nod—a great accomplishment, as everyone was aware.

She was accepted again; beyond that, she was admired. How could she not be? For her second debut, Philippa had chosen to wear to Almack's a gown of white satin with a net overskirt; both its bodice and hem were trimmed with blond lace and an edging of pearls. She wore white satin slippers and long white gloves, with a simple necklace of pearls and pearl-drop earrings. Sir Guy Trent thought he had never seen anyone so beautiful as she and longed to tell her so.

Watching her smiling and laughing happily, surrounded by admirers, he could not quite recall the precise moment when he had fallen deeply in love with her; it had happened so gradually and so naturally. It might have been that he had loved her all the time.

Would she accept him? Would she think him too old, too much of a Londoner? Would she reject his suit as she had rejected that of so many others?

He could not believe his own cowardice, for he had never behaved in such a way before. Of course, he had never felt this way before. He promised himself that, now that Philippa was safely ensconced at Almack's once again, it was time for him to try his luck and tell her of his feelings for her.

God help me, I'm just like Denton, he sighed to himself. *I hope I have better luck with her than he did.*

Lady Jersey watched Sir Guy Trent and the little Somerville girl dancing the quadrille together, and she did so with some interest.

"Smelling of April and May, those two," she said to Mrs. Braithwaite.

"Do you think so?"

"I am very sure of it. I have never, in my whole life, seen

Guy Trent pay any such attentions to any woman as he has to this girl. A kindly man he is, but this is more than kindness, I assure you. He is smitten, and I'll wager you that the girl is as well. How could one not love Guy Trent? I love him very well myself, not that he ever spared a look for me, but at least he tolerates my chattering, which I think quite sweet of him," said Sally Jersey.

"Well, they make a very handsome couple," declared Mrs. Braithwaite, "and I am sure I wish them well."

Lady Jersey replied, approvingly, "I am sure that everyone present at Almack's tonight wishes them both very well, indeed."

Nine

Everyone present at Almack's watching the couple's graceful dancing certainly wished them well, with the prominent exception of Lady Cynthia Protherow. She found the whole fairy tale story not to her liking, and she found Miss Somerville's reascension into society worrisome in the extreme.

For all the fact that her engagement to Lord Denton had already appeared in the *Times* of London, Lady Cynthia could not like having the girl who had driven her fiancé mad with passion, dancing and chatting away happily only a few yards away from him, looking even lovelier than ever before. She felt she could not really trust Lord Denton in Miss Somerville's presence and wished the chit at Jericho.

While Miss Somerville's social career was in eclipse, Lord Denton had been perfectly happy to go along with the general crowd and despise and ignore her. However, now that she had been replaced upon her pedestal, Lady Cynthia could already sense a re-emergence of his former passion.

This worried her no end, for, although she knew that Denton would not renounce his engagement—his manners were far too well-bred for that—the thought that he might embarrass her in public by making a cake of himself over Miss Somerville was daunting in the extreme.

It must have been this fear of mortification before the Upper Ten Thousand that led Lady Cynthia to behave as she did to Miss Somerville on that evening at Almack's.

It happened after midnight. Lady Bergeron and Sir Guy Trent

happened to be deep in conversation, standing to one side of the room, while Miss Somerville had gone toward the windows to enjoy a bit of fresh air. Seeing her victim alone, Lady Cynthia approached her, her smile as wide as the mouth of the Thames.

"So, Miss Somerville, you are back again! I am so glad of it! I was wounded to the quick during your brief absence from our little London world. Welcome back!" chirped Lady Cynthia.

Annoyed that Lady Cynthia had seen fit to mention the incident at all, Philippa replied, in a cool voice, "Thank you so much."

"We all have been talking about the fact that you have become such great friends with the great Sir Guy Trent; it is really very highly amusing!"

"Oh? Is it?" replied Miss Somerville, herself unamused.

"Well, of course, you know his reputation. As a confirmed bachelor, he does not, as a rule, enjoy escorting green girls around town, and we all thought it most gallant of him that he was so kind as to pay his attentions to you, so your errors, as it were, might be wiped away. I am sure it was extremely tedious for him, though he's such a gentleman that he surely did not let you know it for a minute, did he?" Lady Cynthia said brightly.

Miss Somerville began to color, and, feeling very uncomfortable, replied only, "I had no idea that he thought that it was tedious."

"Well, of course, he *would* find such a thing tedious, for he's a grown man, isn't he?"

"Indeed he is," she said, discomfited. "Sir Guy Trent is a grown man, and I am but a green girl from the country. What has that to say to anything?"

"He is used to escorting women of sophistication and wit and great beauty, and considering all that, Sir Guy has a very kind heart, don't you think?"

Philippa could not but agree, and she blushed to remember his many acts of kindness and courtesy toward her. She began to feel like an utter fool.

Lady Cynthia went on, hugely enjoying the tale she was spinning. "The wonder of his kindness is that Sir Guy does this sort of thing on quite a regular basis."

Philippa's face fell, but she tried to conceal it, giving a false little laugh, and saying, "Oh, does he? How singular!"

Lady Cynthia laughed in reply, saying, "Yes, indeed! It's sort of Sir Guy's particular own social charity! He finds some little social outcast, takes her up, and through the magnificence of his regard, he restores her to a place in society. Why, he did it thrice just last year, didn't you know?"

"No, I did not," she whispered, her heart breaking.

"Of course you wouldn't have, this is your first season, isn't it?" said Lady Cynthia brightly.

"Yes, it is."

"That explains it—your not knowing about Miss Hicks, and Lady Elaine Purcell, and Miss Dignam-Parker, and all that he did for them," said Lady Cynthia. Her brow creased, as she added, warningly, "I *do* assume you knew enough not to have taken any of his attentions as being personally meant."

Miss Somerville, who was feeling more desolate than she ever had in her existence, laughed a brittle little laugh again, as she said, "No, of course not. Far from it!"

"It would not do to be misled and take what is meant for show, meant solely as a kindness, as if it were directed at you, yourself, rather than being a show for the ton. One's heart might be broken, and that would not do, would it?"

"Of course not," Philippa agreed. "I would not think of such a thing."

No sooner had she spoken than she realized her words were false. She loved Sir Guy. Philippa began wondering just when her feelings of love for Sir Guy had first really taken root in her. It was a sudden shock to discover that precisely when she was learning that true love had arisen in her toward Sir Guy, she was also discovering that her 'love' was merely a school-girl's fantasy, existing only in her imagination, existing in vain.

"You were just Sir Guy Trent's little charity project," said Lady Cynthia. "Happily for you, it worked!"

By the time she had finished weaving the entirety of her web of deceit, Lady Cynthia could see with great satisfaction that Miss Somerville was very upset.

Philippa felt at once very sad and mortified and very angry at herself for her own youthful blindness. Philippa did not know which of these emotions felt worse.

Without even waiting to say farewell to Sir Guy, who had gone into the next room to procure some refreshments, she called upon Lady Bergeron to take her home, saying she had the headache, was extremely unwell, and must retire to her bed-chamber at once.

When Sir Guy Trent returned to the ballroom, ready to proffer some sandwiches and orgeat, having summoned the courage to take Philippa aside and make his addresses to her, the young lady in question was nowhere to be seen.

Ten

It was a very odd thing, really. All the way home riding in the carriage, her head pressed despondently against the grey squabs, Miss Philippa Somerville was having to face cold, hard reality. The hard fact was that she was desperately in love with Sir Guy Trent. The hard fact was that she had not even known it, not until the moment Lady Cynthia Protherow informed her that she had no hope of ever touching his heart.

She had never really taken his attentions seriously, he being so much older than she and so very handsome and fashionable and distinguished. It was only when Lady Cynthia told her that all the things he had done for her he had done merely out of kindness, and not out of any personal affection toward her, that she realized she had fallen deeply in love with him, and that to be deprived of his presence and his friendship, even for a day, would be insupportable.

A tear trickled down her cheek, and she wiped it away.

"What a fool I have been!" she thought to herself, letting her tears flow without constraint. "How could I ever think someone like myself could attract the affections of a Pink of the Ton like Sir Guy Trent! What arrogance, Father would say! What arrant presumption!"

When Lady Bergeron's carriage arrived at her home, Philippa was handed down, and she immediately repaired to her bedchamber. She allowed herself to be undressed, answered her abigail's intrusive questions as to the redness of her mistress's eyes and nose by saying she thought she had caught cold, and dismissed her maid without letting her brush her hair for an hour, which was their usual practice.

Philippa was already in bed when Lady Bergeron came in to wish her goodnight.

"Is something wrong, dear?" Lady Bergeron asked solicitously, noticing that Philippa was not in good looks.

"Yes, I'm afraid so," said Philippa, ready to reveal everything in a flood of words. "Everything is wrong! Oh, Aunt Bergeron, I've fallen in love with a gentleman who does not love me in return! Whatever shall I do? I want to die!"

Lady Bergeron's face changed completely.

"Oh, my poor dear, I could not have any more compassion for you than I do! I'm afraid I know precisely what that is like! Come here, my dear," she said, and pulled her into a warm hug. "I know precisely what you mean."

Lady Bergeron looked thoughtful for a moment and then began to speak.

"It was while I was a girl in London that I met the love of my life, Lord James Keating. Almack's did not exist at that time, of course, for Mr. McCall had not yet set it up. But when I was with you at Almack's, it reminded me so much of myself, and all the hopes and dreams of young girls of marriageable days. Looking for a suitable partner, wishing desperately that one young man or another would ask one to dance, hoping that the young man of one's dreams would fall in love with one, and take one away into a blissful marriage.

"Lord James Keating was the younger son of a Duke, without any money of his own. My dowry was a mere competence, nothing much, and so ours was not a good match, at least from a monetary point of view. I didn't care about that, nor did he, for we were young and in love with one another, and had that unfettered confidence of youth that can fly in the face of reason.

"Left to ourselves, we would have married, and been happy, I think. But it was not to be. My family would not permit it, nor would James's family. When they saw how serious things had become between us, James was sent away overseas, and I never, ever saw him again."

Tears welled up in Lady Bergeron's thin, lined face, but in her shining dark eyes there was still a trace of the girl she had once been, and of the deep love that still lived within her.

"My father arranged a marriage for me with Lord Bergeron, thirty years my elder, and I was married to the man, whom I heartily disliked, within a month. After two or three years of misery, and no children to be my comfort, I was left as I am now—a very wealthy widow, with nothing but money to console me in the endless nights.

"That has been my life. That is why I became so distracted, seeing all those hopeful young men and women at the parties and the routs, at Almack's, and at the theaters. Seeing what might have been was inexpressibly painful to me, so I beg you will forgive my distraction, and understand why I seemed a little lost.

"It is a terrible thing when love goes wrong. All of this is a long way of saying that I am deeply sorry that your feelings for Sir Guy were not returned, and that if you wish me to make arrangements for you to return to your parents at once, I shall do so."

Philippa thought for a moment and then blurted out, "Oh, dear Aunt Bergeron, in all respects, my season has been a disaster. Thank you so much for sponsoring me, but it is no use, I'm afraid. I am going back home to Shropshire, if you please, at once."

"Just as you wish, my dear," said Lady Bergeron, patting her hand.

The very next day, arrangements were made for Philippa to set off for her home, and she returned to live with her family at the Vicarage.

Eleven

It was only the end of June, but the sultry weather had already arrived, and the air was warm and lazy-making. Philippa was working in the garden at the vicarage, wearing a round-dress with an apron over it, her hair sweetly disheveled, with ringlets of her black hair hanging down to either side. There was a bit of dirt on her upturned nose, and there was muddy loam on the hem of her gown, but when Sir Guy Trent caught sight of her, he thought she looked as fair as ever he had seen, the more so since it had been a whole fortnight since he had last seen her.

Sir Guy had spent that fortnight in solemn meditation, for it had stung him deeply when Philippa fled from London, and he had not known the reason for it. He had made sure he knew his own mind before he made the trip out to Penbury.

When he saw her, all his thoughts came together.

"Philippa," he said, and he heard her gasp when she recognized his voice. She turned around, blushed mightily, and tried to wipe the dirt from her face and her long white apron.

"Why did you leave London?" he said, in a grave voice.

Philippa blushed again, not knowing what to do, or what to say. Why had he come? What could have possessed him to come all the way to Penbury?

"I . . . I could bear it no longer," she said simply.

"What could you bear no longer?" he asked. "My company?"

"No, not at all! How can you say such a thing!" she replied

feelingly. "You must be mocking me, and I think that is most unfair!"

"I am not mocking you," he said grimly. "I was very angry that you left London without telling me."

Philippa sighed and looked at the ground. She shrugged her shoulders, saying, "I—I did not think it would matter so very much. I am surprised that you would care whether I was there or not."

Sir Guy's eyes flashed with anger. He strode over to her and grabbed her by the shoulders, pressing so hard that it hurt.

"Little fool!" he said. "How can you not know of my feelings for you?

"I know," said Philippa, shrugging off his hands.

"Have you no feelings for me?" he demanded.

She blushed again, hating herself for doing so, and said in a shaking voice, "Of c-course I do. I v-value our friendship very highly."

"Friendship? Damn our friendship! I don't want to be your friend, Philippa, I want to be your husband!"

"Oh, no, you don't!" she shot back, angry herself, now. "I know all about your 'charity cases!' "

He stared at her, uncomprehending, saying, "Charity cases? Are you quite mad?"

"I *know* I was your charity case! You were kind enough to go out of your way to help me by squiring me around town and restoring my place in society. No one else could have done as much for me, and truly, I am most grateful to you. I can't imagine why you came all the way out here, however."

"I came 'all the way out here' to ask your father for your hand in marriage!" he said.

She blushed again, furious, and said sarcastically, "I know you are a kind person, but surely you needn't take your kindliness *that* far!"

"What are you saying?" he thundered.

"I'm saying that you shouldn't marry me because you feel sorry for me!" she spat at him. "That's ridiculous! It's a horrid thing to do, and it's terribly demeaning to me!"

"You are being ridiculous beyond permission, Philippa. I want to marry you because I love you!"

"Now, *that's* ridiculous!" she cried. She turned away from him, starting to run back toward her house, trying to hide the tears that were beginning to stream down her face. She had never felt so miserable or alone in her entire life.

Sir Guy went after her, his long legs quickly covering the distance between them. He grabbed her shoulders again, spun her around, and pulled her strongly to him, kissing her roughly. It took no more than a moment for her resistance to melt completely, as she returned his passionate embrace.

By resorting to the classical simplicity of this method, as well as by exchanging pledges of ardor and constancy, the couple swiftly resolved all differences and misunderstandings, and became happily engaged, just in time to take tea with the Vicar.

Epilogue

Sir Guy Trent and Philippa Somerville were married by Philippa's father at a charming little chapel in Kent, not far from Buckley Court. All the patronesses of Almack's were invited, and all seven of them came to wish Sir Guy and Lady Trent all possible joy.

It was not until after their marriage that Sir Guy discovered under what circumstances the Duke of Harwich had beguiled Miss Somerville into accepting that fatal waltz; when Sir Guy confronted the Duke, he made no bones about revealing his motives. He apologized with what Sir Guy thought was real sincerity, and that matter was put to rest.

Once Sir Guy discovered that the real villainess of the piece was Lady Cynthia Protherow, he considered mounting some campaign against her by means of the seven guardians of Almack's, but when he found out more of her circumstances, he felt sorry for her, and thought she had already been punished sufficiently.

Lord Denton married Lady Cynthia, but when he learned that his wife had been responsible for the scandal that almost ruined Miss Somerville, he was furious. He refused to assume any of the Protherow family's debts, and Lord and Lady Denton from that day on lived separate and apart.

At Philippa's urging, Sir Guy used his connections to locate Lord James Keating, Lady Bergeron's old flame. It took a whole year, but he was finally found in Bengal, India, serving as an administrator for a maharaja.

By the time Lord James returned to England to claim Lady Bergeron as his own, Sir Guy and Lady Trent's happy marriage had been blessed by the birth of a son, Phillip James. His doting godmother was the garrulous Sally, Lady Jersey.

WATCH FOR THESE REGENCY ROMANCES